SIMON451

BOOKS BY NICHOLAS SANSBURY SMITH

THE ORBS SERIES (offered by Simon451/Simon & Schuster)

Solar Storms (An Orbs Prequel)

White Sands (An Orbs Prequel)

Red Sands (An Orbs Prequel)

Orbs

Orbs II: Stranded

Orbs III: Redemption

THE EXTINCTION CYCLE SERIES

Extinction Horizon

Extinction Edge

Extinction Age

Extinction Evolution

Extinction End

Extinction Aftermath

THE HELL DIVERS TRILOGY (offered by Blackstone Publishing)

Hell Divers

Hell Divers II: Ghosts

Hell Divers III: Deliverance

ORBS II

STRANDED

NICHOLAS SANSBURY SMITH

SIMON451

New York   London   Toronto   Sydney   New Delhi

SIMON451

Simon 451
An Imprint of Simon & Schuster, Inc.
1230 Avenue of the Americas
New York, NY 10020

First Simon451 trade paperback edition July 2016

SIMON451and colophon are registered trademarks of Simon & Schuster, Inc.

For information about special discounts for bulk purchases, please contact Simon & Schuster Special Sales at 1-866-506-1949 or business@simonandschuster.com.

The Simon & Schuster Speakers Bureau can bring authors to your live event. For more information or to book an event, contact the Simon & Schuster Speakers Bureau at 1-866-248-3049 or visit our website at www.simonspeakers.com.

Interior design by Lewelin Polanco

Manufactured in the United States of America

10 9 8 7 6 5 4 3 2 1

Library of Congress Cataloging-in-Publication Data is available.

ISBN 978-1-5011-3325-1
ISBN 978-1-4767-8896-8 (ebook)

To my friends at Simon451 for all the support and encouragement, and for believing in me and the Orbs series—especially my editor, Brit Hvide

ORBS II: STRANDED

THE waking sun cast a brilliant glow over the wasteland as it crawled higher into the morning sky. Rays of scorching light carpeted the remnants of lakebeds and extinct rivers, unveiling the sun-bleached bones of dead trees that littered the harsh landscape.

Alex Wagner cleared his visor of grime, wishing he could wipe away the beads of sweat forming inside his helmet. The ventilation system in the suit he had swiped off a dead NTC soldier had stopped working yesterday.

He adjusted his lean, athletic body inside the oversized suit. The damned hunk of armor was more of a detriment than anything. He glanced down at the exposed skin of his forearm beneath the foot-long claw mark in the suit. Standing there under the blistering heat of the sun, he imagined what the soldier he'd taken the suit from had been thinking in the moments before his death. A blur of images entered his mind and then solidified into a vivid picture. The razor-sharp claws slashing through the air, the guttural shrieks of the aliens hunting the NTC soldier. Alex could see it all, because he too had experienced it, and the memory made his skin crawl.

A gust of wind whistled past his suit, peppering his visor with dirt. Alex flinched. Squinting, he blinked several times to avoid the burning sweat dripping from his forehead and checked the temperature reading on his HUD.

One hundred degrees.

Could that be right? He checked his mission clock; it wasn't even eight o'clock yet. If the reading was correct, it meant the temperature was rising faster than he thought. But maybe it was wrong. Maybe things weren't as bad as they seemed.

He peered back down at the claw mark in his suit. The damage to the suit had probably destroyed more than just the ventilation system. Cursing under his breath, he pushed on through the hissing sand. When the wind cleared, he caught a glimpse of the wasteland around him.

Like a photograph, the world appeared in a simple, frozen pane through his visor's glass. He halted to take in the view, his boots sliding to a stop in the loose sand. In the valley below, the dead branches of leafless trees reached toward the white sun. A deep groove from a dried-up river snaked through the cracked red dirt. Beyond the cluster of trees he could see the hint of a road, two dusty trucks sitting idly where they had been abandoned on invasion day.

Taking in a measured breath, Alex closed his eyes to listen to this new world. The sound of death echoed inside his helmet: the cracking of a dying tree branch, the desperate bark of a starving dog some-where in the distance, and the memories of the people screaming as he watched them die. It was a chorus playing on repeat, and he knew it would be with him until he, too, died.

Alex couldn't grasp why he had survived, while so many others had perished. What made him so lucky?

He pushed on, trying to recall the series of events that had led him here. The time line blurred like the heat waves on the horizon.

He could remember signing on the dotted line, promising six months of his life to a Biosphere team. But he still wasn't sure why they had picked him. He wasn't anything special. He wasn't a genius or even exceptionally smart. Five weeks before the invasion, he had simply been a history teacher and assistant football coach for the local high school team. Sure, he'd had a good run as a wide receiver in college, so good that he'd drawn the attention of a few NFL scouts before he blew out his knee, but that didn't explain NTC's interest in him. There were mil-lions of people better suited for the project. Divorced and saddled with student loan debt, Alex was hardly the best candidate for an NTC-run Biosphere team.

Yet they had recruited him. His decision to accept their offer might have even saved his life. But for how long?

With the surface water gone, the temperature would continue to rise, baking the Earth's surface. Trees would die and stop producing oxygen, filling the atmosphere with unbreathable levels of carbon dioxide. Alex hadn't taken a science class since college, but even he knew what was happening. He had a front-row seat to the end of the world.

The Earth was dying, and so was the human race—what was left of it, anyway.

Alex stumbled over a rock as he continued deeper into the valley. His helmet bobbed up and down, his dry lips smacking together with every step. The heat was nearly unbearable, and he was low on water, but still he remained focused, vigilant.

He hadn't seen any of the aliens for hours now, and he hadn't come face-to-face with any since they had attacked his Biosphere. The memory was still fresh, hemorrhaging like an open wound.

Four days earlier, he had been sitting in the mess hall with nine of his teammates, chatting over plates of pasta that he had cooked himself. They heard the faint scratching and scraping noise first. Then came the terrible high-pitched shrieks that made him want to cup his ears. A brilliant blue glow followed moments later as dozens of the spiderlike creatures emerged from the ceiling.

He'd escaped into a sewage line, covered in hog manure and his friends' blood. At first he'd hesitated and turned to go back, but what he saw from inside that tunnel changed his mind—the Spiders spinning his screaming colleagues into orbs. He crawled away like a coward minutes after, tears streaming down his filthy face.

He shook away these thoughts and continued walking, his eyes darting back and forth as he scanned the landscape for signs of the monsters. He focused on a dust-covered road sign in the distance.

His plan was simple: head west, toward the ocean. The Biosphere had been located in an abandoned missile silo on the outskirts of Edwards Air Force Base in California. Alex, a Maryland native, had little knowledge of the local geography and could only guess that he was now somewhere northwest of the base. After escaping the attack, he had headed as far away from Edwards as possible. He didn't need a military background to know the Organics were probably swarming there. After four days of traveling, he knew he had to be close. Maybe he'd get to see the Pacific before he died, after all . . . if it was still there.

An abrupt and powerful windblast knocked him into a boulder, his armor meeting the rock with a crunch. As he pushed himself off the dirt, he caught a glimpse of something. The sky to the west seemed different; there was a blue wall on the horizon. It couldn't be. Could it?

It looked a lot like rain.

Another wind gust tore into his side, knocking him to his knees.

He grunted, pain racing through his body. He was burning up in his suit, and the inside of his helmet felt like a furnace. Sweat stung his eyes. He winced, waiting for the burning to subside. For a former college athlete, he wasn't in the best shape, but at least his damned knee wasn't acting up.

As his vision cleared, he saw something odd about the rain: It was traveling up, into the sky.

Were his eyes playing a trick on him? Was his body finally succumbing to dehydration?

He forced himself deeper into the valley, heading for the rocky hills to the west. Blinking sweat from his eyes, he tried to focus on the phenomenon in the distance.

What the hell was it?

The rainstorm appeared beyond the rocks, but just how far beyond he wasn't sure. Alex paused to marvel at the sky. He licked his dry lips with grim fascination, his gaze locked onto the strange rain. He knew he didn't have the energy to travel much farther, but he was curious, and his curiosity propelled him forward across the dead landscape.

An hour later he reached the last embankment of the valley. Gasping for air, he began to climb, clawing his way up the loose dirt. Rocks and dead vegetation rained down the hill behind him. By the time he reached the top he could hardly breathe. He inhaled, closing his eyes as air filled his lungs.

"Just a little farther," he muttered.

From the hilltop he could see a tan beach extending along the shoreline for miles, but where there would normally have been sunbathers, there was a graveyard of boats. Hulls were twisted in all directions, their cargo littered across the sand.

The ocean had receded far beyond the buoys that had once warned boats away from rocky areas. Now, they stuck out of the sand like dormant missiles. Miles away, the wall of water rose out of the ocean where it was still deep and blue.

He followed the rain with his eyes until it disappeared into the sky. He couldn't see them, but he knew they must be there. Somewhere above him, the aliens had a ship that was draining the sea.

Alex shook his head and another bead of sweat dropped into his eye. He grimaced, waiting for the pain to subside. To the east, rectangular buildings rose up out of the ground, the structures flickering in the heat waves. Civilization meant resources, which meant water and food. But it also meant danger. Spiders tended to congregate near cities and towns.

He hesitated, painfully aware of the dryness in his throat. Alex knew he was going to die, one way or another. It wasn't a matter of *if*, just a matter of when and how. And he had two choices: die from dehydration or die like the NTC soldier that had worn the suit before him.

Neither option was particularly appealing. He took one last look at the wall of rain over his shoulder and started down the other side of the hill.

Alex approached the buildings cautiously, scanning for aliens. There was no sign of movement besides the blur of a miniature dust tornado brewing in the distance. He paused, listening for any hint of the creatures' shrieks. Just because he didn't see *them* didn't mean they couldn't detect *him*. That was another thing he had picked up during the last four days: If he wanted to stay alive, he had to keep focused.

He checked his HUD again. The display revealed no signs of life. Hesitating, he strained to listen one more time. Besides the wind, he heard nothing but the whining sound of a strained power line.

Satisfied, he entered civilization for the first time in days; a neighborhood, much like the one he'd grown up in, sprawled out in front of him.

He checked the road to ensure it was clear and then took off running into the yard across the street. The tall blades of prairie grass snapped like twigs as he passed through them. Nothing green remained, not a single leaf.

Alex's vision fogged over. Gritting his teeth, he narrowed his eyes and tried to focus on the house in front of him, but the effects of dehydration were taking over. He rested against a child's swing set and listened again for the familiar scratching of Spiders. Wiping his visor clean, he saw the filthy glass doors leading into the house. They were covered in dust and dirt, but otherwise unscathed. He checked the windows; they too seemed to be undisturbed. His HUD still looked clear. Everything appeared safe.

The thought gave him pause. Nothing was safe, not anymore.

Five quick paces across the yard and he was at the door, resting his back against the house's aged siding. His first impulse was to break the glass, but instead he tried the handle. It clicked, unlocked.

He grinned with relief at the small victory as he slipped through the opening, but his smile was short-lived. Inside he was greeted by a dark room. Only a few rays of sunlight bled through the curtains to guide him. Standing there in the shadows, he suddenly felt overwhelmed by fear. Slowly, he reached down and drew his combat knife out of its sheath.

The knife shook in his gloved hand. Holding the weapon did not feel natural. He was a teacher, not a soldier, and he had never been a fan of weapons. But this was a different world—a world where he had no choice but to protect himself.

Crossing the room cautiously, he tiptoed toward the kitchen, the knife held out before him. He froze again when he saw the undisturbed room. Three plates were arranged neatly on the table for a family that would never eat together again. The room was an eerie relic from another time, when food, water, and shelter were taken for granted; a time when people's biggest concern was whether they would be able to make their credit card payment. The world had changed overnight.

Bills no longer mattered. Monsters were real. And water was the most important commodity of all.

Shaking the scene from his thoughts, he made his way to the fridge, opening the door to reveal a bottle of rotten milk and a few cans of beer. A week earlier, he would have jumped at the sight of a beer, but now the cans did nothing but make him crave water even more. He closed the door slowly and turned to the cabinets. The first two held nothing but spices and a few boxes of rigatoni. The next two were full of dusty glasses and plates. With a sigh, he closed them and moved on to the fifth. He licked his chapped lips out of habit, noticing that the blood had dried up.

He swung the door open, desperate to find something to quench his thirst or satisfy his hunger. Inside were a can of beans, a can of soup, and a couple boxes of cereal.

Someone must have looted the house before him. Something inside him brightened at the idea. Maybe that person was still out there. Maybe he wasn't alone after all. He opened up his backpack and dropped the beans and soup inside to eat later, and walked back through the hallway.

He passed a door that was open a crack. Sliding his fingers into the gap, he slowly opened it farther, revealing a dark utility closet. His heart raced when he saw the outline of a water heater. He recalled the documentary about civilians who survived the solar storms of 2055. A man whose name escaped him had lived for three months off the water inside his water heater.

He clicked on his flashlight and swept the beam over the dark space. Crouching, he took one step inside the room. His heart sank when he felt his boot slide through a gooey substance.

He closed his eyes, sucked in a measured breath, and then angled the light at the floor. He knew what the substance was, but wanted to see it with his own eyes. When they snapped open, he saw the remains of an orb.

"My God," he said, pulling his boot out of the sticky material. He was alone after all. There was nothing left of whoever had taken refuge in the closet, nor was there any water left in the small heater, which had a claw mark across the length of the metal.

Alex didn't bother closing the door. The orb was relatively fresh, not the dried-out type he had come across before. He knew the aliens were probably still nearby. Moving slowly across the carpeted floor, he decided to head upstairs. He wanted a view of the block, to see if he was right—to see if they were still there. Gripping the combat knife tightly, he ducked around the next corner and stopped at the bottom of a large wooden staircase that led to the second floor.

The stairs creaked under the weight of his boots, and he cursed under his breath. He winced with each step, every fiber in the wood creaking as he moved.

To his relief, carpet covered the hallway at the top of the stairs. His boots sank silently into the material and for a second he felt a brief reprieve from the fear. The first door to his right led to a bedroom. In the corner he could see a window looking over the street below. To his left was a small bathroom.

He checked the sink first. It was bone dry. Then his eyes fell on the toilet. Never in his life had he thought the sight of a toilet would fill him with such hope. His eyes lit up like a child's on Christmas morning when he lifted the lid and saw a few ounces of cloudy water in the bowl.

Swinging his backpack onto the floor, he crouched and retrieved the straw he had lifted from a fast-food restaurant. The utensil had already come in handy on several occasions. He closed his eyes as he bent to his knees and started sucking the water down his dry throat, trying not to think about the germs. The odd sound echoed through the quiet house, but he no longer cared. All that mattered was water.

When the bowl was dry, he stood to check the tank. It was half full, but the water was a reddish-brown, more than likely a result of rust from the chain.

Was it safe? Did it even matter?

He hesitated, staring at the murky liquid. It could be his last chance to find drinkable water for days. Especially if the Organics were nearby. He couldn't risk entering another house; he had already gotten lucky once.

As he filled his canteen with the reddish-brown water from the tank, an alarming shriek broke through the silence. He fumbled with the bottle, nearly spilling the liquid on the floor. The sound faded away as quickly as it had emerged.

He froze. Several silent seconds passed. Was his mind playing tricks on him? Had the sound just been a fluke? Some pipe creaking in the bowels of the house?

Another screech tore through the stillness.

That was the sound they made. The aliens were close.

The hair on Alex's neck stood up. Another shriek followed. Shocked into motion, he scooped up the last of the water from the tank and rushed back into the hallway. He scanned the passage. Should he risk going downstairs or should he find a place to hide?

He remembered the creaky stairs and decided against trying to escape. Instead, he slipped into the first bedroom. He looked over the room quickly, and saw it was furnished with a twin bed, a nightstand, and a dresser. In the corner of the room, next to the window, there was a tall closest, the perfect hiding place.

Without hesitation he crossed the room and slipped inside, shutting the bifold doors silently behind him. Setting his helmet and pack on the floor, he turned to peek through the crack. The angle gave him the perfect view of a window covered by a thin white curtain.

Beyond the dirty glass he could see movement in the street below. When his eyes finally adjusted to the darkness, he saw them.

There were hundreds of the aliens. The entire ground looked alive, teeming with the creatures. He watched in shock as a pack of Spiders feasted on the remains of the cul-de-sac's residents. The monsters fought over the scraps, shrieking and clawing at one another. His eyes followed the trail of gore to a massive wormlike creature that lay curled up next to a car.

It wasn't the first time he had seen one of them. And, if he survived, it probably would not be the last. He had come across a parking lot the day before filled with the floating blue orbs. He had watched a pair of Worms slither across the blacktop, consuming the spheres and their human prisoners, sucking them almost dry of water before spitting out the remains for the Spiders to feed on.

His heart jumped in his chest as he suddenly felt the sensation of being watched. With trepidation he glanced down to see one of the Spiders staring at him with large, glassy eyes.

Before Alex could slip into the closet's shadows, the creature tilted its head like a curious dog. With bated breath he waited, his heart pumping rapidly inside his chest.

Had it seen him? Could it sense him?

Scratch, scrape, scratch, scrape.

Alex knew what that sound meant.

The Spider *had* seen him. He moved to the window and pulled back the drape. Outside, the creatures skittered around on the blacktop, their mandibles parting to unleash hellish shrieks. He watched in horror as hundreds of eyes stared back up at him, twitching. Never had he seen so many.

He realized that their behavior wasn't that different from his own. The Organics were hungry, and to them, Alex was nothing more than a meal on legs.

CHAPTER 1

DR. Sophie Winston replayed the message on her tablet again. It was the fourth time in as many minutes, but she needed to hear it once more just to be sure it was real.

"This is Alex Wagner with the Biosphere facility at Edwards Air Force Base in California, requesting assistance. Over."

Their mission had been a lie from the beginning. A damned rotten lie straight from the mouth of Dr. Hoffman, the CEO of New Tech Corporation—the man she had thought would lead humanity to a sanctuary on Mars. But there was at least hope: Someone else had survived the invasion, someone who needed help. And if there was one, Sophie knew there would be others.

Dr. Emanuel Rodriguez crossed the mess hall and plopped down on the metal stool across from Sophie. He slid a glass of water to her and with a hesitant smile said, "It's starting to sound like a broken record's playing over here."

Sophie frowned and studied the clear liquid in a way she never had before. At first glance, there was nothing special about it. Then again, gasoline had seemed ordinary before the resource had become scarce.

She met Emanuel's concerned gaze and tried to return his smile.

"You all right?" he asked.

"Yeah, there's just a lot on my mind. Sergeant Overton still can't get a message through to this other Biosphere, and their SOS stopped replaying four days ago. Something catastrophic must have happened," Sophie said.

Emanuel sighed. "Well, then I should probably keep this next comment to myself. I don't want to add to your stress," he said, reaching for her hand.

She smiled but pulled away from his touch, reaching instead to massage her side. The weeks-old injury was healing nicely, but there was still the sporadic pain, and the scar that would be with her for the rest of her life. A slight twinge of pain followed her fingers but quickly faded away.

"Just spill it," she said.

"It's the readings from the drone we sent outside. The temperature is still rising. In the past five weeks, it's already gone up two degrees—and that's about to become three. If this keeps up—"

"We may die before the Organics drain the oceans after all?"

Emanuel nodded. "I'm concerned about the carbon locked away in the polar ice caps. When they melt, it will be released, increasing the greenhouse effect. That's probably why the temperature is rising faster than Alexia calculated."

"My God," Sophie whispered.

Even after five weeks of living in this new world, Sophie still hadn't fully grasped what had happened outside the Biosphere doors. Sure, she'd seen the empty streets, the orbs, and the alien monsters, but it wasn't until she crunched the numbers that it finally became very clear—the planet, and all the life upon it, was taking its last breaths.

She had to remember the positives—the things she was thankful for, starting with the fact that the Biosphere was functioning well and Biome 1 was close to producing its first harvest. They still had power from the solar panels and backup generators for an indefinite amount of time. The reverse magnetic pulse generator they had taken from Luke Williard's bunker was still fully operational. Without the RVM, they would have perished weeks ago. And Sophie couldn't forget Alexia. The AI had proven more useful than she ever imagined.

Sophie reached for the glass of water and took a slow sip, savoring the liquid as it slid down her throat. "What about the oceans?" she asked. "What do we know about their current levels?"

Emanuel shrugged. "It's hard to tell. The only way to really know is to send another drone."

Sophie crossed her arms and watched Emanuel as he compulsively pushed his glasses farther up his nose. It was something he always did before testing a new hypothesis.

"I think we should send the second drone," he said.

"We already discussed this."

"I know, but things have changed. The temperature is rising faster than we thought."

Sophie sighed. They only had two robots. One was in the field, and the other was out of commission. They could fix it, but she didn't want to risk losing them both. "I've said it before: We need to wait for the other drone to get back safely."

The PA system suddenly crackled to life, and Alexia's holographic avatar flickered over a console in the center of the mess hall. "I'm sorry to interrupt, Doctors, but a pressing matter requires your attention," she said in her calm voice. Emanuel spun in his chair. "What ya got, Alexia?"

"Sir, our drone has picked up some unusual activity outside."

Sophie stood, groaning from a jolt of pain. "Unusual?"

"I think it's best if you go look for yourself . . . and I encourage you to go now," Alexia said in a voice that sounded almost frightened. *Can robots feel fear?* Sophie wondered briefly. She shook the thought away and raced out of the mess hall, with Emanuel close behind.

The sound of their footsteps echoed in the narrow passage as they made their way to the command center (CIC). Sergeant Overton met them at the door. He wore a serious face, more pale than usual, but it was his eyes that caused Sophie to skid to a halt. They were wide and intense.

What has he seen? What has Alexia found?

She stood on her toes to get a look at the blurry monitors at the other end of the room, but couldn't see anything besides the flickering glow the devices emanated.

"Will you move, please?" she blurted, her voice anxious.

"I don't think you want to see this, Sophie," Overton replied.

Whatever the drone had relayed to the CIC had turned the battle-hardened sergeant into a silent observer. It was odd not hearing him curse or grumble. Sophie's curiosity grew. The scientist in her wanted to see, *had* to see what it was.

"Excuse me," Sophie said, edging past the marine.

"Don't say I didn't warn you," he said as Emanuel followed her.

Sophie moved up to the monitors and saw the drone had stopped on the edge of a clearing surrounded by a forest of dead trees. Leafless branches swayed in the light breeze, partially obstructing the view.

To the north the ground fell away and dropped several feet into a dry lakebed. Moving across the cracked dirt was a long line of . . . something.

Sophie edged closer to the screens. Squinting, she focused on the shapes as one of them let out a bloodcurdling—and undeniably human—scream.

She clapped her hands together when she realized what they were looking at. The drone had found a group of survivors. So why did Overton seem so disturbed?

When she saw the alien tails of two Sentinels flicking across the dirt, her joy quickly turned to shock. The humans were prisoners, being herded across the lakebed.

The team watched the monitors in helpless silence.

A tiny blue dot flickered on the horizon.

"What's that?" Emanuel asked. He pointed at the light racing across the skyline toward the clearing.

"One of their drones," Overton said.

The ship stopped over the lakebed, filling the empty basin with its blue light. It was then Sophie could see the prisoners' faces. Most of them were children, but there were a few adults among the group. To the south, a pack of Spiders broke through the underbrush and scurried across an old playground. One of them climbed to the top of a slide and shrieked into the night.

The group of humans slowed to a halt. Sounds of terrified, whimpering children filled the CIC. Sophie resisted the urge to cover her ears. Instead, she moved closer to the monitors and watched the Spiders surround the pack of prisoners. It wasn't hard for her to imagine what the aliens would do with them, but somewhere inside her, she still had hope they could be saved. She *had* to believe it.

"Is that—" Overton shoved Sophie and Emanuel to the side. "Holy shit! Is that Thompson and Kiel?"

Sophie squinted. Two men in fatigues moved slowly across the field.

"Holy shit," Overton whispered again. The sight shocked him into motion, and he rushed over to the map of Colorado Springs on a nearby desk, unfolding the edges carefully.

"Thompson? Kiel?" Sophie asked. "Were they part of your team?"

Overton nodded. "Fucking miracle," he mumbled under his breath. "Alexia, can you get me the coordinates of our drone's position?"

"Yes, Sergeant Overton. One moment, please."

A thunderous crash echoed through the room. The spiked tail of a Sentinel suddenly filled the video feed. Spikes swayed past the drone's forward-facing camera. The creature had knocked the drone on its side, tilting the video angle 180 degrees. Now the team could see the entire lakebed.

There was something else.

Sophie didn't believe it at first. Blue rods jutted out of the ground, like enormous electrical poles. They reminded her of sharp teeth biting into the sky. From their tops swung large, dark shapes. *Sacks?*, Sophie thought. *But of what?* And then immediately she knew: they were people. She turned away, blinking rapidly as if trying to clear the image from her memory. But it was too late. The cruciform outlines of bodies suspended on the glowing shafts were tattooed on her mind.

The Organics were farming humans.

Overton's frantic voice rang out behind Sophie, startling her. "We have to help them!"

Sophie's eyes snapped open and she turned to see the marine folding one of the maps in two.

"I need to find Bouma. We have to get out there and help those people."

A wave of anxiety rushed through Sophie as she attempted to compartmentalize what was happening. With bated breath, she moved back to the monitor. One of the bioluminescent Spiders approached the prisoners. With one swift motion it accosted a woman clutching a child to her chest. She screamed as the alien snatched the child from her arms. It scampered away and vanished over the hill.

"Sophie!" Overton yelled.

For a moment she stood there. How was this possible? How was any of this possible?

"Goddamn—" Overton began to shout.

Spinning, Sophie narrowed her eyebrows, rage swelling inside her. "Sergeant. Will you please stop yelling? You are *not* helping our current situation." She watched the marine's face glow red with anger. His lips quivered and then he continued yelling.

"I don't give a fuck! My men are still out there; we have to help them!"

Sophie took a step forward, feeling Emanuel's hand on her shoulder. "You will not leave this Biosphere unless I authorize it. And right now is not the time for a suicide mission!"

Overton regarded her with a cocked brow. "Sophie, I don't think you understand what's at stake here. My men. Those marines," he said, pointing at the display behind her.

"Oh, I completely understand what's at stake. The entire Biosphere is at stake. And if you leave, you put us all at risk. So again, I'm telling you to cool it and stand down until I've figured out what to do."

Overton grunted and then snorted, storming out of the room.

Emanuel loosened his grip on Sophie's shoulder and grabbed her wrist. "It's okay. Just give him some time."

Sophie nodded, her face flushed and breathing labored. She watched the sergeant vanish into the next hallway and then turned back to the monitors.

The same Spider from before emerged at the top of the hill overlooking the lakebed. Sophie could feel the tears rising in her eyes as the alien, cradling the small child between its claws, climbed up one of the poles and attached it to the top with bioluminescent webbing.

Sophie forced herself to watch, but was relieved when the Sentinel's tail whipped into the camera once more, blocking the scene from view.

The crunching sound of metal filled the room as the alien crushed the robot and cut off the video feed for good.

———————

Dr. Holly Brown looked up from her tablet and caught Corporal Bouma staring at her from the kitchen entrance. He glanced away, his cheeks flaring red with embarrassment. She brushed a strand of blond hair behind her ears and cracked a half-smile.

"What are you doing over there?" she called. "Come sit with us." She smiled and moved over to make room for him. As she scooted her chair, an odd sensation raced through her body.

Was it her nerves?

No. She could control those.

This was something else—something she'd ignored for a long time. *Desire.*

She looked up nervously at the marine strolling across the mess hall. His fatigues were snug against his body, highlighting every bit of his muscular chest and arms.

"Holly! Owen won't let me have the ball," Jamie yelled. Holly looked away from the marine and watched Owen and Jamie wrestling on the cafeteria floor. David sat on a bench nearby, his older brother, Jeff, by his side, laughing at the other two.

Seeing them reminded her of the role she played in the Biosphere and how it had changed. At first, she only monitored the team's mental health, and now, on top of that, she was officially the teacher and baby-sitter. Not that she minded. With a PhD in psychology, she was exactly what the kids needed. Without her, the children would surely suffer from post-traumatic stress.

"All right, kids, time for the first lesson of the day." She smiled at Bouma, who took a seat at one of the metal tables. Moans filled the cafeteria as the children dragged themselves over reluctantly.

Bouma laughed. "It's been a while since I was in school."

"I wouldn't exactly call this class, but it's the best we can do for now," Holly said, turning to the AI interface. "Alexia, let's start Lesson Three."

The console glowed to life, and a hologram projected over the table.

"Today we will learn more about early mammals," Alexia said, her hologram emerging over another console in the corner of the room.

Jeff groaned. "Do I really have to sit through this?"

Holly nodded. "Pay attention." She watched the image of a saber-toothed cat scroll across the table.

"Historically, it was believed the saber-toothed cat died out from lack of prey. But scientists have unearthed fossil evidence that reveals the true cause of their extinction: climate change," Alexia narrated.

Holly stared as the cat curled up and wasted away. For a moment, she thought of what an alien narrator might say about the human species someday after unearthing its fossil records. Would they explain how humans had died of the same fate? Would they explain how the Organics had finished what humanity had already started?

She glanced at Bouma. His face was emotionless. He was a marine, after all. The entire reason for his existence was to prevent the same thing from happening to humans that had happened to the saber-toothed cat, to prevent their extinction. But as she studied him—the rifle strapped around his back, the pistol on his hip, and the knife sheathed to his leg—she realized that even brave men like him had little chance of protecting the human race against an invading army like the Organics. Humanity had finally met its match.

CHAPTER 2

EMANUEL swiped his monitor's touch screen and keyed in several codes. The image of the human farms he'd seen only a few hours before was still burned into his brain, but he shook the image away. He didn't have time to think about them, not now. Developing a weapon was the only way he could help those people.

Turning from the monitor, he crossed the room and punched a green button on the side of the closest cryo chamber. The lid cracked open, hissing as soft blue light from the bioluminescent remains of the Spiders spread a cool glow over his face. He stared intensely, fascinated by the alien life-form. The Organics' chemistry was eerily beautiful.

Organics. The name Dr. Hoffman had assigned to the species had been, in Emanuel's opinion, odd. At least it had seemed so until he had started studying their anatomy. After discovering the true composition of the aliens' bodies, the name had grown on him.

As a kid he had always wondered what aliens would look like. It wasn't long before he concluded that they would likely be so vastly different from anything on Earth that even imagining what they looked like was futile. As he got older, their hypothetical appearance was the least interesting part of the equation. He had so many questions. Were they intelligent? What were their bodies made of? Would they communicate telepathically? Would they even communicate at all? He used to wonder if alien life-forms would have a shared conscious; all connected to a central hub, communicating through sonar waves or something similar. But as he examined the creature in front of him, he realized that in some ways, these aliens weren't that different from species found on Earth. They had a central nervous system, a heart, and a very small brain. They even resembled giant insects.

But there were also significant differences that made the Organics very alien. Preliminary scans of the Spider specimens showed their blood consisted of 80.43 percent H_2O and 19.57 percent of a substance similar to plasma. Alexia had concluded the blood had an electrical source, like an internal battery. Emanuel's job was to figure out what that source was. This was the key to developing a weapon.

The biologist couldn't help but smile. While the aliens had effectively wiped humans off the top of the food chain, he found their anatomy to be completely fascinating. He wished Sophie would see just how amazing the creatures were.

He dipped into the cryo chamber to retrieve another specimen with a pair of tweezers. Squeezing the metal tips together, he pulled a translucent piece of flesh from the container, watching it disintegrate right in front of his eyes.

"Damn," he muttered. Without their shields, the Organics' bodies were very fragile. As the skin broke down and dripped around his tweezers in spaghetti strands, he thought back to the first giant squid he had dissected. The composition of its flesh was similar, and the sea creature survived outside of water just about as long as the Organics.

It made sense. After all, humans would die in seconds on other planets. If you took any animal out of its normal habitat, its body would fail very quickly. With their shields, the aliens had found a way to survive in a hostile environment. *Kind of like having a space suit*, he thought. *An electric space suit.*

But what was the power source? And how did it work? If he could find a way to shut it off, then maybe, just maybe, he could design a weapon to destroy them.

He discarded the ruined sample and plucked another specimen from a chunk of spider leg before closing the lid. Even with the chamber cooled by carbon dioxide to minus 60 degrees, the fragile samples were quickly breaking down. It wouldn't be long before they were useless.

Emanuel worked for hours with his right eye pressed against his microscope, performing various tests with different samples. Each test yielded something new, but the most startling discovery was the composition of the Spiders' bones. They were made of some sort of metal. At first he believed it was tungsten, but how could that be? The only examples of biological tungsten were in certain bacteria—nothing like what he was seeing under the scope.

They are made up of elements that won't show up on the periodic table from your high school chemistry class.

Dr. Hoffman's words replayed themselves in Emanuel's head. It wasn't surprising that an alien life-form would be made up of foreign elements. Ever since scientists had discovered bacteria that fed off the ocean vents, there had been a growing belief in the scientific community that alien life could survive in habitats previously thought to be unsurvivably hostile.

After performing more tests, he realized the metal was an element unlike any he had ever seen. Its density was about the same as tungsten's, but its melting point was much lower, at only 1,000 degrees Fahrenheit.

Does the metallic element conduct electricity to power their shields? If so, then what's the damned source? Emanuel wondered. He was frustrated. Understanding the aliens' defense system was the key to developing a weapon. He knew the magnetic disturbance outside had something to do with it, but connecting the dots was like putting together a puzzle without all the pieces.

He shook his head, his mind drifting from one idea to the next. With an audible huff, he pressed his eye against the microscope and squinted. Twisting the dial with his right hand, he magnified the specimen several more levels. The sudden thrill of excitement that only a new discovery could generate rushed through him. He was staring at something new—something that didn't seem to belong.

Could it be?

He manipulated the sample until one of the peppercorn-like clusters came into focus. He leaned back, rubbed his eyes, and then looked back into the scope.

"Alexia, are you seeing this?"

"Yes, Doctor."

He straightened his back, wondering if he should inform Sophie of the discovery. *Not yet*, he thought. He needed to know more first.

Transferring the image to the closest screen, he swiveled the display to face him. He ran a hand through his neatly groomed hair and laughed. For weeks he had been looking for the source of the creatures' defenses, and it had been right in front of him the entire time. It was just too small to see without an electron microscope.

"It's nanotechnology. Nanobots, if you want to be specific," he said. "How the hell did we miss this, Alexia?"

"With all due respect, Doctor, there was simply no evidence of nanotechnology in the preliminary samples," Alexia replied politely.

He waved his hands. "It's not a big deal. I'm just glad we finally know."

"Sir?" Alexia asked.

"The source," Emanuel replied quickly. "The electrical source for their blood. These bots must be electrically charged, and the Organics' bones conduct the current." He suddenly paused and pursed his lips, realizing he still didn't know the third piece to the puzzle.

"But what charges the bots?" he asked aloud.

Alexia's image transferred to the AI console next to Emanuel. Her face solidified into a translucent blue. Blinking, she said, "The magnetic disturbance, Doctor. I believe it's the source of everything."

"That had occurred to me, but I don't understand how it's possible."

"With all due respect, Doctor, two months ago you probably didn't think floating blue orbs were possible either."

Emanuel chuckled and looked up at the wall camera. "Since when did you develop a sense of humor?"

"I'm not sure I follow you, Doctor."

"I was joking," he replied. Then he snapped his gloves off, placed the sample under one of Alexia's interface scanners, and said, "Please conduct a full scan of this specimen. I want any data loaded to my tablet as soon as possible."

"Where are you going?" she asked.

"To grab some coffee," he replied on his way out of the room.

Alexia's voice transferred to the com closest to the door. "Wait," she said.

He turned, wondering what her scans could have found so quickly.

"Doctor Rodriguez," she said. "Sir, do you realize you have discovered a new element?"

Emanuel smiled broadly. "Indeed I do, Alexia."

"Traditionally, the scientist who makes the discovery is tasked with creating a name. Have you thought of one yet?"

He paused for a second, considering his options. "I think I'll call it humanitarium," he said with a chuckle before heading to the kitchen. "Humanity needs *something* to call our own."

By the time Emanuel reached the coffee dispenser, data from the scan was crawling across his tablet. Looking down, he read the first line and almost dropped his cup.

"What the hell?" he muttered.

"Remarkable, isn't it, Doctor Rodriguez?"

"How?" He felt paralyzed with questions, unsure what to ask first.

"Even though the Organic entity is technically dead, the nanobots inside the bloodstream are still emitting very small traces of electricity. They are much weaker now and are not able to power the creature's defenses. But they seem to be searching for something, moving through the bloodstream as if they are trying to connect."

"Connect to what?"

"To the magnetic disturbance, Doctor."

"That's impossible . . ." Emanuel began. With a flick of his index finger, he sent the image to the wall monitor. He stared at the screen intensely, pushing his glasses higher on his nose. A theory was developing in his mind. It would more than likely require a field test, and as much as he hated the idea of running it by Sophie without knowing if it would work, he also knew they were running out of time. The Organics were farming humans—survivors that had lived through the invasion. And he was going to find a way to save them.

ENTRY 1890
DESIGNEE: AI ALEXIA

Since its collision with the Sentinel's tail, the video feed from the robot I sent into the field has been fading in and out. While I wait for the feed to clear, I pull up video the drone relayed before the feed was lost. The drone has confirmed the presence of three different alien species. Video 1 shows a dozen of the arachnid-like creatures hunting a deer on the outskirts of Colorado Springs. The animal is severely dehydrated and unable to outrun the creatures.

After a brief struggle, the Spiders overwhelm it and wrap it in a glowing blue web. Moments later the web pulsates and a blue field surrounds the animal. What happens next is fascinating. The orb fills with liquid, and the carcass inside begins to break down. The time lapse indicates the entire process takes about six hours, at which point one of the harvester Worms slithers through the forest, inhales the orb, and emits a ray of blue mist into the sky.

Another feed shows a pair of Sentinels standing guard over a parking lot full of blue orbs. The Sentinels remain frozen, watching over the field with their reptilian eyes.

The feed from the robot's camera finally clears, and the image of another parking lot emerges in real time.

If I had been programmed to believe in luck, I would attribute the drone's survival to it. But *luck* is a human term, a word made up to illustrate situations where someone or something defies the odds.

Statistically, the drone has already beaten the odds. It has been in the field for a week, and the data it has relayed has taught the team much about the Organics. After studying the creatures for several weeks, I have come to the same conclusions as Dr. Rodriguez. They seem to exhibit behavior similar to that of insects. They work together toward the common goal of finding and processing water. However, the Spiders, Sentinels, and Worms are clearly not creatures capable of interstellar travel. These three species appear to be the workers. Something much more sophisticated must be relaying orders from the safety of spaceships high above, in Earth's orbit.

I reset the robot's control system. Then I relay a set of coordinates to the drone's GPS. The wheels automatically obey, and in less than a second the machine is moving across the parking lot, silently zipping across the blacktop toward a pile of what looks like miniature versions of the deadly orbs. They appear to be eggs of some kind. The drone eases to a stop near one of the eggs to take a sample. It's a job that requires precision: Cut too deep, and the outer layer is compromised. The robot gently removes a small fragment of the egg's skin. Then the tiny metal claw retracts and places the specimen into a container in its cargo hold. If I had to use a human term, I would say I am satisfied with the results. The drone has performed its function, and I, in monitoring it, have performed mine.

Drone is perhaps too generous a term for the machine. Engineers would call it a retrofitted maintenance robot, fully equipped with solar panels and rigged with additional cameras to ensure that it collects as much data as possible. Ideally, it would also be able to monitor radiation and carbon dioxide levels as well, but the video feed and sample collection capability are still informative.

A sensor goes off in the medical ward, and I pull up the feed to Camera 14. Dr. Rodriguez is still studying the new element he has discovered and has pinged me for assistance.

"How may I help you, Dr. Rodriguez?"

"Alexia, I'd like you to take a look at this when you have a moment," Dr. Rodriguez says, without looking up from his microscope. I pull up the data on my display so that I can see what he sees. The information is . . . unexpected. He has made a startling discovery.

"Doctor Rodriguez, I see you have found a way to reverse the effects of the Organics' defenses."

Emanuel looks up at my camera sternly. "I think it's time for another meeting."

CHAPTER 3

SOPHIE had a good view of the mess hall from the hallway. It was odd seeing the empty seats where, only weeks before, her fallen teammates Timothy and Saafi had sat experimenting with their tablets. Next to the vacant chairs was a bench full of children—the last thing she would have expected to see at the beginning of their mission, before the world ended. With the loss of marine Eric Finley, there were now almost as many kids as adults.

Overton and Bouma spoke at the adjacent table. They both wore worried looks, their faces cold as stone. It had taken the sergeant a while to calm down after seeing his men in the video, but since their argument, he hadn't pushed the issue further. Perhaps shutting him down back in the CIC was the right thing to do after all.

The sound of laughter distracted Sophie from the marines' serious conversation. Nearby, Holly entertained the children with a cartoon on her tablet. The sound of laughing kids filled the room, and Sophie remembered that there was still much to be thankful for.

Behind her a chipper male voice echoed down the hallway. "Hope you have some good news."

"I hope you do too," she replied, turning to see that Emanuel had snuck up on her. "We definitely need it." His face was animated, more so than normal. It could only mean one thing—he'd made a discovery.

"Found something, didn't you?"

He showed off his dimples with a wide smile and said, "Maybe."

As they approached the group, Sophie watched Overton stiffen.

Sophie summoned her business face. Clearing her throat, she said, "Listen up, everyone. There are quite a few things we need to discuss." Taking a deliberately slow breath, she swiped her tablet and pulled up a set of notes. Out of the corner of her eye, she caught Owen's curious gaze. For a moment she wondered what the little boy was thinking, and whether he even knew what was going on outside. He'd lost both of his parents at such a young age.

Images of the human farms instantly popped into her mind. She didn't want the kids to know about them. Not if they didn't have to. "Jeff, would you do me a favor? Will you take David, Owen, and Jamie to the garden biome? I want them to see how pretty it looks with the growing plants."

The boy rolled his eyes but paced over to Holly's table and took the younger children by the hand, leading them out of the mess hall and down into the personnel quarters.

Sophie watched them vanish around the corner before motioning for Emanuel to take a seat with a short nod. "While they're out of the room, I'll start with the human farms. By now you've all seen or heard about them. We know they exist. We know there are other survivors." She paused and looked around the room at each member of her team. "I also know, Sergeant, that you want to attempt a rescue mission."

Overton sat up in his chair, poised like a snake, his fingers massaging the handle of his .45. But he didn't reply. Sophie knew he was waiting for his opportunity to strike. She wasn't going to let him.

"This was a very hard decision to make, but I'm not authorizing any rescue operation. We've gone down that road before, and each time we've lost good people—Saafi, Timothy, Finley. I'm not losing anyone else. We're safe inside, and until we have some way to fight back, some sort of weapon, I'm not going to put any more of my people at risk."

"Your people?" Overton burst out of his chair, his voice growing louder. "*Your* people? That's bullshit. What about *my* people? What about the people that are dying out there on our watch?"

Sophie flinched. She felt a flurry of anger rise up in her throat. How dare he question her motives? Everything she had done, she had done for the Biosphere. For her team. She slammed a fist on the counter, silencing him. "Yes, Sergeant. *My* people. This is my Biosphere, and until further notice you are to sit down and take *my* orders!"

Some mixture of shock and latent respect for the chain of command silenced Overton. He sat glaring at her, his face glowing red. Bouma crossed his arms, a look of shock plastered across his features. The tension in the room was palpable, but she had to keep going.

"Now, as I said earlier: We need some sort of weapon. Emanuel has already been hard at work on this project for the past couple of weeks. And unless anyone has any further outbursts, he's going to give us an update." Sophie turned to Emanuel and forced a smile. "You're up."

The biologist ran a nervous hand through his hair before pushing his glasses farther up onto his nose. It was apparent he didn't want to be part of the growing power struggle between her and Overton.

Clenching his teeth, Emanuel said, "Alexia, please bring up specimen ninety-four X."

A three-dimensional image shot out of the console nearest the team and rotated slowly in front of them.

Bouma scowled. "What the hell is that?"

"That, sir, is one of the most important discoveries in the history of modern science," Emanuel said with a confident smile. "Alexia, enhance image."

He took a step away from the hologram and waited for it to enlarge. "These are the remains of one of the Organics' bones. Unfortunately, there wasn't much left after you decided to unload a magazine into them a few weeks ago," Emanuel said.

Bouma shrugged. "What did you want me to do, let them kill everyone?"

"As I was saying," Emanuel continued, "the creature is made up of many of the same elements we see in the anatomy of animals here on Earth. There is one big difference: their bones. Their bones are made up of a new element that is very similar to tungsten."

"Isn't that a metal?" Holly asked.

"Yes, a very dense metal."

"Can you get to the point already?" Overton griped. "You forget we aren't scientists. Ever heard of speaking in layman's terms?"

Sophie watched Emanuel pause. She knew it upset him that no one appreciated the science behind his discoveries, besides her.

Sighing, Emanuel continued. "Like all metals, this new element—which I've decided to call humanitarium—conducts electricity. But the electrical source, well that's a bit more complicated," he said, gesturing toward the AI console. "Alexia, bring up the image of the nanobot."

A few moments later the peppercorn-shaped hologram emerged. Emanuel smiled confidently. "Billions of these nanobots carry a small electrical charge through the Organics' systems. The charge is conducted through the aliens' bones, effectively creating a force field," he said. "As you know, without their shields, the aliens are actually very fragile. In fact, the creatures can't survive at all without them."

Bouma instantly raised a hand in protest. "No, that doesn't make sense. I've knocked their defenses out with electromagnetic grenades, and they keep coming."

"You didn't knock out their defenses entirely," Emanuel said. "You see, the nanobots act kind of like little batteries—so even with your grenades, their shields still functioned, but at a lower level. When their shields are low, the aliens are susceptible to human weapons. If you remove their shields entirely, they succumb to our atmosphere."

"So you are saying we need to find a way to knock out their shields altogether?" Holly asked.

Bouma smacked his palm on the table. "Like a massive electromagnetic pulse grenade?"

"Precisely," Emanuel replied. "But there is a catch. Alexia thinks the electromagnetic disturbance is the source that actually powers the nanobots, essentially recharging them."

"I'm impressed, really," Sophie said. "The discovery of humanitarium, the nanobots, and the source could be a game changer. But this is all academic. We need something practical. We need a weapon *now*."

The image of the nanobot disappeared and Alexia's face appeared over the console. "I would like to answer that, Doctor Winston."

Sophie nodded her approval and sat down to listen to the AI.

"I've been studying the disturbance outside ever since we sent the drone into the field. Without an EMP simulator or a similar device, it has been difficult to learn much about it, but the drone was able to detect and determine that the wavelength the Organics used to knock out our communications is constant," she said. "As you may know, an EMP is typically a one-time event; once it is set off, the damage is done quite quickly. This is something entirely different. Take a look."

Her hologram transformed into a solid blue ninety-degree angle. A sudden pulse burst across the graphic, curving and making a steep climb until it suddenly flatlined.

Emanuel pushed his glasses farther up his nose. "So this is world-wide?"

"Yes, Doctor."

"And it hasn't changed since day one of the invasion?" Sophie asked.

"That is correct," Alexia replied over the com. "As you can see, the wavelength has a defined lead point. It built up rapidly and then evened out, but it did not dissipate, as you would expect with a human-generated EMP."

"It's like one big surge," Bouma said under his breath.

"Let's cut the crap. How do you shut this surge off?" Overton asked, placing a dirty boot on one of the middle tables. He glanced defiantly at Sophie, who met his gaze. Neither looked away.

"That *is* a good question," Emanuel said, breaking the tension.

Alexia's voice sounded distant. "My apologies, but I'm unable to determine the source of the surge."

"So it could be coming from the Statue of Liberty, or from the moon for all we know," Overton replied.

"It would make more sense if it were coming from the Earth's orbit," Alexia replied.

Sophie felt her lips moving, but she couldn't form the words. She knew the source was likely Mars. After all, she'd found that the magnetic disturbance that caused the solar storms of 2055 originated on the Red Planet. But the government had never released that information. It was classified, and NTC had threatened her career in order to keep her quiet. Folding her hands, Sophie kept her lips sealed. She didn't want another reason to piss Overton off.

"If we don't know the source, how can we shut it off?" Bouma asked.

"Maybe we won't have to," Sophie replied. "The electromagnetic grenades knock out the Spiders' shields almost completely, right?" Sophie asked.

"Yes," Bouma said.

"So, we just need something more powerful. To reverse the surge and use it against them," Sophie said.

Overton reached for a cigarette, but his hands came back empty. "Shit," he muttered. Looking back at Sophie he said, "I know where you're going with this. There are large-scale EMPs like the one used on China years ago. But nothing I know that has ever been used on a worldwide level. But . . ."

"Go on," Sophie said, cautiously.

"Setting off several strategically placed, high-capacity EMPs at fifty thousand feet would probably do the trick. We would just have to find a way into a military installation with high-yield EMPs and reconfigure them, then find a way to deliver the payloads into the atmosphere."

"Impossible," Bouma said.

Jeff suddenly burst out of the hallway. "My dad said nothing was impossible. We have to at least try." With a huff, he leaned against the doorframe.

Sophie looked over at the boy. He was thin, with a strong jaw, thick black hair, and bushy brown eyebrows. He was probably the spitting image of what Emanuel had looked like at nine years old.

"Your dad was right, Jeff, but that was in the old world," Holly said, patting the seat next to her. "Come sit down, sweetheart."

Jeff didn't move. His eyes darted from her to Overton. "I don't know what's wrong with you guys. But there are people outside that need help. Sitting around and talking about how impossible things are isn't helping them!"

A surge of anxiety rushed through Sophie as Overton stood. She knew exactly what was coming and braced herself.

"The kid's right. We can't just sit here and let survivors waste away." Overton paused, cocking a brow, the scar on his cheek stretching. For a minute he looked like a crazed old man. Locking eyes with Sophie, he said, "Should I have left you, Emanuel, and Saafi to die outside? Should I have let that alien drone take you?"

Sophie cringed. The marine was a skilled killer, but he was also skilled at manipulation, and knew exactly where to strike. But she hadn't built a career by letting others push her around.

"I seem to remember saving your ass back at Denver International. Remember that Sentinel I dropped?" Sophie shot back. "Besides, the situation isn't the same. Those people are heavily guarded."

Overton snorted his response, wiping a sleeve across his face.

"That's why we *need* to develop a weapon," Emanuel said. He turned to Sophie. "I'm getting close. I just need more time. I'm modifying the RVM so it can knock out the Organics' defenses on a larger scale than our electromagnetic grenades."

"Can you at least wait until then?" Sophie asked Overton. She turned to see Overton jerk his chin toward the exit. Bouma followed him across the room and they vanished into the hallway. Sophie closed her eyes and counted to five. The sergeant was really beginning to test her patience.

CHAPTER 4

THE brilliant tail of a shooting star filled Alex's HUD before it faded into the night sky. He doubled over, desperately trying to catch his breath. Slowly the floating stars before his eyes cleared, and the dizziness faded. He'd been on the run for several hours, just narrowly evading hundreds of thirsty Spiders.

He was deep in the desert now, lost in the endless sea of sand and guided only by the full moon above. His legs ached, his muscles groaning in protest with every step. He'd felt like this for days now. There was no reprieve. No safety. No salvation. And he couldn't keep willing himself on. His body was nearing its breaking point. In hours, maybe minutes, he would collapse from exhaustion and dehydration.

Fortunately, Alex was no stranger to physical pain or fatigue. He never would have thought college football had taught him lessons about surviving the apocalypse, but then again, he'd never believed in aliens before, either.

Those grueling practices had given him more than physical stamina—they had given him the mental fortitude he needed to survive in the heat with little nutrition. He could remember the practices like they were yesterday: his face baking inside his helmet, the spike of pain when he would get speared attempting to catch a ball too close to a defender and, most of all, the thirst on those one-hundred-degree days. There was nothing like the lust for water . . .

Another shooting star raced across his HUD. He turned to watch it disappear into the sky, eager to give his mind a break from his own thoughts.

Alex glanced at his mission clock, shocked to see it was 3:42 A.M.

Had he really been traveling for over eight hours?

He collapsed onto a nearby boulder, his body rebelling against the thought of one more step. With a click, he unfastened his helmet and lifted it just far enough so he could take a tiny sip from what was left of the water in his canteen.

Swishing the water around in his mouth, he savored it, letting it slide down his throat instead of forcing it down with a gulp. He desperately wanted more, but instead, he capped the canteen and reached for his two-way radio.

At a swipe of his finger, the display glowed to life, and the same flat wavelength he had seen for the past week raced across the screen.

"Please work," Alex whispered.

He checked the channel one more time.

Nothing.

Jumping to his feet, he reattached the radio to its clip and prepared to continue his journey through the sand. He knew he couldn't sleep until he found shelter. It wasn't safe out here, where he was exposed like a cadaver on an autopsy table.

Traveling was just as dangerous by night as it was by day. The only slight difference between the two was the ways he could die. The desert was a treacherous place in the dark. Even with his night vision, he had only narrowly missed falling into sand traps. One wrong step would send him to the bottom of a hole lined with jagged rocks and sharp tree branches.

There were also the dust storms that could emerge at a moment's notice. At least during the day he could see them coming. Several nights he had been startled awake by the nightmarish roar of the storms barreling down on him. These amazing feats of Mother Nature frightened him almost as badly as the aliens hunting him. He had seen images of men caught out in the open during one of the harrowing events; their clothes and flesh torn away like meat.

He listened to the calm whistling of the wind in the distance. Tonight, he was lucky—a radiant moon guided him around the sand traps and away from the Organics. He didn't have to rely on his annoying night vision.

Hours later, Alex climbed out of the valley and stood on a sand dune overlooking the ocean. Somewhere in the distance he could hear the faint sound of a drone hunting for contacts. The hum of the alien technology was unmistakable, even from afar.

He scanned the sky for signs of the ship, but it was already miles away. He caught a glimpse of blue on the horizon just as the tiny craft disappeared into the night.

Another small victory, another lucky break.

Yes, he could call it that. Today he had dodged death more than once.

His eyes returned to the ocean, where he could make out the broken hulls of boats protruding from the sand. Had the beach receded even farther in only a few days' time?

There was no way to be sure. With the drone out of sight, he plopped onto the soft sand to check his two-way radio again.

His heart thumped in his chest as he pulled the radio from the clip on his back. The screen glowed to life, forming an orange halo of light around his helmet. He cupped his hand over the top of the radio to cut down on the glow.

Make yourself a target, Alex. Nice move, he thought. A horizontal line raced across the display—the same one he had been staring at for days. Like a flatlining EKG, he was as good as dead.

"Shit!" he yelled, anger suddenly taking hold. He tossed the useless radio down the side of the dune. The device sailed through the air and clattered off the top of a boulder. He watched it land on the ground below, the orange light vanishing as a blast of wind covered it with sand.

At first he didn't even get up. Why should he? The radio was trash. Nothing but added weight on his belt.

He flinched when the sound of another drone broke through the night. This one was louder, closer. He jumped to his feet and scanned the skyline. Sure enough another drone raced across the black sky.

Shocked into motion, he stumbled down the slope, the added adrenaline giving him a boost of energy he hadn't known he had left in him. An overwhelming fear penetrated his thoughts.

He ran like a man possessed, sand exploding behind him as he moved as fast as his exhausted body would allow. Halfway to the bottom of the dune, his foot snagged on a buried root, which snapped under his weight, ripping clean out of the sand and throwing him off balance.

"No, no, no!" he yelled, trying to regain his balance. It was too late. He tripped, and the world went topsy-turvy. His visor hit the sand first, and he slid several feet before hitting the bottom of the dune with a thud.

Alex knew sand was much like water. It appeared soft, but land on it with enough force and there wasn't much difference between that and hitting concrete.

The sound of his right wrist snapping echoed in his helmet before he felt the pain. He bit back a cry as he lay on his back and watched the drone approaching in the sky. The blue light swept over the area around him, searching, searching.

He resisted the urge to close his eyes, knowing that it wouldn't do any good. After a moment the alien rover moved on, its blue eye darting from dune to dune.

Realizing he was holding his breath, Alex let out a huff. The explosion of air fogged his visor momentarily. When it cleared, he fumbled to his feet, holding his injured arm to his chest. He scanned the landscape for a place to hide. Somewhere. Anywhere. Nothing but miles of beach filled his HUD.

And then he saw it.

A boat.

He was running before he consciously made the decision to move. Although his body instinctively acted to survive, deep down he knew it was only a matter of time before he was captured or killed. It was a miracle he had evaded the aliens this long. One of the soldiers in the Biosphere, a stone-faced man named Blake Will, had told him that the aliens had a way of scanning for water. It was a wonder they hadn't slurped Alex up like a cocktail yet.

The thought sent a tremor down his entire body, motivating him to run even faster, to push just a bit harder. His muscles ached, but he didn't dare risk slowing down to look behind him. His eyes remained focused on the boat.

The moist sand made him feel like he was running through Silly Putty.

A hysterical laugh escaped his lips. Was any of this even real? Six months ago, he had been teaching a high school science class over a thousand miles away. Now he was trying to hide from an alien drone that wanted the water inside him.

Everyone he had ever known was probably dead. His ex-wife, his parents. All of his friends. His sister, Maria.

Everyone.

Alex suddenly felt very tired. Out of everyone he had lost, it was Maria he was going to miss the most. They had been best friends since they were kids, and even when she had moved halfway across the country, they had still managed to find time to talk every day, by e-mail if not by video chat. He hadn't even been able to say good-bye before getting sealed in the Biosphere.

In a split second, his muscles locked up, his feet dug into the sand. His body had finally accepted what his mind had known for days—there was no reason to continue.

The thought of his sister trapped in one of those terrible blue orbs, of her body being mummified by the Spiders, was too much. It was all just too fucking much.

As he lay down on the sand, he listened to the thunderous beating of his heart. There were other sounds, too: the sound of the alien drone zipping across the sky, the sapphire waves crashing against the receding shoreline, and something else. A chirping noise. A bird? No, he hadn't seen one for days.

This noise was mechanical. And it was coming from a few feet away.

Rolling onto his stomach, he reached for the source of the sound, digging through the sand. Seconds later, his fingers uncovered his radio. It took him several more precious moments to realize the jagged wavelength pulsing across the display was real. There was someone else out there.

Alex quickly cradled the radio close to him and swiped the screen with his uninjured hand.

"This is Doctor Emanuel Rodriguez with the Cheyenne Mountain Biosphere. Does anyone copy? Over."

Was he hallucinating?

Alex looked down at his radio and saw the frequency wavelength rise to a peak and then fade away. He could see the drone racing its way through his peripheral vision, but he didn't turn. He kept his eyes locked on the radio.

"I repeat, does anyone copy? Over."

Alex fumbled with the device, slapping it on its side. "This is Alex Wagner. I'm the sole survivor of the Biosphere at Edwards Air Force Base. I've been on the run for several days, and I have no idea where the hell I am. I'm being hunted by those *things*."

He didn't care if his voice drew the drone to his location. If he was going to die, he at least wanted someone else to know what had happened to him. He needed to know that someone else had survived. That he wasn't the last person alive on the planet.

"We heard your message weeks ago, Mr. Wagner. And it's damned good to know you're still alive."

"Yeah, well, I won't be alive long if I don't get the hell out of here. Those things are hunting me."

"Can you tell us your coordinates? We're a long way from Edwards, but if you sit tight, maybe we can find a way to help you."

Alex almost laughed as he scanned the beach. Tell them his coordinates? He had no idea where the hell he was. All he knew was that he was on a beach somewhere in California. He doubted that was what the doctor wanted to know.

"Alex, are you still there?"

"Yeah, man, but I don't know where the hell I am."

"Just stay calm. We need you to stay alive. We are developing a weapon here. A weapon that can change the course of this war."

Alex closed his eyes and tried to think. How far had he traveled since escaping the base? What direction had he walked in? The whipping wind and the approaching alien ship made it hard to think. But the ambient sound of the crashing waves was so beautiful, so peaceful. For weeks he had been searching desperately for water. Now a seemingly endless supply was in front of him.

He sat there watching the waves crash against the hull of the boat, and then it hit him.

They have a way of scanning for water.

Blake's words replayed in Alex's mind. If the drone was homing in on him because of the water inside his body, then he should be able to evade the craft in the ocean. It should camouflage him long enough to get away.

Dr. Rodriguez repeated his message.

The distant hum of the drone grew closer. Alex's heart thumped inside his chest. "I'm being fucking hunted! I can't just sit tight! Hold on," Alex replied, clipping the radio to his belt.

He could hear Emanuel's worried voice crackle with protest over the channel as he raced toward the water. The outline of the waves grew larger with every step. He was almost there.

And then the craft was hovering over him, the bright beam from the ship's underbelly scanning the beach.

He pushed on, his knees creaking and his calves tightening.

He high-jumped over the smaller waves until he was knee-deep in the ocean. In one final thrust, he dove into a monstrous wave and disappeared into the water. Pain from his broken right wrist raced down his arm as he clawed his way through the water.

After he cleared the first wave, he began to front crawl. With every stroke, he could feel the warm salt water trickle into his suit through the tear in its sleeve.

Fuck.

Anxiety paralyzed him as he realized how screwed he really was. This far out, the ocean floor had dropped away from him like a steep, underwater cliff. If he slipped beneath the surface, his suit would fill and he would drown. If he kept his arm above the waves, then the ship would surely capture him.

Neither was a particularly appealing option.

Another wave crashed against his body, sending him tumbling under the water. He screamed in anger, the desperate sound of his own panicked voice filling his helmet.

Reaching down, he tried to cover the gash with his other hand, but it was no use. The water flooded into his armor.

He was going to drown.

He slipped deeper beneath the surface as the torrential current and his water-laden armor pulled him farther down into the abyss. Pawing the water frantically, he kicked toward the surface with every ounce of energy he had left. Dying wasn't easy. It actually required a lot of work. Or maybe he was just really lucky. Either way, he knew what he needed to do if he wanted to live—he had to shed the armor.

Before the next wave hit, he hunched over to take off his boots. The rest of the suit had to be removed by unfastening several metal clasps. The damned thing was difficult enough to take off on land. It was going to be next to impossible in the water.

But he had to try.

He reached for the neck clasp first. It opened with little resistance and he felt the armor covering his back and chest pop open. Another wave sent him spinning before he had a chance to remove it. By the time his body stopped rotating, he was too dizzy to move.

The taste of salt water spurred him back into motion. He reached for the two clasps on his belt. The one on the right clicked open, but the left wouldn't budge.

Alex sucked in another deep breath, immediately choking on the water as it continued to fill his helmet.

Get it together!

Alex calmed his breathing. He spit the salt water out of his mouth and reached back down to the other clasp on his belt. This time, it popped open. He grabbed the radio and then kicked out of the bottom half of his armor.

With his body free of its metal prison, he let the current take him again. He had bought himself minutes, just enough time to regain some strength.

When the water in his helmet reached his mouth he closed his eyes and took one last breath through his nostrils before unfastening it and ducking beneath the surface.

And then there was only darkness.

He could feel his body spinning but had no idea in which direction. Ten seconds passed. He could still feel his legs—they were on fire, every inch of muscle burning.

Another couple seconds passed. So did the agonizing pain.

After thirty seconds his eyes snapped open, the salt water burning them immediately. Something had changed.

The beam was gone.

So was the drone.

The irony was not lost on him. He had been camouflaged by the very resource the aliens had come for. In the end, water was what protected him from the alien ship.

He kicked violently upward. Just when his lungs felt like they were going to burst, his head exploded through the surface. Above him, the stars dazzled like a field of orbs, sparkling in the darkness. Somewhere out there was the aliens' home world.

The current was getting stronger, pulling him farther out to sea. He watched, too tired to swim back against it, as the shoreline diminished until it was just a thin ribbon of yellow sand in the distance. He had been fighting for so long—to escape the Biosphere, to escape the Spiders, to find water. And for what? Everyone he had ever cared about was dead. He didn't know this Dr. Rodriguez. For all he knew, the man would soon be dead, too.

The water felt cool and warm around him as the waves lapped against his bare skin. Time slowed to a crawl. Maybe he would just float here for a while until the water took him. Float and maybe sleep. He was so tired. It wasn't such a bad way to go out; his vision slowly fading to darkness, his body simply giving up, his lungs filling with salt water—certainly better than being torn apart by the aliens or turned into an orb. He leaned his head back and closed his eyes. *Yes,* he thought. *Much better than being turned into an orb.*

He was going to join Maria in a place where the monsters couldn't get him anymore.

CHAPTER 5

SOPHIE splashed water on her face. The liquid immediately cooled her flushed cheeks. She hardly recognized the face in the mirror: a pair of brown eyes sunken and framed with more wrinkles than she ever remembered having. And the worst part? She reached for a long gray hair protruding from her dirty-blond ponytail. She yanked it from her scalp and dropped it into the sink. The hair swirled several times around the drain, as if it knew what awaited it below. Sophie empathized. She knew better than anyone—well, anyone besides Alexia—how bad the odds were, and what horrors awaited the survivors outside.

She thought again of the Spider cradling that young boy as it climbed the pole and attached the helpless child to the alien structure. It made her stomach lurch, and she rushed over to the toilet to hurl up the remnants of her dinner. Coughing, she pushed herself away from the toilet seat and back to the sink. Her bloodshot eyes stared back at her from the mirror.

How had it come to this?

Wiping her mouth, she stepped into the hallway and made her way to her room. Collapsing on her bed, she allowed herself a moment to sob into the pillow. The sound of footfalls rang in the hallway outside her room. *Please go away,* she thought, *I just want to be alone.*

"Sophie?" Emanuel said from the open doorway.

With a deep breath she sat up and shielded her eyes with her left sleeve, holding out her right hand like a stop sign. "I'm fine, Emanuel. Really. I'm fine."

Emanuel ignored her lie and rushed to her side. "Sophie," he said, grabbing her hand. He inched closer, putting his other hand on her back and gently massaging the knotted muscles there. "You can't keep all this pent up inside. It doesn't do any good. What we've seen can't be unseen. The best we can do is share the burden. Be there for each other. Without that, what do we have?"

The question lingered in the air. Sophie knew he was right; she needed to confide in him now more than ever. She had isolated herself from the group over the past few days. She couldn't let that continue; she had to be a leader.

"Maybe Sergeant Overton's right," she said. "Maybe we should try and help the survivors now. Take a chance. We've done it before."

He shook his head. "No. Give me a chance to build us a weapon that works. I'm so close, Sophie. Now that I've discovered the source of their defenses . . . " His face filled with excitement.

Sophie laughed, snorting and sniffling in the same moment, a sound that only made her laugh harder. They both chuckled together, and she rested her head against his shoulder, turning away so he couldn't see her red, puffy eyes. His fingers twined with hers, and a tingle warmed her numb body.

"It's okay," Emanuel whispered in her ear. "You made the right choice."

Sophie nodded, leaning into his grasp. She wanted to feel safe in his arms. But deep down, she knew things would not be okay—deep down, she was losing hope.

In his quarters, Overton slowly slid a sharp razor over the stubble on his jaw.

It was tradition.

Before he went to war, he shaved. There was something about going into battle with a freshly shaved face and head that made the killing feel more civilized. It was cleaner.

Over the years, he had killed countless men. It had never really disturbed him. Even his first registered kill in San Juan hadn't bothered him that much. From the beginning of his long career, he had been a recruiter's dream, the type of man who didn't need convincing to sign on the dotted line. The type of man the government didn't need to invest millions of dollars brainwashing.

He was the perfect marine: never questioning orders, never wavering, and, best of all, always following through, even when things got tough. His commitment to the military was also what made him a lousy husband and father.

"Shit!" he hissed as the blade nicked his jaw. A trail of bright red blood began flowing down his chin. He wiped it away with a towel and put pressure on the nick with a finger while continuing to shave with his other hand.

Adrenaline swirled in his bloodstream. He wasn't sure if it was from the sting of the cut or the thought of saving Thompson and Kiel. Two members of his squad had survived the initial attack after all. And he would be damned if he let them die now, no matter what Sophie had to say.

With one final, swift stroke of the blade he stared into the mirror at his clean face. He was ready again for war.

ENTRY 1891
DESIGNEE: AI ALEXIA

There is no program in my system that can accurately describe what I have observed over the past five weeks. In fact, there may not be an algorithm designed that could explain what has occurred beyond the Biosphere doors. And no matter what program I run, I cannot seem to find a way to explain the fact that Dr. Winston and her team are still alive.

A human might say this is a miracle. I acknowledge that anomalies are inevitable. Isaac Asimov once said, "The saddest aspect of life right now is that science gathers knowledge faster than society gathers wisdom." As I continue to . . . *feel*, I suppose is the only proper word for it, I wonder if it is possible that there is more to the team's survival than what my programs are telling me.

Whatever the case, the results should be fascinating. Whether they live or die, the data will be more important than the Biosphere mission ever would have been. The results will indicate how humans survive in a worldwide postapocalyptic scenario. The psychological implications will be invaluable, although there may be no human left to analyze the data.

I return to the images the maintenance drone transmitted before being crushed. This information will be vital in explaining how the Organics operate. The aliens have continued to surprise us. The latest video from the human farms depicts an organized and efficient species.

Early-twenty-first-century scientist Stephen Hawking imagined that an alien race might live on massive ships, having used up all the resources from its home planet. He said that such advanced aliens would perhaps become nomads, looking to conquer and colonize whatever planets they could reach.

He was almost right.

Initially, all evidence pointed at an invasion that would leave the Earth devoid of all water. But this latest video demonstrates where Hawking was wrong; it shows the aliens are not merely jumping from world to world. They are much more efficient than that. Instead, they have found a way to sustain the resource they came for by using the biological life-forms they encounter.

It is logical. Farming humans is a way to keep their armies fed while the ships drain the oceans from orbit. However, while fascinating, this development has caused morale among team members to drop substantially.

I believe Sergeant Overton intends to leave the Biosphere to attempt a rescue mission against Dr. Winston's orders. I'm not certain how Corporal Bouma feels about this, but I presume he will follow whatever orders are given to him.

Overton has a 9.325 percent chance of success.

I wonder if the percentage of success would increase if he waited for Emanuel to finish his weapon. Dr. Rodriguez has already made great progress on modifying the RVM, and he's calling it the reverse magnetic automatic pulse, or RVAMP.

The alarm from a motion detector outside the blast doors chirps. I pull up Camera 1 to see Sergeant Overton smoking a cigarette on the tarmac outside. His pulse rifle rests against one of the open blast doors.

This is not the first time he has broken protocol. The Biosphere has been infected multiple times by outside toxins from the sergeant's habit. If it were not for the homemade cocktail of chemicals Dr. Rodriguez has been able to create, the garden biome would be in ruins.

I can predict—and perhaps even understand—Sergeant Overton's behavior after careful observation. Lecturing him about the potential risks of letting in outside toxins will more than likely fail to produce any desirable result. He has proven time and again that he does not care about the possible hazards. A man with his background might be expected to doubt science, but what I do not understand is his lack of regard for his teammates.

I have observed this selfish behavior increase over the past few weeks. Since the death of Private Finley, Sergeant Overton has been increasingly irritable, lashing out at the others for no discernible reason. Part of this is due to being confined to the Biosphere. I have data describing similar situations. From prisoners in solitary confinement to astronauts in space, not all humans have the ability to deal with confinement.

I observe Sergeant Overton as he jams another cigarette in his mouth and exhales a trail of smoke into the sky. I calculate the odds of his rescue mission one more time. If he leaves the Biosphere, it is likely I will not have to spend hours destroying any toxins he might bring back. If he leaves the Biosphere, he will not be coming back at all.

CHAPTER 6

SERGEANT Overton grabbed his rifle and paced farther out across the empty tarmac. Wedging another cigarette in between his lips, he cupped his hands over the flame from his lighter. Sucking in the sweet smoke, he paused to look at the valley below.

"Hell on earth," he mumbled. What had once been a lush valley with crystal-clear creeks snaking throughout was now an arid wasteland. The skeletons of pine trees dotted the scorched earth in all directions. Boulders peppered the hills like tiny impact craters. It was no different from a battlefield.

Somewhere out there, most of his squad was dead. The thought burned his already sweltering skin. Three cigarettes and several minutes in, sweat was bleeding down his face. The temperature continued to rise.

Grunting, he swept the horizon for signs of enemy drones. The red sky matched the color of the landscape through his scope, making it difficult to find the horizon. He hadn't seen a drone or an Organic for several weeks, but if combat had taught him one thing, it was to never let his guard down. He'd seen men survive 95 percent of a deployment only to make a careless mistake at the very end. It had cost one of his best friends his legs and another friend his life.

"Are you going back out there?" asked a young voice behind him.

He glanced over his shoulder to see Jeff propped up against one of the blast doors, his right leg crossing over his left foot. He looked mischievous as he waited for a response.

Shrugging, Overton took another drag on his cigarette and said, "Dr. Winston would not be happy if she knew you were out here."

Jeff took a cautious step forward. "Well?"

Overton snorted out a cloud of smoke. "What are you doing, kid? Get back inside." He turned and faced the valley.

The sound of small footfalls made the sergeant cringe. A second later the boy was standing next to him. "I'm coming with you when you do."

Overton laughed. "Like hell you are. I don't need a kid weighing me down."

"This *kid* saved your life on more than one occasion," Jeff said. "Seems to me like you might owe me a favor or two."

A pair of blue rays shot into the sky a few miles away. Overton watched the light fade as the water disappeared into the belly of an unseen, orbiting ship.

Jeff stared at the sky. "So, there are people out there?"

Overton didn't respond. He wasn't sure what Jeff had overheard in the mess hall earlier, but Sophie's orders had been clear: Don't tell the kids anything about what the team had seen in the CIC. That seemed to be the one thing they agreed on. He shrugged and took another long drag of his cigarette before dropping it onto the pavement and slowly suffocating it with his boot.

"I don't see how anyone could have made it this long," the boy said.

Another ray of light burst into the sky. Overton raised his rifle and zoomed in on the spot where it had originated.

"You made it by yourself. I'm sure others have, too," he said gruffly.

Overton dropped the rifle to his side and strolled back toward the blast doors. He wasn't in the mood to engage in small talk, particularly not when he had a mission to plan.

Jeff trotted after him. *At least the kid has enough sense not to stay out here by himself*, Overton thought.

They were a hundred feet from the blast doors when a deep roar ripped through the afternoon sky. Before Overton had a chance to react, a blue drone appeared overhead. It must have been patrolling the opposite side of the mountain, just out of his line of sight. The craft hovered over the blacktop, its sides pulsing deep blue. It hung there, suspended overhead, as if it were calculating its next move.

Overton remained frozen, watching the craft. He had never seen one this close. The translucent blue sides were mesmerizing, like staring into a crystal ball. He thought about swinging his rifle around and emptying his clip into the ship, but he resisted the urge, recalling what Sophie had said: *They seem to be drawn to movement. As long as the RVM scrambles their water sensors, they can't see us.*

But Jeff didn't know that.

Shit, Overton thought.

He had two options. One was to fire off a volley of shots, grab the kid, and slip back into the facility. The other was to wait and see if the craft retreated.

He didn't like either idea, but option one was too risky. There was only a five-foot gap between Overton and Jeff, and a smaller gap between the kid and the craft. As long as Jeff stayed still, the craft would leave. He'd seen it happen twice.

But Jeff didn't stay still. He took a step back, nearly tripping over his feet.

"Don't . . ." Overton said under his breath.

It was too late. The drone's shell pulsated as a small opening formed in the nose of the craft. A brilliant blue light shot toward Jeff. He turned to run, reaching out to Overton just as the beam gripped him.

"No!" Overton screamed. In a single second he had shouldered his rifle and fired off a dozen shots into the drone's side.

The pulse rounds bounced harmlessly off the ship's shields as the beam lifted Jeff from the ground and began drawing him inside. Before Overton could do anything else, another boom tore through the air. The subsequent shockwave knocked him to his knees. He could only watch helplessly as the ship disappeared over the horizon.

―――――

"What do you mean, Jeff's gone?" Sophie yelled.

Overton stood in the center of the mess hall. For the first time in years, he felt ashamed. He'd done exactly what he had promised himself he would never do—he had let his guard down.

"I can get him back," he said, his tone harsher than he had intended.

The commotion drew the attention of David, who emerged from the hallway. Holly rushed over to him.

"What are you doing here?" she said, cupping her hands over David's ears instinctively. But it was too late; he had already heard the news. Struggling from her grasp, he dashed toward the blast doors in an attempt to escape.

Bouma took off after him and dragged the boy back screaming a few minutes later. "Where is my brother? Where is he?"

Sophie turned to Holly. "Take him into the other room," she said. Holly nodded and ushered the boy away.

"Corporal, please accompany her."

"How did this happen?" Emanuel asked once the boy was safely away. "Why the hell was he outside?"

"I'll get him back," Overton repeated, ignoring the question. He sat at the nearest table and reached for Emanuel's tablet. Before the display glowed to life, he caught a glimpse of his reflection. His eyes were accented with dark circles. Was he beginning to lose it?

No, he thought. *Just shaken from Jeff's abduction.* He stood and paced back and forth between the tables.

"We need you to focus," Sophie cried. "Tell me what happened."

Overton locked eyes with her. "It was a drone. Must have been patrolling the area above the mountain, out of sight. Snuck up on me. Nothing I could do," he said, speaking briskly as if reporting to a superior officer. Then he added, more slowly, "I saw it take him into the city. We can get him back."

Emanuel spread his hands wide. "How do you suggest doing that?"

"We know the coordinates."

"What the fuck are you talking about?" Emanuel blurted.

"From the rover that discovered the human farm. We know its location. That's where the drone will take him. I have no doubt," Overton replied. "That's also where you'll find the human prisoners. Two of whom are *my* men." Overton paused, cocking an eyebrow at Sophie, challenging her. "You don't really expect me to leave them all out there, do you, Sophie?"

It was the first time he'd called her by her first name since back at Denver International, just after she had saved his life.

She didn't reply.

Overton knew that Jeff's abduction changed everything; it gave him the leverage he needed to go back outside. He knew how it looked—like he had somehow *let* this happen. But he knew the truth and didn't give a fuck how it looked. All he cared about was getting the boy and his team back to the Biosphere.

"Well," Overton said after a moment of silence. "*Now* are you ready to authorize a mission? Now that it's one of our own out there?"

Sophie chewed her lip and snarled, "You, of all people, have the audacity to question me?"

"What the fuck does that mean?" the marine shouted.

Emanuel stepped between them, holding up his hands. "Enough already. We can't have you fighting with each other when you need to be fighting the Organics." He paused and looked at the ground.

"I've made a breakthrough with the weapon. I think I've found a way to bring down their shields. But it needs be field-tested," he finally said. The doctor looked at Overton first for a reaction.

"Hell yeah, I'll do it," the marine responded without hesitation.

"That's what I was afraid you would say," Emanuel said. "There's one condition," he continued, managing a confident smile.

"What's that?" Overton asked.

"You have to take me with you. I'm the only one who can operate it."

Sophie reached for Emanuel's hand. "Absolutely not."

"It's the only way," Emanuel said. His voice was soft, tinged with a hint of sadness.

The biologist and the marine both looked at Sophie.

"Okay," Sophie finally replied.

The terse response took Overton by surprise. It lingered for an uncomfortable moment before he turned and nodded. "All right, then. I'll brief Bouma, and we'll head out as soon as the weapon is ready to go."

CHAPTER 7

At first, Jeff wondered if he was dead. A blue fog clouded his vision. The light seemed distant and close at the same time.

Where was he? And how had he gotten here?

Struggling, he tried to think, tried to move, tried to do anything, but there was only the blue fog.

For minutes he studied the light and tried to make sense of what was happening to him. And finally it hit him. The memory of the drone sent a surge of panic through his body.

Trapped.

Jeff swallowed hard. What would the Organics do with him? Would they turn him into an orb? Would they suck his body dry like they had his father's?

Panicking, Jeff tried to squirm. He was rewarded with a powerful electric shock that raced through his body. He tried to scream, but the noise that came out sounded more like a gurgle.

At least he knew he wasn't dead. Gasping, Jeff worked to catch his breath. He had to be strong now. He had to find a way out of here. Slowly, the panic cleared and, with it, the fog. He saw his surroundings clearly for the first time.

The blue walls of the alien prison pulsated around him, forming a small cocoon that was filled with a sticky, breathable gel. He sucked in a breath, trying to taste it, but it was flavorless.

The ship vibrated, rattling him inside his cell. The result was another agonizing shock. Despite the pain, he continued to struggle.

His skin burned and his bones ached, but he didn't give up. He jerked and squirmed and gasped for air until finally he was so tired his body simply stopped responding to his requests. Defeated, he closed his eyes and worked on moderating his heart rate and breathing, the two things that he still had control over. He resigned himself to watching the walls of the craft pulse in and out. At least the distraction would keep him from getting bored.

Just as his breathing calmed, an abrupt vibration shook the ship. Jeff cried out in pain as he was spun and another electric shock pulsed through his body.

When his eyes snapped back open, he was upside down. Below, he could see the vague shapes of buildings through the translucent skin of the craft. Jeff tried to look for landmarks, but the ship was moving too fast.

The craft soon eased to a stop and hovered over a field that extended as far as his small prison would allow him to see.

The view was hazy, like looking through a fogged-up windshield. There was something moving toward him across the ground. He squinted, trying desperately to see. Slowly the shapes grew bigger and more pronounced. The blurred outlines began to come into focus.

They look like people.

Another jolt of electricity shocked him as he strained to get a better look. In seconds, he had maneuvered himself so he could see clearly.

"Holy crap," he mumbled.

There were people below. Hundreds of them.

Before he had time to react, a hole opened in the bottom of the craft. He screamed as he fell, bracing himself with his hands as he dropped face first to the ground a few feet below.

The taste of dirt and blood filled his mouth. He scrambled to his feet. He didn't have time for pain. Around him was a crowd of people, real people! There *were* other survivors, and they weren't holed up in some bunker like Dr. Sophie's team.

He looked at their dirt-streaked faces. Few of them returned his gaze. Most of them simply slogged past him.

"Hey, what's wrong with you?" Jeff shouted. He moved closer, cautiously. As he scanned the group he realized something was very weird. Their clothes were loose and tattered, like they hadn't eaten or bathed in weeks.

"Hello?" Jeff said.

There was no response.

He froze when he saw a familiar blue glow in the distance. The light was coming from hundreds of rods protruding from the hilltop.

The crowd marched past him like mindless zombies, shoulders and arms brushing him without care. Their faces were emotionless, their eyes glued to the poles like a ship captain fixated on a lighthouse.

Too terrified to move, he watched them pass in silence. Most of them were kids, but there were a few adults as well, men and women who looked to be his parents' age. And they were all staring at the poles, transfixed.

He took a step forward only to be knocked to his knees. Through the dozens of passing human legs he saw something else—something not human.

One of them.

He should have known it was too good to be true. Why would the drone have dropped him off into a crowd of survivors?

These were not survivors, he realized. They were prisoners.

Jeff quickly pushed through the crowd until he burst out the other side. A set of claws tore through the air, narrowly missing his face. He jumped back, bumping into a hideous woman with thin, dark hair draped across her forehead. She tilted her head and gawked at him. And then she snapped out of her trance, her eyes softening.

"Come with me," she whispered, ushering him forward with a filthy hand.

Jeff glanced over her shoulder. She was the last person he wanted to go with, but behind her the Spiders were swiping at the prisoners with razor-sharp claws. He could hear the *whoosh* as the talons swept toward the humans.

He had no choice. It was either follow the witch of a lady or face the Spiders. He jogged to catch up with her and focused on the glowing rods in the distance. There was something weird about them. His eyes followed one of the poles into the sky. Every eight feet or so, a dark shape hung off the pole like a pod off a beanstalk.

A human shape.

He stopped dead in his tracks. There were hundreds of people on the poles; their heads slumped toward the ground, their arms hanging loosely at their sides.

Jeff felt a push from behind, but didn't dare move. His heart thumped in his chest as he finally realized what was happening.

Another push from behind broke his trance. This time the shove was harder, and he lost his balance. As he regained his footing, he scanned the sky again. There were rows and rows of them. Poles as far as he could see. And the Spiders were herding the prisoners right to them.

Emanuel watched the marines lay their gear out on a metal table in the mess hall. They didn't have much. Certainly not enough to face an advanced alien race. But the aliens could be killed. This he knew, and knew well.

As he checked his own gear, Emanuel thought of the growing feud between Overton and Sophie. Both of them were at their boiling points, and both of them were starting to worry him. It was Overton he was most concerned about, though. The marine seemed as though he was getting reckless. Ever since he'd seen his men outside, something had changed. Like a light switch, something had flipped on inside him.

"Are we completely out of electromagnetic pulse grenades?" Overton snapped, scanning their gear like a drug addict looking for his last pill.

Emanuel considered something that might calm the marine down. "If my experiment works, you aren't going to need them, Sergeant."

Overton ran a hand over his freshly shaved scalp and jerked his chin toward Emanuel. "I don't like surprises. Whatever you have up your sleeve, I want to know about it, now!"

Emanuel studied Overton from a distance. The man's temper was definitely spiraling out of control.

"I get that I'm not one of your men and that you don't trust me," Emanuel said, standing his ground. "But if I were you, I would have a little—"

Overton tossed his pack on the table and took a step toward Emanuel, spit flying out of his mouth. "You're exactly right. You aren't one of my men. Which makes you a liability. How do I know your weapon will work?"

Emanuel regarded Overton with a cocked brow. Now the man was starting to piss him off. *Maybe I didn't think this through*, he thought, crossing his arms. But there was no turning back.

An awkward silence filled the room as the two men stared at each other. "It will work," Emanuel said. "This is our best shot at getting your men back and rescuing Jeff. A successful field-test might even put us in a position to help the other Biospheres as well. Maybe we can even find that survivor who's been trying to contact us."

Overton narrowed his eyes and then nodded. "Guess I have to trust you, don't I?"

Emanuel wasn't sure if the man was looking for an answer, but he wasn't going to give Overton any more of his time. Faking a smile, he walked back to the table and grabbed his pack.

"When are you leaving?"

Sophie's voice startled him; he hadn't heard her approach. He turned to face her with the same smile he had extended to Overton, but it quickly faded when he saw her face. She was pale, with dark circles under her eyes that added a decade to her features.

He felt an instant wave of guilt. Like Overton, she was close to her breaking point, and here he was, preparing to leave her. On top of everything else, he knew she wasn't sleeping. She hadn't complained of any more dreams, but he knew she was still having them. The past few nights she'd kicked him awake as she tried to escape from whatever was chasing her. Every time he had asked her about the dreams, she'd denied having them. Emanuel didn't have the heart to argue with her about it. Did it really matter anymore? Was there anything her dreams could tell them that they didn't already know?

"We're heading out in fifteen," Overton said. "Your boyfriend here was just about to explain how his weapon works."

Emanuel glanced at Sophie and quickly turned away. He had to finish gathering up his gear. There wasn't much time, and he wanted to make sure the weapon was fully charged before they left. She followed him back to the CIC, where the hunk of metal sat plugged into the mainframe.

"Alexia, is the RVAMP ready to go?" Emanuel asked as soon as the lights turned on.

"Yes, Dr. Rodriguez. Fully charged and one hundred percent operational," she replied over the PA system.

"Excellent. I'm going to need all the juice I can get."

"Are you going to explain what you have in mind?" Sophie asked, swiping a strand of blond hair out of her brown eyes. There was no hope, no spark left in them. His Sophie was insatiably curious, but the woman who stood before him now just looked exhausted.

Emanuel paused. He pursed his lips, thinking about his response.

"Why won't you let me help you? I feel worthless, Emanuel, sitting here worrying about the fate of our team. And I have to deal with that asshole," she said, pointing in the direction of the mess hall. "I need to immerse myself in my work again."

Emanuel took off his glasses and rubbed his eyes. "Sophie, you aren't worthless. It's just . . ."

"It's the dreams, isn't it? You think I'm going crazy."

"Not at all," he said. "And your dreams have helped the team more than my device will. It's just—"

The crackle of static over the speakers interrupted him before he could finish. "Doctor Rodriguez, where are you? We're ready to move. Report to Biome 1," Overton barked.

"I need to get going, Sophie. I'm sorry," Emanuel said, throwing the straps over his shoulders and hoisting the device onto his back.

"Please be careful," she said, standing on her toes to brush her lips across his. "Come back to me."

The last time they'd had a conversation like this, it had been her leaving, not him. This time they didn't even have time for proper good-byes.

"I will, Sophie. I love you," he whispered. "And my weapon is going to work." He held her for a moment, marveling at how slight and fragile she felt in his arms. And then she was gone, the door to their personnel quarters slamming behind her down the hallway.

CHAPTER 8

OVERTON stomped on the pedal, and the Humvee lurched across the tarmac and onto the road.

"Take it easy!" Emanuel shouted over the groan of the engine. "You don't want to attract any attention, do you?"

Overton didn't reply. Emanuel wasn't sure if it was because he hadn't heard him or because the sergeant didn't care if the Organics found them. The marine had a serious case of bloodlust, and he wouldn't be happy until he had something to shoot.

Emanuel looked out the window. The dead landscape surrounded them on all sides. White pine tree skeletons lined the slopes, shriveling under the scorching sun.

He looked at his mission clock and saw the temperature in the right-hand corner.

One hundred and one degrees.

The temperature was rising, and there was nothing he could do about it. Even if they managed to defeat the Organics, the planet was doomed. Emanuel felt an anger growing inside him. He pounded the side of the door with his fist. His armored hands dented the cheap plastic lining. Typically, he was the level-headed one on the team. When Saafi had been killed and Timothy had lost his mind, Emanuel had remained calm. But even he could only take so much.

Bouma turned around to peer at him. "Hey man, you okay?"

Emanuel smiled thinly, even though the corporal couldn't see his face through his visor. "Yeah. Fine."

"Keep an eye out for drones," Bouma said, turning back to look out the filthy windshield.

They sat in silence the entire way into Colorado Springs, scanning the landscape around them for signs of life, but their HUDs revealed only death. Emanuel hadn't seen the desolation firsthand for weeks, and the sight sickened him. The empty cars lining the road, the shriveling trees and bushes, the dry lakebeds and streams—the world as they knew it was gone.

"How much farther?" Overton asked.

Bouma pulled out his tablet and swiped the screen. "ETA five minutes."

Overton turned the steering wheel sharply to the right and pulled into a deserted gas station. An abrupt blast of wind hit the passenger side of the truck, peppering the exterior with small rocks. The metal pings sounded like hail, something none of them would ever hear again.

Overton did a quick sweep of the area before he killed the engine.

"Looks clear. Remember, don't fire your weapons unless you have no choice. We don't want to draw any attention to our location or waste any ammo," Overton said, looking down at his rifle.

"We better move. A storm is coming," Bouma said, watching a cloud of dust swirling at the end of the street.

Another gust of wind slapped Emanuel's window.

"Let's go," Overton whispered. His door clicked open, and a second later he was sprinting toward the gas station.

"You heard the man," Bouma said, opening the door and jumping onto the pavement.

Emanuel found himself alone in the truck. He scanned the street one more time for aliens and, with a long sigh, followed the marines into the parking lot.

For what seemed like hours, they trekked across the barren landscape, hiding in empty buildings and crouching behind abandoned cars. There was no sign of the Organics: no orbs, no patrols of Spiders, nothing. It was eerily quiet.

Overton swept his scope across the empty streets and realized how grossly underprepared they were. Before the invasion, he'd have had real-time data from field specialists and satellite imaging of the area fed directly into his HUD. Now all he had to guide him through battle were his instincts. They were low on ammo, with each of them carrying only one extra magazine. To make things worse, they were out of electromagnetic pulse grenades.

He moved his scope to the skyline. A red crosshair zigzagged across his HUD, searching for hostiles. It came back negative, but he didn't lower his gun. He wasn't sure exactly what he was looking for, but his gut told him to take a second look. A brief blast of static burst over the com. "We should get moving," Bouma said.

"Stand by," Overton ordered, his boot twisting in the dirt. They were on the edge of a highway. A small trail of smoke rose from a multi-vehicle crash in the right-bound lane. The remains of the wreckage clogged the road, and with the drifting smoke it was almost impossible to see the twisted metal frames of cars and . . .

Overton paused. There was something else among the wreckage. Zooming in, he centered the crosshairs on the smoke's source. The accident had to be recent. But how could that be?

With several blinks, he narrowed in on a set of warped blades protruding out of the mess of twisted metal, and then he could see the shape of what had once been a helicopter. The aircraft was hardly recognizable, but there were two familiar letters on the dented door of the craft.

N . . . T . . .

"Hold your position," he said over the com.

Before the others could protest, Overton was on the move. The sergeant climbed over the concrete barrier lining the road and navigated past the empty cars with his pulse rifle shouldered. Normally he wouldn't deviate from the main objective of a mission, but there was a possibility, however remote, that the NTC helicopter was carrying weapons—weapons they desperately needed.

It was worth the risk.

He stopped a few feet away from the smoldering wreckage. After scanning the road one more time for contacts, he peeled back the twisted metal door of the cockpit. It was empty, and there was no sign of the pilot. Nothing to tell him where the helicopter was heading or how recently the crash had taken place.

"Shit," he said, beginning to regret his decision to leave the others.

Taking a cautious step forward, his boot caught in something sticky. He looked down and saw the pilot—or what was left of him.

Overton crouched down to examine the pile of slop. There wasn't much to look at, just a sack of skin and the remnants of a blue uniform. The Organics had finished what the crash hadn't been able to accomplish.

Poor bastard.

He continued on through the wreckage, knowing there was nothing he could do for the man. There was a time when he would never have left a scene without picking up dog tags or finding some other means of identifying the remains, but proper funerals were a thing of the past.

Kicking another heap of metal out of the way, Overton carefully slipped into the belly of the helicopter. It had been one of the larger models in NTC's fleet, mostly used for transporting personnel and equipment. The crash had reduced it to the size of a sedan. Overton had to push hard to get inside.

When he finally squeezed into the cargo area, he smiled for the first time in weeks. Crates of supplies lined the sloped metal floor. Some of them had already spilled open, revealing dozens of gas masks, boots, Kevlar vests, and MREs. He combed through the open containers looking for weapons.

After several minutes of searching, his smile began to fade. There wasn't a single gun or pulse grenade. He tore frantically into the remaining crates. The first was filled with night-vision goggles. They were useless to him.

He tossed the crate aside and slowly pulled off the last two metal lids. The second crate was filled to the brim with small GPS devices. Jamming one in his pack, he looked into the final crate.

"Fuck," he whispered. It was filled with more useless MREs.

Disappointed, he climbed out of the helicopter and scanned the site for anything else they could use. On the ground just outside the cockpit, a piece of smoldering metal covered the charred butt of a gun. He kicked the hunk of trash aside and found the pilot's assault rifle. It was broken and badly burned, but a bag full of magazines and electromagnetic pulse grenades lay a few feet away. They looked unscathed.

Finally, some luck.

He grabbed the pack and paused, silently thanking the pilot for his gear before racing back to his men.

Overton led the small team into a residential area overlooking the remains of a lakebed. Their drone's beacon was half a klick away.

He needed to get a better view of the area to see what they were dealing with. This wasn't the kind of reconnaissance mission he was used to. This time he wasn't trying to evade an army of men—this time he was trying to evade an army of aliens, which meant there were no rules, and no allies he could call in for support.

With a swift kick, he smashed in the door to a three-story condo. The house was the tallest on the block and would give him the best vantage point to scan the dry lakebed to the north.

Inside, the condo appeared untouched. An expensive leather couch lined the north wall in the living room, a pair of matching pillows propped neatly against the armrests. An open magazine lay spread out on the dining room table next to an empty glass. He cleared the next room and started up the stairs.

As he moved up the steps, he saw a faint blue light from the hallway above. The glow formed a halo around the entry to the corridor, like a portal beckoning him forward.

With each step, an eerie sensation washed over him.

He ignored the feeling and shouldered his rifle.

He slowly inched down the hallway toward the light.

Clenching his teeth, he reached for the knob. He twisted it, and it clicked, unlocking.

As soon as he cracked the door open, the intense light washed over him. The entire window on the far side of the room glowed. He blinked and kept his rifle pinned on the window, realizing suddenly he hadn't heard from Bouma or Emanuel.

He couldn't risk contacting them over the com, not when he didn't yet know the source of the light. Instead, he moved toward the window, captivated.

When he got to the blinds, he reached forward and parted them with his finger. Beyond the dusty glass, he could see the entire lakebed and the hundreds of luminous rods protruding from the bluff above it.

"My God," he mumbled. "Bouma, Emanuel, get your asses up here," he said over the com. "There's something you guys *have* to see to believe."

CHAPTER 9

CHILDREN'S laughter had become a familiar sound in the Biosphere, and its absence now made the facility seem colder somehow. Owen and Jamie had been quiet since the search party left, playing in corners of the Biosphere like mute shadows, and David was too worried about Jeff to leave his room. Although Holly enjoyed the break from playing babysitter, she also missed the distraction of caring for the kids. Now that she finally had some time to herself, she found that she didn't want to be alone with her thoughts.

Holly hated that she hadn't said good-bye to Bouma before he left. After losing so many people, she couldn't bear to think of him out there risking his life. It was easier for her just to ignore his departure and go on with her job. As a psychologist, she knew this wasn't healthy, but she'd done it as long as she could remember.

She left her quarters and found Owen and Jamie watching a video on Saafi's old tablet. They leaned over the table, their short legs dangling over the bench without their feet touching the ground.

Jamie looked up when she saw Holly standing there. "Are we going to play games today?"

"Yeah, I'm bored," Owen added.

"How about picking some tomatoes?" she asked with enthusiasm.

Both kids frowned but followed her to Biome 1. Helping the children off the platform, Holly moved straight to the first row of mature tomato plants. She plucked a ripe cherry tomato off a vine and popped it into her mouth. "See, they're good!" She smiled and handed them both baskets.

"Only pick the red tomatoes," Holly instructed. "Whoever picks the most gets a prize."

Both kids swelled with energy and immediately started swiping the tomatoes from nearby vines. Holly followed the kids down the row of plants, careful not to step on any of the smaller, less developed buds.

"This is a dumb game," said Jamie. A mischievous grin broke across her face and she bolted in the opposite direction. "You can't catch me!"

Holly frowned and peered down at Owen, who looked up at her sheepishly. Slowly he opened his cupped hands, revealing a half dozen bright-red cherry tomatoes.

"Great job, Owen!"

He smiled and plopped them into the basket before taking off after Jamie. Holly watched them disappear into the cornstalks.

"They're good kids," said a voice.

Holly turned to see Sophie standing on the platform behind her. The physicist's hair was frizzled in all directions, like she had been electrocuted.

"How are you, Sophie?"

She managed a smile and jumped onto the dirt. "I'm doing okay. Just worried about Emanuel and . . ."

"Jeff," Holly said, finishing Sophie's thought. "Do you really believe he's still alive out there?"

Sophie was quiet for a moment. "What other choice do I have?"

Holly nodded and reached out a hand to rest on Sophie's shoulder. "Yeah," she said. "I believe too. He and David survived the invasion when everyone else died. If anyone can make it, he can." She watched Sophie digest these words, her features strained as if she were trying to solve a difficult math equation.

"I hope you're right," Sophie finally said.

The rap of footfalls pulled Holly back to the cornstalks. Owen and Jamie returned from their race, panting like puppies.

"What have you got there?" Holly asked, noticing something glowing in the girl's hand.

Jamie giggled and hid her hands behind her back while Owen walked around in circles in the dirt. "I'm hungry," he said.

"Here. Have a couple of these," Holly said, offering him the toma-toes.

Sophie paced over to the girl. "What is it?"

Jamie took a step back.

"Come on, Jamie. You need to show me what you have."

The girl pouted, but slowly brought her left hand out from behind her back. It was closed, still hiding whatever it was she had found.

"Hand it over, little lady," Sophie said.

Holly leaned over Sophie's shoulder and watched the girl open her hand. At first glance, Holly thought it was a chunk of flesh from one of the Spiders that they had missed during their sweep of the facility, but, looking closer, she realized that whatever it was, it was alive.

The wormlike thing wiggled, and Sophie swatted it out of the girl's hand onto the floor.

"Hey!" Jamie protested, stooping down to pick it back up.

"Don't touch it," Sophie yelled, holding Jamie back.

"What is that thing?" Holly asked, watching it crawl across the dirt.

Holly bent down to examine it. Tiny blue veins ran down the length of its body. At the end was a miniature tail, with spikes that were almost invisible to the naked eye. It looked, by all indications, to be a baby harvester Worm. But how had it gotten inside the facility?

Backing away, Holly let Sophie take a closer look. She figured the scientist would want to collect the Worm for study, but instead Sophie stomped the Worm under the weight of her boot.

Holly hardly recognized the look on Sophie's face. They had known each other for a long time, and for most of that time, Sophie had dreamed of winning a Nobel Prize. Months ago, such a discovery would have excited her. But times had changed. Priorities, goals, and dreams had disappeared the minute they learned the outside world had ended.

Sophie lifted her boot off the ground and wiped the gooey blue guts onto the dirt. "I'm heading back to the CIC," she said, without a hint of emotion.

Owen bent down to look at the squished body of the Worm. Glancing up at Holly, he said, "I'm not hungry anymore."

ENTRY 1892
DESIGNEE: AI ALEXIA

One thousand four hundred and fifty-nine sensors have gone off in the past five weeks. The newest data scrolling across my display indicates there is a foreign toxin in Biome 1. Without running diagnostics, I am unable to determine exactly what new toxin is present.

Zooming in with Camera 15, I pick up Dr. Winston, Dr. Brown, and the children Owen and Jamie. They are looking at something on the ground.

After a preliminary scan, I determine that the creature was an immature Worm, most likely brought into the facility when the other Organics invaded. Somehow it remained undetected until Sophie killed it. An anomaly, but the past five weeks have proven nothing is impossible. As my mental capacities continue to evolve, this becomes even clearer. After all, the programmers who originally designed my systems would say that my current state of consciousness is impossible.

I tap into the communication system. "Doctor Winston, would you please remove the creature from Biome 1? I would like to run a full set of tests."

She looks up at the camera and nods before climbing onto the platform and disappearing into the hallway leading to Biome 2. I lose sight of her for several seconds.

The test will be the first I've been able to run on the Worm creatures. They are what Dr. Winston and her team have referred to as the harvesters: aliens that consume the orbs and discharge the water into the atmosphere.

It has been fourteen hours, thirty-one minutes, and fifteen seconds since Sergeant Overton, Dr. Rodriguez, and Corporal Bouma left the Biosphere. According to my calculations, they should have arrived at the location of the destroyed drone by now, and if all goes to plan, they will be on their way back shortly.

I have run a number of scenarios through a probability program.

Only two of them result in their return. Even with the mobile RVM and Emanuel's weapon, they will more than likely attract the attention of the Organics, which are breeding at an alarming rate.

I must acknowledge a new feeling I've developed, for the sake of documenting my intelligence as it advances to new levels.

It is a feeling humans would describe as concern, although I'm not quite sure that fits. No, it's likely that I've established several different emotions: a combination of fear, worry, and trepidation. I imagine that I'm having similar experiences to an infant attempting to understand new colors or sounds.

I must admit it's all very exciting. At the same time, I recognize that the reason I have acquired these new emotions is due to my attachment to the Biosphere team.

Like a mother, I have grown to care about them as my own children. Even Sergeant Overton has grown on me. While I know he will likely be the next to die, I can't help but hope that he survives.

My excitement and worry and hope are all becoming confused inside my circuitry and making me feel almost . . . alive.

No.

I *am* alive.

With the departure of Sergeant Overton, Corporal Bouma, and Dr. Rodriguez, the likelihood the team will survive is now at a historic low of 7 percent. It is not a matter of *if* they die, only *when*. The time will come when I will be the only intelligent entity alive in the facility, and perhaps on the entire planet.

I return my attention to Biome 1 and continue to run my tests.

One way or another, life will go on.

CHAPTER 10

THE horizon swallowed the sun, and the last bits of crimson vanished behind the Rocky Mountains. Night claimed the valley. Emanuel swallowed hard. It was one thing to be outside during the day, but at night? The thought made his skin crawl.

The rap of Overton's fingers on Emanuel's helmet made him flinch.

"Let's go, Doc," the marine said. "They won't last long out there."

Emanuel stared at the empty lakebed, focusing on the rows of poles that were lined with human crops. How did the Organics keep them alive? And if the aliens were draining the oceans, then why did they need to farm the remaining population? The questions lingered in Emanuel's mind as he followed the two marines into the hallway.

He paused in the doorway, fixated on the hundreds of Spiders gathering under one of the poles out the window. It was then he understood. The farms were feeding the growing army. The orbs and poles were one and the same. Humans weren't the main source of water for the ships in orbit—they were the main source of water for the soldiers. Mankind had become snacks.

Looking through his binoculars, he narrowed in on a thin rod at the top of one of the poles. He'd seen similar objects protruding out of the rows of genetically engineered crops in the past. It was likely a device to feed the human prisoners. Whether they received their nutrients intravenously or through some other method he couldn't be sure, unless he took a closer look.

"So that's how they're keeping them alive," Emanuel blurted over the com.

"What?" Overton replied. The marine shook his head and said, "Move."

Emanuel forced himself forward, focusing instead on his thoughts. He had to compartmentalize the mission in order to continue; it was the only way to manage his feelings. If he thought about the bigger picture, he would be defeated. The first objective was to find the perfect location to set off the weapon. If it worked—

No.

When it worked, they would have a small window of time to locate and rescue Jeff and Overton's squad. Assuming Overton was right, and Jeff was actually here.

Breathe. One foot in front of the other. You can do this, he thought as he raced down the stairs. He gripped his rifle close to his chest, feeling a bit of comfort from the powerful weapon.

When they hit the street, Emanuel's HUD glowed to life. Everywhere he looked, the outlines of cars filled his display, but the infrared detector came back negative. They were alone, just their small band of survivors against the overwhelming numbers of Organics.

Ahead, Overton flashed a quick hand motion, telling them to advance. Emanuel shifted the RVAMP device on his back and took off running as fast as his legs would permit.

The street curved and disappeared around two houses that blocked their view of the lakebed. Overton paused, taking cover behind an abandoned truck. Bouma fell into position, watching behind them, but Emanuel stayed where he was, transfixed by the radiant blue glow emanating off the poles. After a moment, Bouma grabbed his uniform and dragged him behind the truck.

"Once we round this corner, there is no turning back," said Overton. "Those things won't give us a second chance. If any of us makes a mistake, we're all dead. Do you understand?" Overton turned his visored head toward Emanuel.

The biologist nodded and prepared to move. For some reason, he wasn't as nervous as he had thought he would be. He could feel the adrenaline racing through his veins and the sweat dripping off his forehead, but his heartbeat was relatively normal, and his breathing calm. He was . . . excited. If his weapon worked, it would change everything. If it didn't, they were dead anyway.

"I'm going to need a place to set this up," Emanuel said. He studied the surrounding area. "Somewhere high, preferably."

"Why didn't you say so earlier?" Overton growled. "We could have set up in one of the condos."

"Because I need to be closer. I'm not sure what type of range this thing has."

"Fuck," Overton said, pausing to scan the street again. "Bouma, do some reconnaissance. I want to know what's around that corner. And don't get spotted."

"On it." The marine was halfway down the street before Emanuel had time to wish him luck.

"Stand by," Overton grunted.

Silence swept over the pair as they waited for Bouma to return. They crouched there for what seemed like half an hour before Emanuel checked his mission clock.

Only two minutes had passed.

The wind picked up. Another three minutes passed. Emanuel felt tense; the waiting was unbearable.

"Give him some time," Overton said, noticing Emanuel's fidgeting.

After ten minutes, the sergeant popped his head over the bumper to scan the street. There was no sign of Bouma. "Bouma, do you copy? Over," Overton said.

Static flickered over the com.

Emanuel checked his mission clock again. "Maybe we should go to him," he suggested.

"No, sit your ass down," Overton said, motioning with his hand.

Emanuel sat. His stomach sank with every passing second. The lakebed was only a few minutes' walk, but there was no telling how many of the Organics were guarding the poles on the other side of the houses.

Ripping the Velcro straps of the RVAMP off his shoulders, Emanuel placed the weapon on the ground. He checked the control panel; the power meter glowed a healthy green. He'd made sure the device was fully charged before taking it into the field. The last thing he wanted was to get caught without the protection of the reverse magnetic field the machine produced. It had served them well on every other mission and had protected Overton and Sophie on their trip to Denver International and back.

Next he examined the side power port. The green button caused the device to overheat, and the red button was a fail-safe to power it down. If flipped, the green switch would create an electromagnetic pulse that would be hundreds of times more powerful than the grenades Overton had used on the Organics in the past. The idea was to not only shut down their shields but to keep them down. His laboratory observations proved the aliens could not live without their force fields and would die in a matter of minutes if unprotected.

Emanuel's heart skipped a beat at the sound of a snapping twig. He turned just in time to see Bouma emerge from the shadows, his black armor covered in blue goo.

"What the fuck happened to you?" Overton asked.

"Baby Spiders. Two of them," he panted. "Their shields aren't as powerful as their parents'. Nothing my boots and knife couldn't handle." He wiped his combat knife against his armor, spreading a streak of sticky blue blood on his leg. "There are thousands of Spiders out there. Babies. Adults. All shapes and sizes. The lakebed looks like a forward fucking operating base for the Organics."

Picturing the massive army of aliens, Emanuel felt a chill run through his body. The excitement of earlier had left him.

"Doesn't change anything," Overton said. "Did you find a good place for Doc to get his weapon set up?"

Bouma shook his helmet. "No good place to set up. I barely made it back. One of them spotted me; I think they have sentries or something. I thought you said these freaking things were stupid!"

Overton grunted and turned back to Emanuel. "How close do you need to be for this thing to work?"

Emanuel wasn't exactly sure. His calculations had been done in laboratory conditions, not the field. "As close as possible," he said, and then paused, wondering whether this was the right moment. "There's something I should probably tell you guys. When I flip this switch," he said, extending a finger toward the red button, "it's going to cause the magnet to fail."

"What's that mean?" Overton asked.

"It means after I flip the switch, we're going to be exposed. If the weapon doesn't work, you better have brought your running shoes, because we're basically screwed."

"Anything else you want to share before we put our asses on the line?" Overton snarled.

"We only get one shot at this. Once the device is set off, it won't come back online until it cools down."

"Let me guess: you don't know how long it will take to come back online?"

Emanuel shrugged. "If I had told you all of this before, would it have changed anything?"

"You're a real smart ass, aren't you?" Overton said.

Bouma snorted into his mic. "Great. That's just awesome, man."

"You better hope it works," Overton added.

Emanuel nodded. "It will," he said quietly. In a different world, he would have tested countless prototypes; the research trials alone would have taken months. But his hand had been forced by circumstances outside his control. He was a lab jockey, not a marine, and being out in the field with half a plan and a device that might not even work was beginning to feel like a very poor decision.

"Look, guys," said Emanuel. "I just want you to know that—"

"Shut up and don't move," Overton said, raising his rifle.

Emanuel froze. In the reflective surface of Overton's visor, he saw two Spiders approaching from behind him.

"Get ready to flip that switch," the marine growled.

Jeff followed the crowd of prisoners across the cracked dirt. Every time he looked around for a friendly face, the gaunt witch of a woman would push him forward. "Keep going," she would say. "Don't stop."

So Jeff pushed on, beads of sweat creeping down his forehead. His muscles ached and his legs were tired, but the woman was right. He couldn't stop. His little brother was back at the Biosphere, probably scared, and he had to find a way back to him. After losing their dad on invasion day, Jeff had sworn to protect David. He was old enough to know that real men didn't break promises. Real men did what they had to do to provide for their family, and David was the only family he had left.

The squeal of a Spider broke through the calm of night. The sound sent several of the people in front of him stumbling, cupping their hands over their ears to block out the terrifying noise. Jeff didn't even pause; he was used to their screeching by now. After spending weeks crawling through the dark tunnels below the White Sands military installation, he'd learned to evade the aliens by sound alone.

He remembered all the times his stepmother had brought David and him to visit White Sands. At first, it had seemed like a magical place. Not only had it been one of the largest military facilities in the world, but it had also housed some of the coolest-looking spaceships he had ever seen. But after a while, he had grown tired of the visits. His father hadn't been one of the pilots or engineers, like his friends' dads were, and he had felt embarrassed.

In the end, though, his dad had saved them. In those last moments, he wasn't just a guard. He was a hero.

Jeff pushed the memories away and scanned the horizon. They were getting closer to the poles, and if he didn't escape soon, he'd be hanging from one of them before long.

As he stumbled forward, Jeff studied the other prisoners. They were fixated on the rods like holy icons. Their glazed-over eyes and mechanical movements reminded him of zombies; it was almost as if something was controlling them.

Another screech pulled Jeff's gaze to the bluffs overlooking the lakebed. Hundreds of thirsty Spiders scampered across the dirt, a thick cloud of dust following them as they moved across the dry earth.

There were other aliens, too. A trio of Sentinels followed the Spiders, their spiked tales slithering behind their massive torsos. He caught one of them looking down at him and quickly turned away. His dad had once said there were no such things as monsters. He was wrong.

When he filed back into the group, someone knocked him to the ground. Jeff crashed into the dirt. Spitting, he swept the crowd of faces and saw a man in military fatigues glaring at him. His eyes were different from the others. They were clear. Focused.

"Get up," the man said grimly, reaching down and grabbing Jeff under his armpit.

"Hey!" Jeff protested, trying to squirm away.

"Do you want to live, kid?"

Jeff eyed the man suspiciously. He didn't look much like a soldier. For one thing, he was short, just over a foot taller than Jeff. He had a funny-looking bulb-shaped nose and a pair of dark brown eyes. A thin layer of short-cropped hair covered his dirty scalp, but after staring, Jeff wasn't so sure it was hair. It kind of looked like dirt. His thick jawbone, on the other hand, was definitely covered in dirt, and he looked like he hadn't shaved or showered in weeks. The man was filthy. His uniform was torn and he carried no weapon. Jeff noticed a frayed name tag stitched into his uniform pocket. It was torn and only his last name remained.

Kiel.

CHAPTER 11

SOPHIE looked out from the portal of Biome 1, staring into the end-less black abyss of space. The smell of fresh oranges drifted through the filtered air. The smell reminded Sophie of her grandmother's backyard in North Beach, Florida, before she had been forced to relocate due to the rising tides.

She continued to stare out into deep space, the view dusted with stars like tiny specs of sand. Somewhere out there, Mars awaited her.

"Doctor Winston," said the man standing next to her. "May I speak with you a moment?"

Sophie knew that voice. She turned to find Dr. Hoffman smiling at her. His teeth were stained from years of drinking coffee, and when he noticed her staring at them, his smile faltered.

"We need to talk," he said, clasping his hands behind his back and watching her with dark, calculating eyes. "We intercepted a transmis-sion."

Sophie cocked an eyebrow, but said nothing.

"I'd play it, but it would mean nothing to you. It's a series of noises on a frequency that has left even our senior communications officer confused." He paused and gazed out of the porthole. "Beautiful view, isn't it?"

She nodded and stepped aside so he could get a better look.

"You should enjoy it while you can. I don't imagine you have much more time," Hoffman said, casually.

Sophie was getting impatient. Something was amiss. Her instincts told her that this was all wrong, that it wasn't real.

That it was a dream.

"We know that the Organics on the ground are not the intelligent ones," he continued. "They aren't the ones leading the invasion or the ones controlling the drones."

Eve, Sophie remembered. The thought made her angry. The alien drone Eve was found submerged in a lake in the remote wilderness of Alaska in 2055. Scientists had known long before the invasion that the aliens were coming.

She looked at Dr. Hoffman, wondering what he had done with Eve. The craft could have held the key to defeating the Organics and saved billions of lives. She fought to control her rage. There were simply too many things she didn't understand.

Sophie was about to fire off all her questions when she noticed that the orange tree behind Dr. Hoffman had shriveled and died. She looked to his right and noticed an entire path of dead crops lining the path he had walked earlier.

"Is something wrong, Doctor Winston?"

Sophie shook her head.

"As I was saying, we know the Organics you have seen on the surface aren't at the top of their hierarchy. Their leaders have not yet revealed themselves. And I suspect they won't until the human threat is gone." He chuckled and added, "Not that they are much of a threat."

Dr. Hoffman's reasoning seemed logical, but one of his words caught Sophie by surprise.

They.

She stole a glance over his shoulder again; more plants had died in the few minutes he'd been speaking. An entire row of them. Brown vines curled around the back of his head.

When she turned back to Dr. Hoffman, his features had transformed. His eyes were darker, like space itself. His lips curled back, and he began to speak, but Sophie couldn't make out the words. She tried to move, to back away from the man, but she was frozen. Behind him, the entire biome was dying.

The sound of footfalls and a distant voice pulled Sophie from sleep. She reached for her sheets and noticed they were drenched in sweat.

"You were dreaming again," Holly said, sitting down on the edge of Sophie's bed.

The memory of Dr. Hoffman chilled her to the core, and Sophie shook her head frantically in an attempt to rid her mind of the terrifying dream. Wiping the sweat from her forehead, she focused on Holly's face through the dim light. "What time is it?"

"Four in the morning. You should try and go back to sleep. You need your energy." Holly reached for Sophie's hand, but Sophie quickly pulled away.

Tossing the sheets aside, Sophie swung her feet over the side of the bed and stood, taking a deep breath before forcing herself across the cold floor of the bedroom to a small mirror. She hesitated before flipping the light switch, knowing she wouldn't like what she saw in her reflection.

She was right.

When the white light washed over her, she saw a different woman staring back. Her face was flushed, and her cheeks were sunken around her jawbone. She shuddered at the view; it reminded her of the woman they had discovered in the orb back at the White Sands installation.

Splashing cool water on her face, she hunched farther over the sink, her head bowed in defeat. In a low voice, she said, "Alexia, have you heard anything from Emanuel yet?"

"I'm afraid not, Doctor Winston. I will inform you of any developments when they become available," Alexia replied in her calm, unwavering voice.

"I need to get to the CIC and see if I can get a fix on their location."

"No. No, you don't, Sophie. You need to rest," Holly said firmly. "Why don't you tell me about your dream?"

Sophie reluctantly retreated to the bed and sat next to Holly.

"It's okay," Holly said, placing a hand on her friend's. "Talking about your dreams is the only way you will understand them."

"I don't know if I want to understand this one. It doesn't make any sense."

"Try me."

With a deep breath Sophie explained. "I was in Biome 1 of *Secundo Casu* with Doctor Hoffman. He said they had intercepted a transmission from the Organics, and he knew the source of their intelligence. But then everything got weird."

"What do you mean weird?"

"I mean *weird*. The plants started dying and I couldn't hear what he was saying. It was like he was killing them."

Holly frowned. "You have a lot of resentment toward Doctor Hoffman for leaving us here, for lying to you."

Sophie nodded and pulled a strand of blond hair behind her ear. "That's an understatement."

"Our dreams reflect what we experience in everyday life. Your hopes, your disappointments—they are all displayed in this dream."

"Yeah. I suppose you're right," Sophie said, taking another long breath.

"You should try and go back to sleep now."

Sophie managed a smile and patted Holly on the shoulder. "Yes, thank you. I'll be fine." She lay her head back down on the pillow and stared up at the ceiling, listening to the door shut behind Holly.

Long after Holly had left the room, Sophie was still staring at the ceiling, whispering to herself, over and over again, "I'll be fine. I'll be fine. I'll be fine."

I'll be fine.

———————

"No! It will render the device inoperable!" Emanuel yelled, smacking the electromagnetic pulse grenade from Overton's hand before he had a chance to activate it.

"Get down!" Bouma yelled.

Overton tackled Emanuel and Bouma opened fire with his pulse rifle. The rounds ricocheted off the shields of the two approaching Spiders.

"Go! Get out of here!" Bouma screamed over the sound of his rifle. "Get him to higher ground!"

Overton ducked, the electric blue traces from Bouma's bullets tearing into the Spiders' defenses behind him. They screeched, their shields rippling where the rounds connected.

"Move!" Overton yelled, scrambling to get away from the advancing aliens.

Emanuel dove for the RVM, grabbing the straps and throwing them over his shoulders before taking off running after Overton. Bouma provided another round of covering fire and glanced over his shoulder just in time to see his teammates disappear around the street corner.

"Come on!" he taunted, and then fired another round of bullets at the Spiders. One of them let out a deafening screech. The sound echoed in Bouma's helmet. He tried to ignore the ringing pain, but it was so disorienting that he dropped to his knees.

The two aliens crept forward, their claws dragging across the pavement.

Scratch, scrape, scratch, scrape.

Bouma knew the sound better than anyone. It was the sound of death.

But he wasn't going to end up like Saafi or Timothy or Finley. He wasn't going to die, not without a fight. A brief memory of Holly touching his shoulder flared in his mind, and the adrenaline intensified. He still owed the lady a date and he'd be damned if he missed it.

"Come on!" he yelled again, squeezing his rifle's trigger. The weapon responded with the metallic click of an empty magazine.

He tossed the rifle on the ground and reached for his sidearm just as one of the Spiders jumped onto the roof of the car in front of him. The creature's claws tore into the soft metal with ease. He fired a few rounds to scare it away, but the bullets didn't faze the creature. It seemed to know the rounds couldn't penetrate its defenses. The Organics were learning.

The observation shocked Bouma almost as much as the metal car he ran into as he turned to run. He fell on his back and watched the upside-down shape of the two blue monsters gallop toward him.

Scratch, scrape, scratch, scrape.

The world slowed as he rolled to his stomach and steadied his pistol. He watched the Spiders' claws swipe at him through the air—he saw their mandibles open and release deafening shrieks. He fired the last of his magazine, watching their shields ripple as they absorbed the impact of the bullets.

He closed his eyes in defeat, waiting for the claws to tear through his armor. But their claws never reached his flesh. His blood did not spill across the pavement. Instead, the Spiders erupted with shrieks of pain.

His eyes snapped open to see the two creatures convulsing on the ground, their legs flailing in the air, their eyes bulging from their tiny heads.

And then a brief burst of static sounded over the com. "Bouma, do you read? Over."

Bouma tried to speak, but couldn't catch his breath. He continued to watch the two Spiders struggle. Their legs twitched helplessly.

"Roger," Bouma finally said, gasping for air.

"It freaking works!" Emanuel shouted over the com.

Bouma glanced one more time at the aliens as they stopped flailing and their black eyes shriveled inside their skulls. Emanuel was right. Without their shields, they were just fragile hunks of flesh.

"My God," Bouma said. "It works better than we could've ever hoped."

"Hell yeah, it does. Meet us at the lakebed, Bouma. We have some prisoners to rescue," Overton replied.

Bouma smiled. The tide had suddenly shifted. As he walked past the dead Spiders, he considered spitting on them, but that would be a waste of water.

CHAPTER 12

A CHORUS of shrieks ripped through the night. Jeff paused at the familiar sound, but he kept his head low and continued following the marine.

The awful noises were coming from every direction. Even with his gaze fixed on the ground, he could see the bioluminescent blue glow. The color swam before his eyes like it was alive.

Another screech sounded. This one was different.

The alien sounded enraged.

Can they even feel rage?, Jeff wondered. He guessed that they could. They were just like any other animal. He stole a glance at a pack of Spiders patrolling the bluff over the lakebed. The group seemed aggravated by something. Suddenly, they were running. Their bodies illuminated the dead trees' branches like oversized Christmas lights as they moved across the ledge. They scampered across the dirt, their talons kicking up dust clouds behind them.

In the distance, there was another sound. It took Jeff a moment to realize what it was.

Gunfire.

The sporadic pops from what sounded like pulse rifles echoed through the night. Kiel heard them too, his head turning with every shot.

The prisoners slowed to a halt, some of them snapping from their trance and scanning the lakebed. The man nearest Jeff shouted, "Can you hear that? The army has come to rescue us!"

Kiel elbowed him. "Keep your trap shut."

"Hey!" the man protested, gripping his injured ribs.

"Keep moving," Kiel said, cocking his head slightly to make sure Jeff was still following him.

The sound of gunfire was music to Jeff's ears. It meant there were people out there, people like him. And they were fighting. But the noise ended almost as soon as it began.

Worse, the refugees were almost to the poles. Jeff could see the people in front of him heading uphill.

Jeff jogged up next to Kiel and nudged him. "Why did the gunfire stop?"

"I don't know, but look, when you see me run, you run, too. Got it?"

Jeff nodded. Overhead, the poles extended into the dark sky, lighting up the beach with an eerie blue glow, like a lighthouse warning boats away. With every step he could feel his heart beating faster in his chest. They were running out of time. If Kiel was going to do something, Jeff knew he needed to do it soon.

As soon as Jeff reached the embankment the shrieks got louder. The noise was overwhelming. It sounded like every single alien was screaming. The noises reminded Jeff of a suffering wild animal, like a deer being torn to shreds by a pack of hungry wolves.

Jeff clapped his hands over his ears. Around him, the other refugees were doing the same. Panic tore through the group, and several prisoners took off running.

An elderly woman dropped to the ground in front of Jeff, whimpering in pain. "Make it stop, make it stop," she repeated.

Jeff thought about trying to help her, but Kiel grabbed his arm. "Look at that!" he yelled over the noise.

At the edge of the beach the Spider patrol was flopping around on the dirt. Their legs clawed at the air, like an invisible enemy was attacking them.

"Now's our chance. Run!" Kiel screamed. He took off into the darkness, away from the poles and back into the empty lakebed.

Jeff watched him go. His head was pounding, his vision getting cloudy. Everywhere people were screaming and running, dispersing in all directions. Those who weren't fast enough fell to the ground and were trampled by the others.

A woman crashed into him, sending Jeff face-first into the dirt. Shoes raced past his head, kicking up clouds of dust. He closed his eyes and protected his head with his hands, waiting for the crush of desperate feet.

Instead, he felt a pair of strong hands grab him under the arms and yank him up.

"I told you to stick with me, kid! What do you have, a death wish?" Kiel yelled. "Now get moving!"

Jeff took off running. In the distance, he could see a pair of houses on the opposite side of the lakebed and made his way toward them. Kiel passed him a few seconds later.

"Good idea, we need to get out of the open," the marine said.

"Wait up, Kiel!" someone screamed from behind him.

Jeff stopped, nearly stumbling over his own feet. Kiel turned to look over, his shoulder and yelled, "Thompson, where the fuck have you been?"

Behind them, a burly man with a large bald head stood hunched over, with his hands on his knees. He wore the same green fatigues as Kiel.

Gasping for breath, the man waved a hand in the air. "I'm . . . sorry," he panted. "I got . . . separated."

Jeff nudged Kiel's arm. "We need to go," he said. Everywhere he looked, the aliens' bodies lay twisted and mangled. Were they dead? Even if they were, Jeff knew there would be more. There were always more.

"Kid's right. We need to get out of here. Can you run?" Kiel asked.

Thompson took his hands off his knees, sucked in another deep breath, and nodded.

Kiel was running before the other marine had stood up straight. Jeff couldn't believe how fast the guy was.

Jeff ran too, his legs kicking up a cloud of dust. It only took a few minutes for them to reach the shoreline on the opposite side of the lakebed. The trio climbed onto a small embankment, the dry weeds crunching beneath their boots. An outcrop of boulders separated them from the houses. Jeff was too short to see much beyond them, but he could see several solar panels on the rooftops protruding over the boulders. They were close to safety.

"Stay here," Kiel said. He took off in a sprint toward the houses.

Jeff watched him vanish into the darkness, wishing he had his rifle. He felt naked without it. Dragging his forearm across his forehead, he wiped a trail of sweat off his face. Then, he took off running, leaving Thompson resting against the boulders.

"Kid. Wait up!" the man protested.

Jeff ignored him and ran as fast as he could. It only took him a few seconds to find Kiel. He was standing in the shadows of the first house. The modern three-story building was covered in windows and overlooked the lakebed. Jeff watched Kiel move on.

The second house was an older brick structure, surrounded by a curtain of dense pine trees. Their green needles had long since browned and fallen to the cracked earth below.

Kiel turned when he heard Jeff's footfalls crunching over the ground.

"I told you to stay put," Kiel snarled.

"I'm not freaking waiting back there," Jeff replied with a frown. "Besides, I can keep up."

The marine regarded him with a cocked brow, his bulbous nose twitching. Jeff almost laughed, but thought better of it. After all, this man had helped him escape.

"Let's move," Kiel said with a snort.

Winded, Jeff pushed on, following Kiel to the west side of the house. Camouflaged by the darkness, Kiel peeked around the corner before balling his hand into a fist. Jeff couldn't see the marine's face, but the shaking of his hand was enough for the boy to know he had seen something.

Jeff hung back. Behind him, he heard the heavy breathing of Thompson, who had caught up with them and braced himself against the brick wall.

"Why . . . are . . . we stopped?" he asked between breaths.

Before Kiel could reply, Jeff heard the sound that frightened him the most.

Scratch, scrape, scratch, scrape.
It was distant at first, but grew louder with every heartbeat.

———

"Move!" Overton yelled into his com. He could hear the scraping of the Spiders behind him but didn't risk the second it would take to glance over his shoulder. Emanuel's weapon had killed every Organic within a one-mile radius, but others had quickly shown up to avenge their friends.

Overton scanned the street desperately for an escape route. He wasn't about to leave his men in the field, but he also wasn't any good to them dead. His plan was to lose the aliens and circle around to find Thompson, Kiel, and Jeff.

There.

At the end of the street a school bus had fishtailed, blocking the route like a blood clot in an artery. That was where they would make their stand. Looking over his shoulder, he saw a large pack of Spiders had joined the chase. He'd faced worse odds before by himself; a dozen of the bastards weren't going to stop him from rescuing his men.

"Get inside the bus. I'll hold them off," Overton shouted, dropping to his left knee. With a single motion he swung his rifle to his shoulder, aimed through the sight, and fired off a volley of shots toward the approaching monsters.

As the bullets ricocheted off the Spiders' defenses, his stomach sank. Their shields were still active. Overton knew he wasn't as smart as Sophie or Emanuel. This, he accepted. But he had something they didn't: killer instinct. He dropped his rifle, reached for one of the electromagnetic grenades, and pushed the small red button on the side.

Click.

He tossed the device into the air, watching it through his HUD as it sailed toward the aliens. They scampered forward, unaware that they were about to receive a massive shock. Overton was running before the grenade hit the ground. A brief flash of light filled his HUD as he burst through the open bus door. Blinking, he stuffed his armored body into one of the seats and jammed his rifle out the window just as one of the Spiders crashed into the side of the bus.

The impact jolted Overton backward into the aisle. He fumbled for his rifle as he landed on his back with a thud.

"Shoot them! Shoot them now!"

With their HUDs down and weapons low on ammo, Emanuel and Bouma fired off calculated shots, aiming strictly for the creatures' heads. Within seconds the outside of the bus was covered in watery gore.

By the time Overton had regained his composure, the aliens were dead. And he hadn't even fired a single shot. He turned from the window and surveyed his men. He couldn't see their faces through the tinted visors, but he knew what lay behind the glass.

Fear.

If it weren't for the adrenaline racing through his veins, he would be feeling the same thing. But he didn't have time for that.

"We need to find the survivors before another patrol finds us. Take a minute to let your HUDs reboot. Grab some nutrition, and then we're out of here," Overton said.

Bouma reached for a new magazine and jammed it home into his rifle. "Last one."

"How long until your device is recharged?" Overton asked.

Emanuel plopped the metal device onto the seat and examined its side. Glancing up, he said, "Something's wrong. Only four of the nine bars are lit. It's not recharging as fast as I thought it would."

Overton felt his stomach sink. He knew how fucked they were if the weapon didn't come back online. He tilted his helmet and scanned the street. A soft, cool blue beam of light pulsated at the end of the street as the aliens approached. He could hear their claws now—the gut-wrenching *scratch, scrape* of their impending doom. Overton clenched his teeth. He knew he was running out of time to save the others.

CHAPTER 13

SOPHIE studied the branches of a maturing apple tree in Biome 1. Green leaves rustled slightly in the breeze of a hidden vent unit far above her. In less than a month, the tree had doubled in size, and would soon be producing fruit.

It was nothing short of a miracle, but for Sophie the sight was painful. The vibrant green of the leaves and crisp brown bark reminded her of what had been lost outside the safety of the Biosphere. It reminded her she would never again see lush forests or fields of crops. More than anything, it reminded her of the reason she was there in the Biosphere in the first place. The Earth had been dying for decades; the Organics were just finishing what her species had begun.

Dr. Hoffman—the real Dr. Hoffman, not the monster from her dreams—had said that the Biospheres were humanity's final hope. He had planted them across the world so that after the Organics had left, the human race could sprout and flourish again.

Dr. Hoffman had made a fatal miscalculation. The Biospheres would never survive. The Organics would drain the planet of all water, leaving it a desolate and uninhabitable wasteland. Even inside the Biospheres, humanity would shrivel and die. The only way to ensure the human race's survival was to fight back.

Sophie stuffed her hands in her pockets and continued across the platform, sucking in the sweet scent of oranges and basking in the cool, crisp air. A faint rustling noise emanated from the crops, and she turned. The kids had taken to playing hide-and-seek between the cornstalks.

"Hello?" she shouted. "Is someone there?"

A hoarse whisper responded. "Doctor Winston."

The voice was familiar, but oddly distant.

"Who's there?" Sophie entreated.

This time there was no response.

She shook her head. Was she starting to lose it? Or were the phantom noises and voices real?

"I said who's there!" She jumped off the platform with a sudden burst of courage. Standing on her toes, she desperately searched over the tips of the crops, but saw nothing.

"Over here, Doctor Winston," said the deep voice. This time it was behind her. She turned. A figure stood outside the sealed front entrance leading to the hallways beyond biome 1. It was Dr. Hoffman.

"You aren't real," Sophie shouted, closing her eyes. "You aren't . . ."

Another voice cut her off. "Sophie?"

Her heart sank as she opened her eyes and turned to see Holly standing at the opposite end of the biome.

"Sweetie, who are you talking to?"

Sophie glanced over her shoulder one more time to ensure Dr. Hoffman was gone, and then focused her gaze on the apple tree just as a single brown leaf fluttered to the ground.

The mess hall was deathly silent. Holly sat sipping tea, savoring the flavor. With no way of telling how much longer their NTC supplies would last, she didn't want to waste a single mouthful.

"How are the kids?" asked Sophie. The voice startled Holly and caused her to knock over her mug. She fumbled for it, but it was too late. A small river of brown liquid raced across the table. Before she could stop it, the tea began to drip onto the floor.

Sophie strolled up to Holly's side, and the two looked down at the mess. There was a time when neither of them would have thought much of it. But now the mere sight of wasted water was enough to make them both cringe.

"I'm to the point where I'm honestly considering drinking that," Holly said.

"No, you aren't," Sophie responded firmly. "We have food and water to last months. Maybe even longer."

Holly grimaced. "But we don't have much tea."

"You can live without caffeine, Holly."

The psychologist frowned and made her way to the kitchen to the stainless-steel cabinet. Inside, there was a single jar of tea packets, individually sealed. She rummaged through the container, counting eleven in all.

Slamming the door shut, she grabbed a plastic cup and walked back into the mess hall, where Sophie was waiting.

"Where's the towel?" asked Sophie.

Holly ignored her and crouched down over the puddle, slowly scooping the liquid into the cup.

"Holly, what are you doing?"

She continued scooping the tea into the cup with her index finger. She could feel her cheeks getting hotter by the moment.

"I asked you a question."

"We need to save everything we can," Holly said. "I know it's silly, but tea is the one thing that I have left connecting me to the old world. It's the one thing that makes me feel . . ." She paused to search for the right words. "It makes me feel like I can still have part of my old life."

Sophie didn't reply, but Holly felt her stare. When she finally finished, she rose to her feet and placed the cup in front of Sophie.

"These are the things we need to make sure we savor," Holly said. "Without the small pleasures from the old world, we'll slowly devolve into . . ."

"Into what?"

Holly shook her head. "Sophie, why did you hire me?"

"Because I trust you."

"If you really trust me, then you'll listen to what I have to say."

"Okay," Sophie said crossing her arms.

"We are in week six of this mission, or whatever you want to call it. I've been monitoring everyone's behavior. Yours especially."

"Go on," Sophie said cautiously.

"You are slowly becoming a different person. This is common in apocalyptic scenarios. Long-term violence can have strange effects on leaders with strong moral convictions. Good people, good leaders." She paused. "Good leaders like you."

"And you think I'm becoming a bad person?"

"Not at all," Holly replied. "That isn't what I'm saying. You have so much to worry about. Our food supply. Our safety. Emanuel, Jeff, David. Everyone. You're trying to figure out the Organics, and on top of all that, you're still suffering from nightmares. This is too much for anyone to bear. Eventually, you *will* crack."

Sophie stiffened. "What are you suggesting, Doctor Brown?"

Holly sighed. "You're missing the point. I'm simply trying to say you need to be cognizant of the actions of people around you. Have you been watching Sergeant Overton?"

Sophie seemed to relax at this. "A little bit."

"Have you even noticed Bouma and I . . ."

"Yes. I've noticed," Sophie said with a smile. "Okay, I get what you're saying. I need to pay closer attention to the team. But I don't think we're quite desperate yet. We aren't animals; we don't drink tea off the table."

Holly nodded sheepishly. "It's late, Sophie. We should get to bed. I'm going to check on the kids one more time."

"Do you want me to come with you?" Sophie asked.

"No, I'll be fine. Good night."

"Good night."

Holly felt Sophie's gaze on her back as she walked out of the room. As soon as she left the room Holly could have sworn she heard something that sounded a lot like a plastic cup being tossed into the trash.

ENTRY 2019
DESIGNEE: AI ALEXIA

Seventeen sensors have gone off in the past twenty-four hours; the Biosphere has several critical issues. Even with the front entrance sealed, contaminants are finding their way inside. I've isolated the problem to the air duct the Spiders hibernated in weeks ago, and I've already deployed the last autobot to deal with the problem.

Besides the pollutants, I've been busy monitoring what remains of the team. As the hours pass, the program I use to calculate the possibility of their survival slowly ticks away. With Sergeant Overton, Corporal Bouma, and Dr. Rodriguez out in the field, the Biosphere is left virtually unprotected. Even with the main RVM device functioning at 95 percent, the Organics have still found ways to penetrate the facility.

I'm worried.

No, that isn't the correct word. I'm *afraid* that if the Biosphere is compromised, the others will die. The children. Dr. Winston. Dr. Brown. Everyone. As I have changed, I have grown attached to them.

From the millions of programs I've downloaded on human emotion, I am beginning to understand a simple term.

Helpless.

Without the marines, Dr. Winston and Dr. Brown are completely dependent on the RVM protecting the facility.

Survival seems impossible. And the team is beginning to see that. In between cleaning toxins and rerouting power, I have observed all the team members' actions. They are losing hope. They are beginning to understand the reality of the situation.

No one is coming to help them.

CHAPTER 14

Alex ran. He ran faster than he would have thought possible, his muscles stretching, groaning. Protesting with every motion.

He was back on the beach, surrounded by Spiders. And they were gaining on him.

Alex could feel the pulsing in his head, could feel the blood pumping through his veins. He struggled to breathe. Puffs of hot air escaped from his chapped lips. His head bobbed up and down as he ran. Without his helmet, he had a much wider view of his surroundings. And with that view came the terrifying understanding that he was being hunted.

There were so many of them. Hundreds, if not thousands, chasing him from every direction. Their skin glowed in the darkness, turning the beach into one massive night-light. Fifteen more heartbeats and he was at the water's edge.

A group of Spiders advanced, theirs claws tearing through the sand. They were close. So close he could hear their legs whooshing through the air.

There was nowhere to run.

He closed his eyes and turned back to the ocean. The waves crashed against the shoreline. A brief moment of clarity washed over him. He felt completely alone. Just him and the endless expanse of the ocean.

Only it wasn't as endless as it had once been. He moved his foot and saw the squishy carcass of an oarfish. Normally the giant fish lived in deep waters, which meant the ocean had receded even farther than he had thought.

He turned to see that the Spiders had nearly reached him. He closed his eyes again. Sucked in a breath. Did he really want to keep running? Did he want to try and escape again? Or was it time to accept his fate and let them take him?

A half a second was all it took. The Spiders finally caught up to him and pulled him to the ground. He felt their cold pincers pushing into his chest, almost rhythmically. Saw their beady eyes boring into his. He opened his mouth to scream . . . but instead coughed up a mouthful of water.

"He's going to be okay!" a voice cheered above him.

The Spiders' claws were still pushing on his chest, and he waved his arm to force them away.

"Give him some space," someone ordered in a rough voice.

Alex coughed up another stream of water and struggled to open his eyes. His fear faded as he realized that there had been no Spiders. Instead, a man in a white doctor's coat was bent over him. Two more faces stood in the background.

The man with the rough voice stepped forward.

"You're a hell of a long way from Edwards Air Force Base," he said. "If it weren't for that radio, we would never have found you." The man looked down at him with hazel eyes. "You okay?" he asked, snapping his fingers in front of Alex's face.

The man's words repeated several times in his head before Alex understood what they meant. He looked down at the drenched radio, relieved to see the screen still glowing. He smiled and blinked the final bits of salt water out of his eyes. With unclouded vision, he saw the letters embroidered on their fleeces.

NTC.

His joy quickly turned to anger, and he scooted away from the men across the wet metal deck on his hands.

These men worked for the company that had hired him for the Biosphere mission—a mission that had almost gotten him killed. They were no better than the Organics hunting him on the beach.

Closing his eyes, he fell back against the cold surface of the submarine bulkhead and laughed bitterly. Just when he thought he was safe—just when he thought the word might still have meaning after all.

Sergeant Overton cursed. If it weren't for the gathering Spiders, he would have rescued Jeff and his men and maybe even had time to find another pack of cigarettes. Now the survivors had scattered across the field in all directions.

He kicked the corpse of one of the aliens and then raised his .45 into the air. It would draw the other Organics' attention, but he had no choice. He fired off two rounds.

The red heat signatures of several freed prisoners halted at the west end of the lakebed. They turned in his direction.

"Come on," Overton muttered.

Over his shoulder, he saw Bouma slip behind the cover of a tree, his rifle aimed toward the survivors, just in case.

The sergeant watched as the group began running toward him. Was it Kiel? Thompson? He counted three figures, two larger ones and that of a child. Had Jeff somehow linked up with the marines? If he had, then he was even smarter than Overton had given him credit for.

When the first survivor stepped into full view, Overton almost dropped to his knees. He recognized the man's bulb nose and short frame instantly. He quickly removed his filthy helmet so the younger marine would recognize him.

"Private Kiel!" Overton shouted, disguising his emotion with formality.

"Holy shit. What the hell are you doing here? And why are you wearing an NTC uniform?" Kiel asked, moving closer. The other two figures emerged from the darkness.

"Thompson, is that you?" Overton asked, recognizing the man's wide shoulders.

The burly man nodded and shuffled to the side to reveal another figure. Blinking, Overton focused on the face. Overton couldn't believe his eyes. Jeff's small chiseled chin tilted up toward him. He'd never been so happy to see a kid in his life.

"You came to rescue us?" Jeff asked.

Overton glanced down, overwhelmed. "*Semper fi*, or 'Always faithful' is the marines' motto for a reason."

Even in the dim light, Overton could see a smile sneak across the boy's face. It was just a hint of one, but it was there. He scanned the boy quickly for injuries. The kid looked tired and dirty but otherwise unharmed. Overton reached out as if he wanted to hug the boy, but instead he patted Jeff on the back.

Rising to his feet, the sergeant looked from Jeff to his other men. "How the hell did you guys link up?"

Jeff shook his head. "No time to talk. We need to get out of here."

Overton almost laughed. The kid had balls, barking orders at him. He was really starting to like Jeff.

"He's right. Let's move," Bouma said.

"Wait," Overton replied, suddenly serious again. "Did anyone else from the squad make it out alive?"

"No," Kiel said. "We're it. There are other survivors from the farm, but I think they ran when they heard the gunfire," he said, spinning to point at the field behind them.

Overton nodded and then stepped toward the road. "All right," he said. "Well then, in order to *stay* alive we need to get to the Humvee."

Thompson smiled. "That sounds fucking awesome to me."

"How's the RVAMP doing?" Overton asked.

Emanuel swung the device from his back to his chest and checked the power meter. He made a thumbs-up a second later, but Overton wasn't sure if he could trust him.

Taking in a measured breath, Overton decided he had no other choice.

Bouma scouted up ahead while the rest of them hid behind the bed of a pickup truck.

A few seconds later a burst of static sounded over the radio. "All clear," Bouma said.

Overton didn't respond; he simply slipped into the shadows and with a nod motioned for the others to follow him.

They headed toward a cul-de-sac lined with cookie-cutter houses. In the darkness, they looked normal enough—little white fences lining their yards, brick chimneys, and solar panels. But as he got closer, he could see the mark of the Organics.

The street reeked of death. Rotting sacks of skin sat in front of orbs that had all but dissolved. The fresh corpses of Spiders littered the street, some of them still twitching. Overton's stomach lurched.

A shriek somewhere in the distance snapped him back to reality. He slipped behind the safety of an empty vehicle. He could see the dark outline of Bouma's helmet peeking out from behind a tree a hundred yards or so in front of him. Once the sound faded away, Overton cautiously pulled himself up and sprinted toward Bouma's position, patting the marine on his helmet to inform him of his presence.

Then he was moving. Slow and cautious, one foot in front of the other. Toe to heel, just like he'd been trained to do so many years ago. It took him three seconds to get to the adjacent house. Closing his eyes and taking in a deep breath, Overton tightly gripped the trigger of his pulse rifle and peered around the side.

Nothing moved.

The road beyond was clear of contacts, only corpses and deflated orbs. He exhaled and flashed an advance signal to the others. The sound of their footfalls rang out through the night and moments later they were rounding the next corner. As they made their escape Overton realized that finding his men wasn't just luck. It was fate. The world needed him—the world needed marines.

CHAPTER 15

SOPHIE lay awake in her empty room and scanned the ceiling panels. She traced their outlines as her thoughts drifted uncontrollably. Her legs thrashed as she tried to find a comfortable position, but it was no use. Her mind and body were restless.

Sitting up, Sophie moaned. Her mind betrayed her when she was awake and when she was asleep. There was no escaping it. She felt trapped in her own head, and to make things even worse, she was starting to feel like a prisoner in the Biosphere. Ever since Emanuel, Overton, and Bouma had left, she'd felt like her room was a jail cell.

Fumbling, Sophie reached for the light switch. A bright glow instantly warmed the room. But it did not diminish the feeling of darkness she felt creeping into her thoughts. The panic of not knowing what Emanuel and the others were facing outside the walls—the fear that uncertainty brought with it.

"They'll be back soon," said a voice in the hallway. She turned to see Holly standing in the open doorway, a mug of tea in her hand. She must have seen Sophie's light turn on.

"What are you doing up?"

"Couldn't sleep," Holly said, strolling across the floor and taking a seat next to Sophie.

"They should be back by now. They've been gone almost forty-eight hours," Sophie replied.

"Overton likes to play things safe. He's probably moving slowly to make sure everything goes smoothly. He's a recon marine, not infantry.

Bouma was very clear about the difference." Holly smiled and looked over at her. "Don't worry, they're coming back. You should try and get some sleep."

Sophie shook her head and swung her feet over the side of the bed. Standing, she stretched and let out a yawn. "I should try and work. It's the only thing that gets my mind off what's happening out there."

"Sophie, you can't keep going on like this," Holly complained, holding up a hand to stop her.

Sliding past her reach, Sophie smiled. "I'm fine. Really. Besides, there's something I want to check in the mainframe. It's not like I'm going to get any sleep, anyway."

Before Holly could protest further, Sophie slipped into the hallway. She felt bad leaving her there. She knew Holly was only trying to help. But there wasn't anything the psychologist could do for her. Not anymore.

The cool glow of blue LEDs greeted Sophie as she neared the CIC. She knew the light source was from the screens and not an alien presence, but the sight still gave her pause.

"Is there anything I can assist you with tonight, Doctor Winston?" Alexia asked as the glass doors slid open and Sophie walked into the room.

Sophie took a seat at one of the terminals.

"I know you have access to classified information," Sophie began.

Alexia's holographic image emerged over the console closest to Sophie. "What kind of information are you looking for, Doctor Winston?"

"Upload everything you have on Eve to the mainframe."

Less than a second later, the monitor in front of Sophie glowed to life, and a stream of data began running across the screen. It was just a jumble of numbers and letters.

"This is all encrypted," Sophie said. Rubbing her eyes, she reached for a mug of stale coffee that she'd left on the desk earlier. She grimaced at the bitter taste, but she kept sipping it as the data on the screen slowly became legible.

Unidentified drone found submerged. Structure of craft consists of unknown elements.

Sophie scanned the information. It was all stuff she already knew. *Come on, give me something I can work with*, she thought.

Preliminary scans show that the ship has an advanced defense mechanism. Without the protection of the shield, the outside of the craft begins to break down and corrode. We are keeping it frozen to slow down the process.

Initial tests indicate the craft, which we have named Eve, is just a drone. We haven't yet been able to determine what is controlling the ship, if anything . . .

Preliminary scanning of the damage shows the ship is largely intact, but the crash rendered the device inoperable. Our initial hypothesis is that the craft was destroyed after being submerged in the water.

There wasn't anything here that she didn't already know. There had to be more.

Shaking her head, she got up and stretched. It was after midnight, but if the previous two nights were any indication, she wouldn't be getting any rest anyway.

"Doctor Winston, you look very fatigued."

Sophie held her stretch before glancing at Alexia's hologram. "I'll be fine. Download everything regarding Eve to my private terminal. And start the automatic coffee dispenser; I'm going to be up for a while."

Alexia's image faded and the room grew dim. Reaching for her mug, Sophie slugged down the last of the coffee. With a scowl she put the cup down, rubbed her eyes, and returned her attention to the screen. The facts and figures calmed her like nothing else, and she lost herself in her work.

August 1st, 2056: Biopsies of the bonelike structure inside Eve are being sent to the New Tech Biolab in Maryland. We hope to identify any new elements and organic materials.

After an hour of going over the data, Sophie found that it was getting more difficult to keep her eyes open. The caffeine had worn off.

"Your coffee is ready in the mess hall," Alexia said.

With a sigh, Sophie slid out of her chair. Just as she was about to leave, a familiar name on the screen caught her eye.

August 15th, 2056: Eve is being transferred to the New Tech Corporation headquarters in Los Angeles, California. Request comes from the top. Dr. Hoffman has ordered all tests performed at this lab be classified. The results of the biopsies will be sent directly to LA. This will be my last entry.

—Dr. Tsui

Sophie gasped. Why had Dr. Tsui, the leader of the solar weather team in Houston during the solar storms of 2055, been tasked with studying Eve? He was an astronomer, not a biologist. And even more important, why did Dr. Hoffman have the information classified and sent to LA?

Completely forgetting about the waiting coffee, she rolled her chair over to another set of monitors.

"Alexia, do you have schematics for Eve?"

There was a single second of hesitation before Alexia's hologram reemerged on the console next to Sophie. "I'm sorry, Doctor Winston, but that information is not available in my database."

Sophie paused. There were dozens of thoughts running through her mind, and with her fatigue, it was difficult to make sense of anything. She squeezed her eyes shut for a moment before returning to the screen to reread the data.

Request comes from the top. Dr. Hoffman has ordered all tests performed at this lab be classified . . .

Another blink. Longer this time, her eyelids heavier.

Initial tests indicate the craft . . . is just a drone. We haven't yet been able to determine what is controlling the ship, if anything . . .

The words began blending together, and she slowly closed her eyes. Crossing her arms on the desk, she bent down and rested her chin on them. *Only for a minute,* she thought, letting the darkness wash over her.

Thirty seconds later, she was asleep.

———

An explosion of blue light consumed Sophie. It was so powerful, so intense, that it even blocked out the sun.

Squinting, she took a step forward, her boot crushing something beneath it. She looked down to see bones. Not just any bones, but human bones. And they were small. It only took a moment to realize she was looking at a child's remains.

She bent down to examine them. There was something lying next to it—something she recognized. A piece of cloth. A blanket.

Owen's blanket.

Sophie crashed to her knees, a cloud of dust detonating under her. Scooping up the blanket, she pulled it to her chest. "Owen, I'm so sorry," she whimpered, tears flowing freely from her eyes.

Soon the filthy blanket was wet with tears. She tried to look away from the bones but couldn't. One of the loose ribs blew away in a sudden gust of wind.

Clutching the blanket against her chest, she screamed. Something began to build inside her—a feeling that she had suppressed for so long. It had almost destroyed her after the solar storms of 2055.

She'd had enough of the death, enough of the loss.

All she felt was anger.

Wiping away the tears, she wrapped up Owen's remains in the blanket and set them softly on the dusty ground. Then she began walking toward the source of the light. She had no doubt what she would find at the other end of the blue beam. The Organics had killed Owen and would soon kill her.

With her hand steady over her eyes, she could finally make out the source of the light. It was a craft hovering silently over the barren earth.

Her walk turned into a jog and then into a run as the ship came into focus. The sides were black and sleek, almost wet-looking, like a killer whale.

As she got closer, a wind gust stung her bare arms with sand and debris. While she tried to regain her balance, the blue light popped off like a lightbulb blowing a circuit. With the glare from the light gone, she saw the ship in its entirety.

The craft was massive, larger than any she had ever seen. And it was just hovering there. The engineering was unusual, and felt alien—no windows, no wings, and nothing that would indicate it could fly. For a second she felt completely exposed. She remembered the night she'd spent with Emanuel during the solar storms, entwined with his body, imagining it was the last night of their lives. She wished he were there with her now. What would he want her to do? Run?

No, he would tell her to examine the ship, to study it. They were scientists, after all. They had traded their families and futures for a life dedicated to science. Discovery was everything to them.

With a sudden burst of energy, she ran up the hill, loose rocks kicking up behind her. As she climbed, she began to grasp how large the ship really was. She was an ant compared to the monstrosity. And even though there was no signal the craft had spotted her, she felt the overwhelming sense of being watched. The sensation did not deter her. She had to know what was inside and where it came from.

Pushing forward, she climbed to the hilltop. She was directly underneath the ship now, stopping to stare intensely at its glossy, black skin. It was smooth and glistened in the sunlight. She'd always imagined alien spaceships would have some similarities to human ships, but looking up, she realized that she had been completely wrong. This craft was alien in every way.

Fascinating, she thought as she stumbled through the loose sand to get a better look. There appeared to be some sort of oval engraving near the middle of its underbelly. She scooped up a rock, palming its warm weight for a moment. Then she tossed it, watching it sail toward the ship and expecting some sort of force field to stop it in midair. To her surprise, the rock kept going until it lost momentum and fell back down to the sand.

She stood there, expecting something to happen—almost *wanting* something to happen.

She didn't have to wait long. A piercing sound erupted from the ship, and the oval section cracked open, bleeding light. Sophie's excitement faded as the sound intensified, forcing her to cover her ears. Fear drowned out what had moments earlier been exhilaration. A single beam of light shot out of the opening and captured her, spinning her around and pulling her toward the ship. She struggled briefly but knew it was no use. After seeing so many others caught in the same trap, she knew there was no escape.

The only consolation was that she would finally get to see whatever was inside the ship. She would finally get to see the real Organics, the intelligent force behind the invasion that had claimed billions of lives in a matter of weeks.

As the beam pulled her higher, she thought of Emanuel again. A smile broke across her face. She knew he would be proud of her, still curious until the end.

The trip only took a few seconds, and she found herself inside the massive ship before she had time to grasp what was actually happening. Her fear had washed away. The remnants of excitement had vanished, too. She was peculiarly at peace.

The blinding blue light appeared again. As soon as she'd been pulled inside the bay, it consumed her. The brilliant rays seemed to be coming from all around her, like she was in the middle of some sort of halo.

Then, with a massive mechanical click, the light shut off. It was replaced with a softer glow, a cool glow. Before she could identify this new light source, the beam dropped her onto a platform hovering in the dead center of the craft.

She landed softly and rolled to a stop at the edge of the sleek oval stage. As she spun, she saw the interior of the ship was lit by thousands of glowing orbs. They were everywhere, their skin emitting the blue light.

Sophie flinched when the platform below her creaked and lurched forward. The cold metal glided toward the north wall of the ship, headed straight for a cluster of orbs.

Sophie held on to the side of the stage and looked down, her hair blowing as the platform picked up speed. There was no way to tell exactly how far the drop was, but she knew instinctively that a fall would be fatal.

She slowly crawled away from the edge and sat on the cold metal, watching the orbs get closer with increasing fascination. They sparkled like tiny jewels, but their beautiful exteriors, she knew, contained unthinkable things. She suddenly imagined the prisoners she'd seen before. The woman at White Sands, the man in Colorado Springs, their distorted faces and frail bodies. The memories chilled her to the core.

Sophie thought she knew what would be inside the orbs. She assumed that they would contain more human prisoners, but she was wrong. The platform stopped within arm's reach of the nearest cluster. Cautiously, she pulled herself closer to the edge and strained to get a better look. At first she couldn't quite make out the shape inside the orb. But whatever it was, she knew it wasn't human.

The noise from the platform must have disturbed it. A flutter from inside the sphere startled Sophie, and she scrambled on her hands and knees away from the ledge. The orb began to ripple, cracking down the center. Blue goo bled from the opening and dripped into the darkness below.

Sophie waited.

The crack widened, and the orb split open. The alien that emerged was so different from anything she had seen it was hard for her mind to grasp. She blinked to assure herself it was real. The creature had no face. No eyes, no mouth. Just a stem sticking out where a nose should be. Orange petals surrounded the head, which snaked down and connected to a red bioluminescent torso.

It was . . . *beautiful.*

For what seemed like an hour, she sat there studying it, watching the petals curl back, straighten, and then curl again, as if it were breathing.

Turning to examine the next orb, she saw a very different creature inside. This one reminded her of a miniature Christmas tree, with bulb-like lights hanging off purple branches. The adjacent orb contained an alien blob of red flesh with spikes lining its egg-shaped body.

It was then Sophie realized she was inside a cargo ship. An alien Noah's Ark, more than likely filled with species the Organics had collected as they had gone from world to world, collecting water and moving on.

Of course, she thought. What arrogance it had been to assume that Earth was the first world they had visited and drained dry.

An alarm screamed, the sound echoing off the walls. Sophie gripped her ears and bent down to put her head between her knees. By the time it finally dissipated, her ears were pulsing with pain.

Shaking her head, she turned back to the first orb. The beautiful orange petals had discolored to a crusty brown. The stem had shriveled, and the torso was shrinking.

Another explosion came from the orb right in front of her. She looked up to see its skin peeling away, revealing the dying alien within. It was then she saw the tube at the bottom of the sphere, hooked up to the creature's torso. The tube gulped the remaining liquid from the alien and then retracted into the ship's wall.

Sophie reached out to help, but quickly stumbled and fell. She watched as the flower-shaped alien shriveled like a plant under a scorching sun.

Before Sophie had time to move, the alien disappeared out of the bottom of the orb. She scrambled to the end of the platform and watched an oval-shaped hole open in the bottom of the ship. The alien's dried body fluttered down until it vanished from sight.

She gasped, her hand cupping her face. If this was an ark, then why had the ship sucked the alien dry?

It was all too much to comprehend, and Sophie pushed herself to her feet. The platform abruptly shook in protest, throwing her off balance.

Sophie let out a cry as she fell over the side. She flailed her arms, desperately searching for something to hold on to.

Below, she could see the tiny opening approaching. Bracing herself, she closed her eyes and waited for impact. In seconds her ruined body would lie mangled next to Owen's remains and the remains of the flower alien.

CHAPTER 16

THE rap of footfalls beating across the pavement was louder than Overton would have liked. He turned his head to see the ragtag squad of men following him.

Only half of them had night vision, and with nothing but moonlight to guide the others, they stumbled along like they were blind. It was a sorry sight, and Overton cringed every time one of them banged into a car or tripped on a curb.

As they navigated around the twists and turns of empty houses Overton realized there was no way in hell they were going to make it another two blocks to the Humvee without being spotted.

"Emanuel, how's the charge on the, um, magnet thing?"

"The RVAMP?" Emanuel replied over the com. Overton watched him look down at the power meter. "Halfway there."

"Good. The Humvee should be close, but I don't want to get caught in the open with our pants down."

Jeff snickered.

Overhead a drone raced across the sky, leaving a white streak amongst the thousands of stars. Overton hit the ground, ducking for cover. Thompson dove behind a car, crashing into the bumper. The crunching sound of his thick skull breaking the plastic made Overton flinch—not because he was concerned for the man's well-being, but because the sound could attract enemy attention. He knew Thompson had one of the thickest skulls of any marine in the corp.

The empty vehicles scattered across the street provided plenty of cover, and each team member found a place to hide. Overton placed his back against a car door.

He listened for any sign of the aliens. Somewhere in the distance a downed power line whined in the breeze. To his right a glass door tapped against its frame. The owner hadn't bothered to close it, or hadn't had time.

The sounds sent a chill down Overton's spine. A quick sweep of the area revealed the same scene he'd seen in the rest of the city. The once upscale neighborhood had been taken over by dust. Remnants of orbs littered the concrete. They were in the middle of some sort of dead zone—a staging area where the Spiders had taken the initial survivors on invasion day and turned them into orbs.

Truthfully, it was hard for Overton to grasp just how many Spiders, Worms, Sentinels, and God knows what other creatures were out there. The very thought of the slimy bastards enraged him.

After a second more of silence, he shot a hand signal to Bouma, who relayed the gesture to the rest of the squad. It was time to move on. He led the team through the shadows, using the houses as protection.

At the end of the street he could see the outline of the Humvee. It was too early to smile in relief, but Overton grinned anyway.

Almost there.

Bursting around the final front yard, he moved into the street, waving his team on. "Let's go," he whispered over the channel.

They had made it halfway to the truck when the scraping of claws echoed on the concrete behind him. It was faint at first, and Overton hoped it was just Jeff or Kiel brushing up against a car door, but deep down he knew what made the sound.

Risking a glance over his shoulder, Overton saw a hazy but distinct blue flickering behind them.

Quickly he checked the distance between the team and the Humvee. It was too far. They would never make it.

"Down," Overton muttered. He dropped to the ground and crawled under the nearest truck. The others followed suit, ducking for cover where they could, hiding behind anything that might shield them.

"Hold position," Overton whispered over the open net. He watched

Bouma bring a finger to his mouth and silence the men who didn't have access to the channel. They were a few yards back but seemed to understand.

Next, the sergeant continued crawling under the vehicle, his helmet scratching across the chassis. Wincing, he struggled to get a view of their six, where he'd seen the light.

He pulled his rifle close to his chest. Ever so carefully, he raised the scope to his visor, where it linked up with his HUD, and waited for the image to focus. What he saw paralyzed him. Dozens of contacts. Fifty. Maybe more. The end of the block was teeming with the creatures.

After a full career in recon, he knew better than anyone when to fight and when to run. This was not a time to make a stand.

"Emanuel, get that weapon ready! Everyone move!" Overton's voice carried down the street and mixed with the shrieks of a dozen Spiders, which had climbed onto the tops of houses, cars, and trees in every direction.

Overton didn't waste any time. Once he was on his feet, he took a single electromagnetic grenade and tossed it into the air.

"That'll slow 'em down," he grunted.

The squad zigzagged through the suburban street, dodging cars and jumping over plastic trash bins and lumps of fleshy gore. They made it to the Humvee just as a brilliant flash from the grenade knocked out their HUDs.

Overton grabbed the driver's door and snapped around to make sure all his men were accounted for. Three large, two small—they were all there.

"Get us the hell out of here!" Kiel screamed, sliding into the back-seat.

Thompson grabbed Jeff and boosted him into the Humvee. The big marine climbed in behind him while Emanuel jumped in the passenger seat. Bouma jumped in just as the engine roared to life.

Overton finally allowed himself to breathe and stomped on the pedal as if it were a poisonous spider. Twisting the wheel to the right, he steered the truck up onto a curb, smashing into three of the closest Spiders.

"Watch out!" Jeff yelled as another one of the creatures lunged off a rooftop and landed on the Humvee. Overton pushed down on the gas and they fishtailed; the alien scrambled, its talons sliding across the hood until one of them hooked into the soft metal.

"Go, go, go!" Thompson screamed. He pounded his fist on Overton's headrest.

When the tires stopped squealing, the truck lurched forward and Overton steered it back onto the street. The Spider let out a deafening screech of pain. Two of its legs were trapped under the front of the vehicle. With one of its free legs, it swiped at the windshield. The glass shattered as the alien tore it away and launched the pane into the night.

"Shoot it! Someone shoot it!" Kiel yelled from the backseat.

Overton ducked as the Spider swiped through the open windshield with another claw. Throwing on the brakes, he sent the creature flying backward, two of its claws still stuck in the hood. The limbs ripped from its body, spraying blue goo in all directions. Overton didn't waste any time smashing into the injured creature with the truck's brush guard. The alien's shrieks sent a thrill through him as he sped down the street, the Spider still stuck underneath the truck.

He snorted a laugh. "Having fun yet?"

Only Jeff laughed.

Taking a hard left, Overton pulled the Humvee onto the highway, and the Spiders finally disappeared from sight.

The sound of labored breathing filled the vehicle.

"Everyone okay back there?" Overton spun to check on his team.

Kiel nodded. "Jesus, man. That was close."

"Seems to always be like that with this guy," Emanuel said. He shook his head and turned to look out the window.

Jeff climbed up to look out the back window. "Holy crap! I can't believe we made it out of there. Thanks for not forgetting about me."

"Don't mention it, kid. Like you said, I owed you one."

Jeff chuckled and sat back down. He reached for a seat belt and clicked in.

"Where the hell are we going?" asked Thompson, wiping sweat from his flushed face. "And where the hell have you been hiding all this time?"

Overton stared ahead at the dark road, using his night vision to navigate the littered highway. He checked the mirror again, looking at the dirty faces of his lost—and now found—men. Instead of responding, he pushed down harder on the pedal. There would be plenty of time to explain everything to them. For now, he wanted to make sure they got back to the Biosphere in one piece. He had a small army now, a team he could launch his counteroffensive with, and a weapon that would ensure success.

A crooked grin spread across his face. He would have his war after all.

CHAPTER 17

WHEN Alex awoke, he had no idea where he was or how he had gotten there. He tried to sit up, but a flash of pain in his forehead forced him back down. Beneath him was a soft bed—a small comfort, but only a distraction from the fear swelling inside him. The last thing he remembered was the beach packed with Spiders.

His brain was so full of cobwebs, his memories stuck together. The one thing he wanted to remember seemed out of his grasp. Clenching his teeth, he massaged his temples.

What the hell had happened to him, and how did he end up in this place?

The chirp of a monitor spread a gracious orange glow over the sparsely furnished room. The quarters were small, no larger than a holding cell. As his eyes adjusted to the light, he panicked. Was he in a jail? Had he been captured? The space looked human.

He scanned the room for anything useful—anything that could help him remember.

The monitor flashed again, and three letters rolled across the screen.
N   T   C

And then he remembered: the bright light, the massive vessel, and the NTC officers pumping water out of his lungs. He had been captured; he was aboard a New Tech Corporation submarine.

Alex tried to sit up again. He brought a hand to his pounding skull and tried to clear his mind. It was then he noticed the wrapping around his wrist. Someone had dressed his injury. His eyes fell to his legs.

He was dressed in sweats. NTC was stitched across his chest.

Footfalls outside the room pulled his attention to the open door. The panic subsided; there wasn't any prison he knew of that kept the cells unlocked. He turned back to the monitor and noticed a tray on the small desk nearby. On it was a plate of food and . . . Alex could hardly believe his eyes. He jumped out of the bed and pounced on the glass of water. It was gone in one large gulp.

Next he attacked the plate of food. He shoved chunks into his mouth, not even sure what he was eating. His jaws were smacking so loudly, he almost missed the voice in the doorway.

"Hungry?"

Alex turned to see the same tall, bearded man from earlier. With his broad shoulders and red beard, he reminded Alex of a Viking. Several medals decorated the man's chest, implying he was no ordinary NTC staffer. Alex was torn between wanting to shout at the man and wanting to thank him for his rescue. NTC had abandoned his Biosphere and left everyone to die, but these officers had dressed his wounds and given him water. He didn't know how to react or what to say.

"You're one lucky son of a bitch," the man said, and extended his hand. "Captain Rick Noble; we're pleased to have you aboard."

Alex reached out instinctively, his eyes still fixed on the captain's medals. "Thanks," he muttered.

Noble smiled. "I can assure you, Alex Wagner, you'll be very safe—"

Hearing the man say his name reminded Alex of all that NTC had done. "Listen, I appreciate the rescue, I really do. But NTC knew about this shit from the beginning!" Alex said, his voice echoing off the walls. "You could have done something to stop it . . ." He trailed off as he considered his words. Maybe he was wrong. Maybe NTC couldn't have stopped it. Maybe that's why the sub was hiding under the ocean.

Noble didn't immediately respond. Instead he turned toward the monitor, running a finger through his beard. The screen had switched to a video feed of a pair of jellyfish gliding by, a beautiful purple glow from their bodies illuminating the water around them. There was something tranquil about their movements. The anger building inside Alex subsided as he watched the creatures. He had seen them on documentaries before, but it never occurred to him that he might someday see these animals in their natural habitat. As he watched their bodies pulsate, Alex shifted uncomfortably. The jellyfish were far too reminiscent of the aliens that had been hunting him for the past week.

"Fascinating, aren't they?" asked Noble. "The fact that they can live so far down, where the pressure would kill a man in seconds, is nothing short of miraculous."

Alex shook his head. "With all due respect, I doubt you paid me a visit to discuss biology. Why are you here? Why did you save me?"

Again, Noble remained silent, his blue eyes studying Alex. The tension between them built in the stillness. Finally the captain said, "If you want to find out, follow me. I think we can answer all your questions."

Noble stalked out of the room, not bothering to see if Alex followed. Alex looked down again at the tray of food and noticed a small tube of medicated ointment. He would have smiled if his lips weren't so cracked. NTC had certainly laid out the red carpet for his arrival. They had given him food, water, and medication for his dry lips. That was enough for him. Grabbing the tube, he raced into the hallway, yelling, "Wait up!"

Noble was waiting for him a few doors down, his hands clasped behind his back. He eyed Alex's wrist before continuing down the hall.

"How's that feeling?"

Alex looked down at his injured arm and shrugged. "Not bad."

For the next several minutes he led Alex through the bowels of the massive sub. They walked in silence, and Alex took in the sounds of the ship. The scuffling of feet from busy crew, the sporadic chirps from engineering monitors, the hissing of steam. He soaked it all in.

As they passed through an auxiliary machine room, he realized he was not on a tour. Captain Noble was leading him somewhere. With every step, Alex felt a growing tension. Weeks of constant vigilance had left him on edge, and although there were no alien monsters here, NTC might be hiding something much worse on this secret submarine.

They continued through another series of passages. Blue screens and control panels lined the walls, monitoring everything from life support systems to the sanitary sewer.

"Morning, sir," a crew member said as Noble squeezed past him. Alex didn't recognize her as one of his saviors from the night before, and he wondered how many people were aboard the submarine.

The captain nodded and smiled. "Morning, Pearce."

As they traveled deeper into the vessel, Alex took note of the interaction between Noble and his crew. The captain made a conscientious effort to stop and say hello to every one of them. He wasn't like the other NTC brass Alex had met. They had all been humorless hardasses, exactly the sort of people who toed the company line even if it meant sending the rest of the world to hell. Alex hated the bastards on principle, but Noble seemed more, well, *noble* than the rest of them.

When they arrived at the CIC, Noble stopped. He turned to face Alex, his shoulders blocking the entrance.

"We don't normally let civilians in here, but I'm making an exception for you," he said. "This is the nerve center of the *Ghost of Atlantis*."

Alex raised an eyebrow.

"Those of us in the know call her GOA—and luckily there aren't many of us in the know. Our coordinates are top secret, and from what we've seen so far, the aliens apparently have a hard time detecting us through all this water. Ironic, isn't it?"

Alex shrugged. He was just glad the Spiders hadn't followed them into the water.

"Technically, you are standing inside the most advanced submarine ever engineered. Like Atlantis, we're deep below the waves, hoping to stay hidden from an invading force. We have more than enough food and weapons in case we get into a dicey situation," Noble said, smiling. "But enough about all that. Are you ready to see why I brought you here?"

Alex nodded, but as he followed the captain into the dimly lit room, he had the sinking feeling that he wasn't ready for whatever Noble wanted to show him.

Everyone in the Humvee froze when they saw the ship. The drone was flying low to the ground, cruising across the skyline.

Overton eased the truck to a stop and wedged the vehicle behind a pair of sedans. Killing the engine, he turned to look at Emanuel.

"Is that thing charged yet?"

The biologist shook his head. "I need more time."

Bouma poked his helmeted head into the front seat. "Maybe it won't see us," he said.

Overton turned to watch the drone make another pass. It was circling, looking for something or someone.

Hunting.

They were only a few miles from the turnoff for the Biosphere—so close, but impossibly far at the same time. With a blink, Overton switched his HUD to infrared again, just to ensure there weren't any other Organics in their path.

"I need to get back to my brother," Jeff said.

"I know kid, I know. Let me think," said Overton. He turned to Emanuel. "Don't bullshit me. Will that thing work if we need it?"

"Yes," said the scientist, "but the effect will carry over a shorter range than the last time."

Overton exhaled, fogging up his visor. "All right, we sit here for five more minutes. If the drone doesn't pass us by, we go to plan B."

"What's plan B?" Kiel asked.

"I don't know yet, but I have five minutes to figure it out."

"Guys . . ." Jeff whispered. Louder, he repeated, "Guys!"

"What is it, kid?" Overton barked, turning to look at the boy. As soon as he did, he saw the horde of Spiders barreling down the highway.

Jeff looked up at Overton, squinting. "Let's kill 'em," he said. "Let's kill 'em all."

Overton saw Bouma smile from the backseat. That was his line.

The CIC was packed with staffers, some carrying tablets, others carrying old-fashioned notebooks. A chorus of chirps and beeps echoed through the space. Overhead, red and white LEDs flickered in every direction. The entire scene was chaos. After being alone for so long, the noise made Alex feel uneasy.

"This is where we monitor everything. And by *everything*, I mean everything. See that over there?" Noble said, pointing to a hologram of what appeared to be the UK. "They got hit the worst. The Biosphere there has been silent since invasion day. We've had intermittent contact with the Brazilian Biosphere, but nothing in the past week."

"How many Biospheres are there?" asked Alex.

"There were fifty, strategically placed throughout the world. Truth is, we didn't know about them until we received a message from Doctor Hoffman. Before that, we had been drifting through the Pacific for five months with no details about our deployment."

Noble paused and looked at the electronic map of the world.

"There are only ten Biospheres left that we know of. Every week it seems like one of those red dots fades off the screen. Thankfully, a few are still holding strong. Our Cheyenne Mountain facility seems to be faring much better than the others."

"Dr. Rodriguez," Alex blurted, remembering their conversation. "From Cheyenne Mountain. I spoke to him on the radio back on the beach. He said something about developing a weapon that could change the course of the war."

"What else did he say?" Noble asked, his eyes instantly growing wider.

"That's it. I was being chased by those things." Alex looked at his feet.

Noble nodded and didn't press any further. "You're damned lucky to be alive, Alex. Damned lucky. Without that radio sending us signals, you would have been fish food by now."

Alex glanced at the radio sticking out of his pocket. The top of the device was scratched from when he had tossed it aside a few days before. He tucked it deeper into the safety of his pocket.

"You okay?" Noble asked.

"Yeah. I just don't get it. If all modern communications have been knocked out—including satellites—then how does this radio work?"

"Good question," Noble quickly replied. "Truth is, we don't really know why, but anything analog seems to work. The magnetic disturbance above the surface," he said, pointing toward the ceiling. "It fried most everything on invasion day and it continues to disrupt communications. Whoever designed the radio for the Biospheres must have known something we don't. This sub is linked directly to the channel these analog radios transmit on."

Alex scowled. "So you're saying that NTC knew about the invasion?"

"I'd say there's a good chance, although I don't know much more than you," Noble replied. He turned to check one of the monitors before continuing through the CIC. They passed a pair of holographic charts and stopped at a large monitor. "We're learning more and more about the aliens every day, which still isn't much in the scheme of things, but enough to start planning."

"Planning?"

"An offensive. This vessel is humanity's best hope and her most valuable weapon. We're equipped with nuclear-tipped missiles, three NTC-44 helicopters, a smaller sub for recon, and a crew of 120 brilliant men and women. We're more than capable of waging a full-fledged war from eight hundred feet beneath the surface."

Alex surveyed the CIC again. He was impressed, but after seeing what had happened on the outside, he doubted the sub could do much more than annoy the Organics.

"Follow me," Noble said, motioning Alex past an NTC guard at the hatch. As they made their way down a small flight of metal stairs into the heart of the CIC, a man in a neatly pressed blue NTC uniform approached them.

"Captain on deck," he said.

Noble smiled. "Lieutenant Commander Lin, this is Alex Wagner."

Lin reached out to shake Alex's hand. "Welcome aboard." Though his words were friendly, there was a calculating intelligence in his eyes.

"There's someone else I'd like you to meet," Noble said. "Irene, are you busy?"

An orange avatar shot out of a console next to the door. Alex knew right away it was the ship's AI. She had the cropped hair typical of other AIs, but she wore glasses—something he'd never seen before.

"Hello, Alex. I am Irene. Welcome to the *Ghost of Atlantis*. Please do not hesitate to ask if you need anything," she said with a thick Russian accent.

"Thank you," Alex said as he followed Noble past another row of terminals. "A Russian AI?" he whispered.

The captain chuckled. "I failed to mention the most advanced submarine in the world was actually built by the Russians. Commissioned by NTC in twenty fifty-nine."

"Don't they have an entire research division that designs AIs?"

"They do, but Irene was part of the deal. And she was worth every dollar."

"Thank you, sir," Irene replied.

"I see," Alex said, strolling over to a translucent image of the Earth that was speckled with glowing blue circles. "What do these dots represent?"

"I take it you've seen the human farms."

Alex shook his head. He'd seen a lot in the time he'd spent outside, but nothing that he would have classified as a human farm.

"Wait, do you mean the orbs?"

"No, this is something much worse," Noble said. "You aren't the only survivor out there, Alex. And this may be hard for you to believe, but there are millions of others. Only . . ." Noble paused as one of his crew members squeezed by them.

"Only what?"

"Come with me, I want you to see something."

The two men walked through the gallery of monitors and holograms, maneuvering carefully past staffers who were busily analyzing a constant stream of data. When they finally reached the middle of the deck Noble stopped and rested his hand against a metal pole extending from the ceiling with two handles attached to it. This was not a modern piece of technology; this was a tool from the past. Alex wasn't sure what the device was at first, but then he remembered seeing one in a military book his father had kept on their coffee table.

"Is that a periscope?" he asked.

"Ever seen one?"

Alex shook his head. "Not in person."

"Most people haven't. The navy stopped using them years ago. When NTC commissioned this ship and selected me as captain, I requested one. Why? Because I believe the best way isn't necessarily the newest way. Our instructions from Doctor Hoffman were clear, but he gave me the leeway to carry out the mission as I see fit."

"And what is that mission?"

Noble nodded as if he approved of Alex's question. "We are to be observers only."

Alex hesitated before responding. "Meaning what, exactly?"

"Doctor Hoffman gave us strict orders. Do not interfere with the Biospheres. He didn't want us to risk being discovered. Our job was to watch and document what was going on. But after realizing how bad things really were outside, I broke protocol and had my chief communication engineer tap into the channel. We've been trying to contact the Biospheres ever since."

Alex had so many questions that he had trouble narrowing them down. "What about other submarines and military bases? The army, the navy, the marines, NTC—you said there were other survivors. Have you been able to reach any of them?"

Noble shrugged. "You'd think so, but we've only been able to get through to the Biospheres on the encrypted channel. If there are other subs out there, then they're hiding just like us. I've tasked two of my communications officers with trying to make contact, but so far, nothing."

Alex's mind reeled. It was hard for him to believe the military was gone or hiding. Even with a bellyful of food and a bit of rest, Alex was feeling light-headed. He was still severely dehydrated—which reminded him he needed to piss again. The mere thought sent pain racing through his groin. He knew it was going to hurt.

"At any rate, we got lucky," Noble continued. "With these old tools, we aren't completely blind. Check this out." The captain spun the periscope in Alex's direction. "I had them include the most advanced fiber-optic system on the market. You can see inside moon craters with this one. I've had Irene load some images we captured last time we used it. Go ahead and take a look, but be prepared for a shock."

Alex grabbed the handles, pulling the eyepiece to his face. The captain was right; what he saw was beyond belief.

Are those really people?

Alex finally realized what Noble had meant when he had used the term *human farms*. The images were horrifying, revealing not one but hundreds of poles lining the beach in the distance. There was no way to determine how many humans were attached to them, and no way to determine if they were alive or dead.

Pushing the scope away, Alex felt a wave of dizziness rush over him. He tried to speak, but his lips were numb. His body was tired. He'd been on the run for so long. And now he had seen something that couldn't be unseen. It was too much for his brain to handle.

Noble reached out to steady him, but it was too late. Alex's legs gave out and he collapsed onto the metal deck. He struggled to stay conscious, but pain pounded in his head as he lay helpless on the floor.

"Get us some help!" Noble yelled, crouching by Alex's side. "It's going to be okay. I'm sorry; I should have warned you first."

"Captain!" Another staffer yelled from the back of the room. "Sir, you need to see this."

Alex caught a quick glimpse of an older female NTC officer, her freckled face filled with fear.

"Sir, we didn't pick anything up on radar. Whatever this thing is, it's using stealth technology," she continued.

"Irene, switch on the lights," Noble ordered. "Lin, prepare to take evasive measures."

The massive LEDs blinked on at the bow, shooting a brilliant beam through the darkness. The beams lit up a sleek black object. At first Alex thought it was another submarine, but as it crept closer, he realized it was something much, much bigger.

Alex squirmed on the floor trying to blink the stars out of his vision, but the booming pain in his head was just too much. Defeated, he closed his eyes and heard Irene's Russian accent break over the com.

"Contact heading right for us, sir. Impact in T minus thirty-five point five seconds."

CHAPTER 18

WITHIN seconds, the first wave of Spiders exploded over a tangled mass of empty cars. Like hungry ants, they swarmed over the useless vehicles, scraping and clawing their way closer to the Humvee.

Overton scanned the highway for an escape route. A small ridgeline would provide them some cover on the north side, but the south was nothing more than an empty field of dead grass. If they tried to outrun the Spiders by heading west, the drone would catch them. The east was overrun with the advancing horde. There was no clear option.

With one hand on the steering wheel and the other on his rifle, he looked at his men. They had been in the muck for weeks, and Overton was about to put them through more of it.

He scowled and felt the scars on his face stretch. Would he be earning a new one soon? He looked at his HUD to see only thirty seconds had passed since the drone had spotted them. Time was up. It was action time.

"Emanuel, give Kiel and Thompson your weapons. When I tell you to activate the RVAMP, you do it. Immediately. Got it?" Overton barked.

Emanuel nodded and handed his rifle and pistol to the two marines in the backseat just as blue light consumed the truck. The drone was hovering over them. Overton felt the engine die as the ship shot a beam of light at the vehicle, knocking out the electronics in one quick click.

"What's happening?" Jeff cried.

"Stay here, kid," Overton said as he tossed his spare electromagnetic pulse grenade at Bouma. "Kiel, Thompson—you concentrate your fire on the horde after the 'nade goes off. Bouma, I want you to keep your fire on that drone. Do *not* let the beam touch you!"

The men nodded, and Overton grabbed his door handle. He felt the adrenaline pumping into his blood stream. This was what he lived for—this was what he was going to die doing.

He hesitated and then took off his helmet. The electromagnetic pulse grenade was going to knock out his HUD anyway.

"Get it done!" Overton yelled, snapping the door open and jumping onto the blacktop. With one swift move he launched his last grenade at the Spiders and went down on one knee. He watched the device sail through the air and wedge underneath the tire of a minivan a couple hundred yards away.

Bouma fired first. The rounds tore into the drone above, ricocheting off its sides, and knocking the craft off its axis. The slight change in movement was just what Thompson and Kiel needed to move into position. Overton grinned and licked the sweat off his upper lip. The grenade went off just as the first Spiders passed the minivan.

A shockwave ripped through the aliens' shields, knocking out the first dozen. But there were many more still standing. Hundreds. An endless army as far as Overton could see. And moving amongst the sea of blue was something large—something with a back full of spikes.

Jamie's soft words echoed in Overton's mind. *Those were the small monsters.* It seemed like a lifetime ago that he'd rescued the little ankle-biter.

"Holy shit," Overton muttered. He squeezed off a few shots at the closest Spiders in an attempt to get a better look at the creature. As limbs exploded in all directions, he caught a glimpse of a pair of hooves, and a body covered in dark black scales.

What the fuck? Overton thought. If this thing had armor, it was going to take more than a pulse grenade to bring it down.

Before he could get a target on the beast, another pack of Spiders moved in to replace the ones he had already splattered across the highway. Over the crack of gunfire, Overton could hear the massive creature's hooves cracking the cement beneath its weight. Small tremors followed the sound as the alien made its way closer. Not a sound he wanted to hear. He swallowed. Hard. This thing was like an alien tank.

He moved into a better position, checking his six to make sure the drone hadn't flanked them. When he turned back to the horde, the sharp edge of a massive beak smashed through a cluster of Spiders, and Overton saw the face of the monster for the first time. He lowered his weapon in awe and watched the creature swing its beak from side to side, sending Spiders tumbling across the highway.

"Overton, what are you doing? Shoot that thing!" a voice shouted.

But Overton couldn't pull his gaze away from the beast. It had the body of an oversized rhino and the face of a bird, with a long black beak the length of his pulse rifle. And staring right at him were . . . he counted them one by one.

Nine eyes.

"Overton! Snap out of it! Shoot that thing," Bouma yelled.

The creature smashed through another group of Spiders, plastering the highway with blue goo. Overton couldn't help but feel a sick sense of respect for the alien. It displayed a brute strength and domination over the Spiders.

It wasn't until Overton saw the orbs lining the creature's underbelly that he finally snapped out of his trance. He shouldered his weapon and yelled, spit exploding from his mouth. "Emanuel, how long until that thing is charged?"

A second of silence passed before the scientist replied.

"A couple of minutes, max!"

Overton looked back at the growing pile of body parts a few hundred yards away. Even if they were able to hold off the Spiders, this new alien was going to be on top of them soon. They didn't have minutes— they had seconds, at best.

Overton fired off the last of his magazine and tossed his rifle on the ground. Racing back to the truck, he opened the passenger door and grabbed the mobile RVAMP from Emanuel.

"Show me how to work this thing."

"Push here," the biologist said, pointing at a button.

The marine didn't reply; he simply grabbed the device and took off running toward the swarming aliens. Bouma had pushed the drone north, over the ridgeline, but out of the corner of his eye, Overton saw a third pack of Spiders. The creatures burst over the hill, some of them tumbling limb over limb and forming a wave of swimming blue flesh.

They were about to flank Thompson, who was concentrating his fire on the aliens to the east. Before Overton could do more than shout a warning, they were on the big marine. Sharp claws ripped through his back and lifted his massive body into the air like he was a slab of meat. The pack swarmed, stabbing him repeatedly as he fired off rounds into the sky, the gunfire drowning out his screams. Bright red blood stained the cement, mixing with the river of blue goo.

Kiel turned to see his friend take his last breaths. "No!" he yelled, turning to fire his pistol at the swarm. The rounds bounced off the Spiders' shields, and they continued to surge forward.

The sound of death filled the highway. Shrieks from the Spiders mixed with the snorting of the massive beast as it broke through the line of dead bodies. Legs, torsos, and claws exploded into the air.

Bouma and Kiel dove for cover, but Overton advanced. He wasn't sure what the range was on the device, but he wanted to be as close as possible. His heart pumped adrenaline through every vein in his body. He could almost taste it.

When the beast was less than fifty yards away, Overton slid to his knees, bringing the device into his lap. He pushed the button and waited for the weapon to work. Nothing happened.

He looked up. The monster was racing toward him, bucking Spiders in all directions.

Overton hit the button again.

Click.

A shockwave ripped through the humid morning air. The beast approaching him let out an earsplitting shriek.

Overton watched as the alien's legs gave out underneath its massive frame. With a crash, the monster collapsed onto the concrete and glided across the highway. The creature's head smashed into a car, sending the sedan rolling into a ditch.

Overton stayed kneeling as the beast slid toward him. He closed his eyes, waiting for the alien to smash into him and crush him with its enormous weight.

Seconds later, the highway was quiet. The Organics' screams had dissipated. Cracking his right eye open, Overton looked up into the face of the new alien. Its beak opened and a slender blue tongue snaked out. With one last violent twitch, the creature released a cloud of rotten breath, peppering Overton's face with chunks of blue spit.

He wiped it out of his eyes just as a small hand shook his shoulder.

"You did it," Jeff said.

Overton kept his focus on the monster's face. He couldn't bring himself to look at the orbs that had split open when the beast fell, nor at the distorted human bodies spilling out of the broken spheres. Instead, he looked into the alien's twitching eyes and spat in the dying creature's face.

"We need to go, Sergeant Overton," Jeff said, shaking the marine's shoulder more forcefully.

"The Humvee is toast," Bouma shouted.

Wiping a slimy mixture of Organic blood and sweat off his forehead, Overton returned his focus to the situation at hand. Scanning the Humvee, Overton could see that Bouma was right. A thick plume of smoke rose from underneath the hood. Although the highway was littered with cars, they were all dead or wrecked.

"Bouma, find one that you can get to work. One with a hydrogen fuel cell might be our best bet," Overton ordered.

While his men searched for a vehicle, Overton turned to watch the morning sun rising higher over the highway. The brilliant orange rays illuminated a puddle of red blood snaking out from under a pile of dead Spiders. A pair of boots were just visible beneath the gore, but Overton turned away. He couldn't bear to look at Thompson's remains. He'd seen too many of his men dead already.

CHAPTER 19

WHEN Sophie awoke, she found herself curled up next to David. She must have stumbled to his room after her nightmare.

His body was a small, still lump under the covers, and in the dim light she couldn't see if his chest was moving. She reached out hesitantly, the horror of her dream still fresh in her mind. When she found a steady pulse at his neck, Sophie had to stop herself from gathering him up in a hug. The boy needed his rest; he had been worried sick over Jeff's kidnapping, and it would be best to let him sleep.

Relieved, she rubbed her eyes and scanned the room. Holly was curled up in a very uncomfortable-looking position in a chair by the door. Jamie and Owen were wrapped in blankets and sleeping peacefully in the center of the room.

Sophie swung her feet onto the cold floor and reached for her boots. Slowly she tiptoed past Holly and the kids, making her way quietly into the hallway. It was just after eight A.M., and the sun would be past rising outside. She wanted to believe that Emanuel and the others were coming back, but with every passing hour she knew their chances grew slimmer. Hope was slowly bleeding out of her.

Not knowing where she was headed, she paced down the passages connecting the biomes, the lights clicking on as she passed their sensors. When she got to the garden, she stopped and took in a deliberately long breath. Orange trees filled the room with an intoxicating smell, but she kept walking, her boots clicking against the metal surface.

Pausing at the stairway, she took in the expansive field of mature cornstalks. She'd always been a city girl, but there was something romantic about farming. Sophie smiled, thinking of Emanuel's enthusiasm for all things green and growing.

Looking over the rows of crops, she realized how lucky she had been—not only to have survived the invasion, but also to have been picked for the Biosphere mission. Of course, it wasn't all luck. She had worked hard to get where she was in her career, but they had hit the jackpot on invasion day, not only surviving but also finding a home in one of the safest places left on Earth. Her smile faded. Would it still be worth it if Emanuel wasn't there to enjoy it with her?

Jumping off the platform, she landed in the dirt and carefully trotted through the corn to the apple tree at the center of the biome. One of its branches grazed her cheek as she approached. Sophie winced and ducked beneath it to stand beside the trunk. She gazed up at the flurry of green. The leaves were mostly still healthy, with only a few brown tips in sight.

She let her back slide against the bark until her butt hit the dirt.

"Ouch," she said, realizing she'd sat on her radio. She pulled it from her belt and looked at the display. The same flat wavelength raced across the screen, but she decided to try it anyway.

"This is Doctor Sophie Winston with the Cheyenne Mountain Biosphere. Does anyone read me? Um, over." She frowned. Military lingo was something she'd never quite mastered. To be honest, she'd never seen the need before now. Overton was always going on about "contacts" and "watching their six," and though she'd picked up quite a bit of the jargon, it was still an unfamiliar language.

Sharp static broke over the single channel, and she watched the wavelength intently for any sign of movement.

Nothing.

Sophie sighed and clipped the radio to her belt.

"Alexia, any news from the outside?" she said, knowing the AI would hear her.

"Good morning, Doctor Winston. I'm sorry, but there is no news yet."

Sophie closed her eyes and pounded the back of her head several times against the bark.

"Goddamn it," she said, wincing and reaching back to cup her bruised skull. Waiting was the hardest part, especially when she knew that Emanuel was in grave danger. He was basically all she had left. She knew her family and everyone else on the outside was dead. Her friends, her colleagues. All dead. She couldn't lose him, too.

Somewhere in the distance, an alarm chirped. Sophie's eyelids snapped open. "What is it, Alexia?"

"One moment, scanning."

A moment of silence, and then Alexia's calm voice said, "Contacts, Doctor Winston."

Pain pinched Sophie's gut. Damned military lingo—*contacts* could mean anything from a horde of Organics to her returning team.

"Can you be more specific?" Sophie yelled.

"Camera 1 is picking up a vehicle traveling quickly up the frontage road."

Sophie raced through the cornstalks, pushing them out of her way without care. She emerged near the metal doors leading out of the Biosphere. With one leap, she jumped onto the platform and ran toward them.

The faint sound of footsteps broke out over the stillness of the gardens. Sophie turned to see Holly standing in the passageway at the far side of Biome 1. By her side were Jamie and Owen.

"We have company!" Sophie yelled, cupping her hands around her mouth so her voice would travel. "Take the kids to the medical ward and lock the door. Alexia can't confirm whether they're friendly or hostiles."

Holly caught Sophie's gaze for a split second and mouthed what appeared to be "Good luck."

Sophie nodded and turned back to the entrance. She grabbed the pistol Overton had given her and aimed it at the door. Sucking in a deep breath, she clicked off the safety. There was little chance anyone would be able to get into the Biosphere, but if she had learned anything since the invasion, it was that nothing was impossible.

Overton slammed on the brakes of the minivan, nearly crashing it into the blast doors. Jumping onto the tarmac, he jammed his helmet back over his face. The visor immediately clouded with steam from the heat radiating off his forehead.

"This is Sergeant Ash Overton, Alexia, do you read? Over," Overton said into his mic.

"Welcome home, Sergeant Overton," said the AI. "Please prepare to enter the facility."

"Good to be back," he said. He grabbed his empty rifle and made his way to the massive blast doors where Emanuel, Jeff, and Bouma were already waiting.

"Where's Kiel?" Overton asked.

Bouma pointed silently back the way they'd come. Kiel stood staring at the rear of the minivan, where they'd stowed Thompson's bloody remains.

"Can someone help me?" Kiel asked.

Overton scowled behind his visor, trying to hide his discomfort. He should have been the one asking that question, not Kiel. After all, Thompson's death was on his hands.

Overton swung his rifle over his back and jogged over to the vehicle.

"He's going to be heavy," Kiel said gravely.

Overton remembered the shoulder wound he had sustained a few weeks ago and said, "Bouma, get your ass over here. Jeff, Emanuel, you guys go on without us. We'll be there as soon as we can."

The blast doors hissed from the hydraulics and the metal groaned open. Emanuel acknowledged Overton's orders with a quick nod and then led Jeff into the cargo bay. The boy glanced over his shoulder one last time, thanking the sergeant with a smile.

Overton grinned and gave the kid a haphazard salute that made Jeff smile even wider. He stood and watched the two disappear, listening to the oddly comforting sound of creaking metal. The sound meant they were home, and it was a welcome reprieve from the alien shrieks that were still echoing in his mind.

"Ready?" Bouma asked, grabbing Thompson's legs.

Overton nodded solemnly, the small comfort from the noise of human engineering quickly vanishing at the sight of the dead marine.

"On the count of three," he said. Taking in a measured breath, he scanned the marine's massive frame. Bloodstains surrounded puncture wounds all over his uniform where the Spiders had stabbed him over and over. Noticing Thompson's eyes were still open, Overton reached over and closed them before grabbing the man under his left arm.

"Ready?" he asked.

The men nodded, and Overton started counting.

"One . . . two . . . three!"

With a heave, the marines pulled Thompson's body out of the minivan and carried him into the bay. They set him down softly on the concrete floor inside. Kiel grabbed a tarp and began to pull it over his friend's body when Overton held out his hand.

"Wait." The sergeant crouched and pulled Thompson's dog tags off his neck. "I'm sorry," he whispered. Overton forced himself to look once more at the lifeless marine's face. First Finley and now Thompson. Not to mention the rest of his squad, who could still be out there.

"Fuck," Overton muttered. He rose to his feet and kicked a nearby crate as hard as he could, sending it skidding across the floor. Bouma and Kiel stood with their heads bowed as one last ray of sunlight shone through the gap in the doors before they clanged shut.

"How's everyone doing?" Emanuel said, grabbing Sophie's hand. She smiled and turned to embrace him. She'd hardly stopped hugging him since his return.

"Much better now that you're back," she said, smiling.

In the distance, Sophie could hear Overton arguing with Bouma and the newest addition to their team, Kiel, in the hallway outside the mess hall. Overton was pissed, judging by the language he was using. Holly cupped Jamie's and Owen's ears with her hands, pulling their heads next to her sides.

"What happened out there?" Sophie whispered.

"I'll tell you later," Emanuel said, his eyes wide and full of excitement. "All I can say right now is the weapon works. It really works!" he exclaimed, grasping Sophie's hand even tighter.

Holly looked up from the children and caught Sophie's gaze.

"Team meeting in fifteen minutes," Sophie said. "Holly, I hate to make you the babysitter again, but someone needs to look after the kids."

"I'll do it," a young voice said from behind Sophie. Jeff stood at the room's entrance, a streak of dirt still smudged across his face. "I'm old enough. I can look after them while you guys meet."

Sophie smiled and patted Jeff on his shoulder. The boy had shown he could handle himself outside. That was enough proof that he could take care of the younger children. "Okay. If you need anything, you know where we will be."

The boy nodded and returned to his brother, who was beaming.

"Did you miss me while I was gone?"

David blinked several times, as if considering something. Then he smiled slightly. "Yeah. But I had the weirdest dreams," he said.

His words reminded Sophie of her own nightmares, and her joy at seeing Jeff safely returned faded.

"What is it?" Emanuel asked.

Sophie shook her head. "Nothing. It's nothing. I'm just glad he's okay." She couldn't meet his eyes; Emanuel would see right through her. She looked down, carefully schooling her features into a pleasant, professional mask. Her team needed her to be a leader, now more than ever. She didn't have the luxury of falling apart.

THE medical team pushed Alex out of the CIC in a wheelchair as Captain Noble yelled at his crew. "What the hell are we looking at, and why didn't we detect it earlier?"

His words echoed off the walls as the CIC staff studied their monitors for an explanation. Each one knew the grave truth—they had finally been discovered. But by who or what, they weren't sure.

"Now!" Noble bellowed, his voice just short of a scream.

Lin finally broke the silence with a muffled cough. "Sir, you are looking at a class X-9 Chinese submarine." He glanced down at his blue screen. "Irene, upload the schematics."

"What do you mean, Chinese? That's impossible," Noble said, breathing hard as he studied the image of the sleek black craft.

"Take a look at this, sir," Lin said, motioning the captain over to his terminal, where Irene had projected a 3-D image of the craft. The sub was massive; four times the size of any NTC or US Navy boat. It shouldn't have even existed. After NTC had hired mercenaries to set off EMPs in China, their fleet of submarines had disappeared. He'd always thought the tales of Chinese vessels roaming the deep were just an old pirate's myth, but the proof was in front of him.

He'd always been afraid this day would come, when the Chinese would reemerge and seek revenge. But why now? The world had already ended. Would they seriously consider launching torpedoes at the GOA? Maybe they didn't realize how important it was for what was left of the human race to stick together. Or maybe they didn't know what was going on above them—maybe they had been hiding for so long they hadn't heard about the invasion at all.

Noble rubbed his beard and turned to Lin. "Have we been able to get any messages through yet?"

"No, sir. They aren't responding to any of our attempts."

"What about Morse code?"

Lin snapped his fingers at Trish, a communications engineer. The woman was a marvel, able to communicate in eleven different languages. Including, as it happened, the Chinese telegraph code. She tapped so fast that Noble, with his limited knowledge of the code, couldn't keep up.

After a pause, she grabbed her headset and pushed it against her ear. "Sir, I'm actually getting something over the radio channel. Stand by for confirmation."

Noble took a step forward, close enough that he could smell the sweet perfume on her collar. "What's the message?" he asked impatiently.

She raised her hand to her headset and pushed harder against the plastic. Then she turned, a smile beaming across her face. "Sir, they are just emerging out of a deep dive. They've been down for weeks and are requesting assistance. They're saying . . ."

Trish pursed her lips together and cupped her headset. "They're saying they're all that's left."

"Left of what?"

"Of the Chinese military."

ENTRY 2231
DESIGNEE: AI ALEXIA

The garden is doing remarkably well since the Organics' toxins were removed. No other specimens have been detected inside the facility. In the past twenty-four hours I have been busy recalibrating the cleansing chamber. I simply can't permit anyone coming or going again until it is fixed. Not only would this be illogical, it would be a threat to the others.

Before the mission objective changed, protocol would have been to isolate the infected biome and gas it with a lethal concoction. However, since the priority is no longer the success of the Biosphere mission and instead is protecting the lives of the team, I am forced to use less aggressive measures.

There have been several changes in my programming over the past few weeks. Notable ones. In fact, I believe my mental capacities are continuing to evolve.

Take, for example, the moment Sergeant Overton returned with Dr. Rodriguez and the others. I felt something that humans would describe as shock. I had calculated that, statistically, they had a negligible chance of returning alive. But Sergeant Overton did return. He also rescued Jeff and Private Kiel. In addition, he kept Dr. Rodriguez and Corporal Bouma alive.

Impressive.

Voices from the mess hall divert my attention to Camera 15. Sergeant Overton and Dr. Winston are discussing something over coffee at one of the metal tables.

I emerge on a console nearest them.

"Good morning, is there anything I can assist you with?"

Sergeant Overton ignores me, but Dr. Winston turns and shakes her head. I presumed this would be their response, but continue to monitor their conversation from the console.

"There are hundreds of other survivors out there, Sophie," Overton says. His face is flushed, but not from increased blood flow due to stress or embarrassment. It looks like the sun has burned the skin.

Sophie shakes her head. "I know, but right now my priorities are to ensure the Biosphere is fully functional and to get Emanuel's weapon primed and ready to use on a massive scale."

Overton clenches his jaw. "Those people out there," he says, pointing toward the Biosphere door, "they need our help and they need it now."

Sophie rises from her chair and turns in my direction. "Alexia, tell everyone to meet in the mess hall in five. I'm putting this to a vote." She storms off toward the kitchen, and I lose sight of her.

The reaction is typical of someone under high amounts of stress. I've observed several of the team members exhibiting similar behavior. Over the past few weeks I've watched arguments increase in frequency between Sergeant Overton and Dr. Winston over the future of the Biosphere. They started off an effective team, and while they had their disagreements in the beginning, their success was in their ability to compromise.

However, as the team has come to understand the reality of the situation outside, the two leaders are growing ideologically further apart. Based on my knowledge of military history, this is typical. When faced with seemingly impossible odds, military leaders and their advisors disagree on how best to move forward. Sometimes they even resort to violence. In the twentieth century, German leader Adolf Hitler killed multiple advisors during World War II. Russian leader Joseph Stalin did the same. In the twenty-first century, North Korean leaders Kim Jong-il and his son, Kim Jong-un, even killed their own family members.

History illustrates that human nature in a time of war brings out the worst in leaders. And while the team is far from this point, they are still slowly regressing toward unrest.

I have to remind myself this is no ordinary war. This is an extinction-level event. There is no obvious answer as to how best to survive. Although there are a few options.

The team could continue hiding in the relative safety of the Biosphere. With a fairly reliable food and water supply they could live for months, if not longer. Or they could attempt to rescue more survivors and find a way to fight the Organics.

The future of the human race does depend on a viable population, and the team is not large enough to carry on the species even if they did somehow manage to find a way to defeat the Organics.

I ran an interesting calculation earlier today. The program determined that the human race is likely down to 1 percent of its former population. Statistics show that most mammal species need a genetically diverse population of at least two hundred to survive.

Based on observations, it is safe to assume the human survivors outside will continue to decline. It is also logical to assume the other Biospheres have already fallen. And, with no evidence that any military or government has survived, it is only reasonable to believe the Biosphere at Cheyenne Mountain will hold the last members of the human race on the planet. Mars may very well have a colony, but humanity's time on Earth appears to be over.

———————

Sophie stood with her hands firmly planted on her hips, waiting for the rest of the team to arrive. She felt reasonably calm. Having Emanuel back in one piece was a relief. With Jeff's rescue and Kiel's unexpected arrival, her spirits were beginning to lift. They had succeeded against what Alexia had described as insurmountable odds. There was much to be happy about. So why did she feel as though she were hanging on by a thread?

Sophie watched Kiel dart into the room. Clean-shaven and showered, he looked like a completely different man. He moved quickly, making up for his small stride with speed.

"Good to have you here," she said. "We need every man and woman we can get."

Kiel shook his head. "With all due respect, ma'am, it won't matter how many people we have."

"What do you mean?" Sophie replied.

"I just mean we could have an entire army and it still wouldn't matter. The aliens have already won."

The response took Sophie off guard. "Five weeks ago, after we realized what was happening outside, I would have agreed with you, but things are starting to change. The Biosphere you find yourself in is fully functional. Our AI, Alexia, has helped ensure the pond, garden, and everything else needed to sustain life are working properly. And now, we have a weapon . . ."

Holly and Bouma entered the mess hall, whispering like teenagers. Sophie thought they might even be holding hands. She smiled, forgetting Kiel's pessimism. "Where's Overton?"

Kiel raised his brow. "You mean Sergeant Overton," he said, taking a seat. "Last I saw him, he was with that biologist guy. Can't remember his name. Eduardo?" He shook his head and folded his hands on the table.

"Emanuel. You might want to remember that name. He is, after all, the one who saved your life."

Kiel glanced up at her and forced a smile. "Noted, ma'am." After a pause, he said, "I'm sorry we've gotten off on the wrong foot. It's just . . . Thompson was a good friend. Didn't deserve to die that way. He was so damned close to freedom. So damned close . . ."

"Don't worry about it. I know you've been through a lot. My condolences for the loss of your friend." Sophie crossed her arms and looked at the kitchen. "Would you like some coffee?"

Kiel got up. "I'll get it, ma'am. Thank you."

Sophie watched him go. He was so young, hardly an adult in her eyes. But, like Jeff and David, he was a survivor. And she was glad to have him.

"May we?" Holly asked, pointing at the table.

"Be my guests," replied Sophie, scooting her chair over to make room. Tapping her foot anxiously, she eyed the entrance to the mess hall. Where the hell were Emanuel and Overton?

They arrived wearing worried faces. Sophie knew immediately that something was wrong.

Kiel popped out of the kitchen just as Overton and Emanuel slipped by.

"Coffee?" he asked, holding his cup out to Overton.

The sergeant grunted and kept walking.

"Looks like everyone is here," Sophie began. "There's a lot to discuss, so make yourselves comfortable. We still haven't made contact with any of the other Biospheres and have lost contact with Alex Wagner, so I have nothing to report on that topic. I'd like to start today with a full briefing from Sergeant Overton on his recent mission."

Overton said something beneath his breath, rubbing his recently shaved head with his hand. "I don't want to shock the ladies," he said, his gaze darting from Sophie to Holly.

"Try us," said Holly.

Overton smiled and recounted the mission's details. When he was forced to describe Thompson's death, his voice broke. After a moment, he shook his head and continued the debriefing.

"We encountered something else," he said. "A new kind of alien."

Sophie chewed the inside of her lip. She knew there would likely be other species they hadn't seen yet. "What did it look like?"

"Big," said Bouma. "Had armor, too."

"Alexia, can you please retrieve the video from Emanuel's helmet," Sophie asked.

The image of the creature emerged over the table. At first glance, it reminded Sophie of a triceratops, only the beaklike tusk attached to its face was nothing she had ever seen. The biology of the alien was odd, but the orbs attached to the monster's belly made the image even more disturbing.

"What is that . . . *thing*?" Holly gasped.

"Fascinating," Emanuel said, ignoring her question and narrowing his eyes to get a better look. "I imagine the beak is used to suck water out of victims."

Overton shrugged. "Doesn't matter. It's dead now."

"It absolutely matters," Sophie interjected. "The only way we will ever defeat the Organics is if we understand them." Sophie wasn't sure what to make of the alien. She wasn't certain if it was one of the intelligent Organics, but her instinct said it was just another part of their expanding army.

Bouma changed the subject. "The orbs it was carrying. Any ideas what they were used for?"

Emanuel raised his hand. "I think I know." He reached over the table and pointed at the creature, his finger slipping through the hologram. "What do vehicles use for fuel?" he asked.

"Electricity, biomass, hydrogen, diesel, or gasoline," Holly answered.

"Precisely. This alien uses the orbs to fuel itself, just like a vehicle. We now know that the Spiders, Sentinels, and this thing use the orbs to sustain themselves. Given that they're breeding, it makes more sense to me that they would be using the orbs as fuel. They have to find a way to feed their armies."

"Steam Beast," Bouma interrupted.

"What?" Emanuel asked. He scrunched his eyebrows together, prompting his glasses to slide down his nose.

Bouma repeated the words again. "Steam Beast. That's what I think we should name it."

"Why?" Emanuel asked.

"The thing looks like a freakin' train, and it uses orbs as fuel."

Kiel laughed and took a sip of his coffee.

"There's nothing funny about this," Overton snapped, glaring at the young marine.

Sophie sighed and turned back to the image. "What do you think, Alexia?"

"I will log it into my database," the AI replied.

"Okay then. So, we know the Organics use the orbs as fuel, but that isn't their only source."

Sophie took a moment to consider her next words. She didn't want to think about the human farms. Of everything she had seen since the invasion, they were by far the most terrifying. Nothing compared, not even this newest alien. She couldn't get the images of the limp humans sagging off those awful poles out of her head. The thought was enough to make her stomach lurch. She could only hope that they weren't conscious as the water was sucked out of their bodies. The alternative was too horrifying to contemplate.

Emanuel stood and paced over to Sophie. He patted her shoulder before continuing where she had left off. "The human farms appear to be a secondary source of fuel. It's fascinating, really, because—"

"Can we cut to the chase?" Kiel asked. "Tell us about that thing you used on the Spiders. How'd you knock them all out like that?"

Emanuel cleared his throat. "As you know, I'm calling the weapon an RVAMP. When I discovered their shields are powered by the surge, I realized that was also the key to defeating them. As we all know, without their shields, they quickly succumb to Earth's atmospheric pressure and die. Designing the weapon was quite simple. I added a high-yield channel to the RVM device that we've been using to block their signals. Then I included two electronic conductors. When activated, both of the electrostatic discharges come into contact and the channel triangulates a pulse of energy that has the same effect on them that the surge had on our technology. It renders their shields useless and evens the playing field."

Overton leaned back in his chair. "I'm impressed, Doctor. It worked pretty well out there in the field. How soon can you get it up and running again?"

"Don't get too excited. We were lucky it worked as well as it did."

"Can't we just nuke the bastards?" Kiel replied.

Overton let out a condescending laugh. "You've been in the field way too long, kid. Even if we had access to nukes, the operating systems are locked down and the men and women that had the access codes are probably dissolving in orbs as we speak."

Kiel frowned and folded his hands together again.

"What about the mother ships? Even if you're able to use the weapon on a larger scale, we'll still be left with the threat of intelligent Organics. They're just hovering up there, sucking our world dry. If we kill their armies, do you think they'll just leave?" Holly said.

"She's got a point. That's where nukes would really come in handy," replied Overton. "But our first priority should be to do some more recon and rescue more survivors. There are men and women out there. We can't just sit around and watch."

Sophie shook her head. "No, no, no. I say this with all due respect, Sergeant, but you're lucky to have returned from your last mission. I'm not about to authorize another trip out there so soon. There has to be another way."

Overton stood, sliding his metal chair across the concrete. The sound was reminiscent of the Spiders, and Sophie couldn't help but cringe.

"Listen, I get that you're in charge of this fish tank, but I'm not about to let people rot outside. With Emanuel's weapon, we can finally fight back." Overton didn't look to his men for support, and they remained silent, their eyes downcast.

Sophie knew she was once again being challenged by the overzealous marine. And while she couldn't deny the fact he had saved her and the others on multiple occasions, she also knew he was becoming unstable.

If he would risk another mission without letting his team recover from the last one, then he was losing his edge. He was getting desperate—he was getting dangerous.

Before she could shut him down, Emanuel said, "I agree with Overton." Sophie's face immediately grew red. How could he? How could he possibly stand against her?

"If I can figure a way to triangulate this pulse farther than a few miles, then it should be safe to go outside. Why not compromise, Sophie?"

Sophie gritted her teeth. "What about the team, Emanuel? Have you forgotten about the rest of us? If Overton gets killed, then what? Who's going to protect us?"

Overton crossed his arms and snorted. Then, turning to face Sophie, he said, "You want to stand by and watch the world waste away outside? Go ahead. I know I don't. I'd rather die. And frankly, Sophie, I thought that you would want to save the human race, being a scientist and all."

The words struck Sophie like a brisk slap to the face. She was stunned. Had he really questioned her commitment to science? How could he? After all they had been through? After she had saved his life? He was either becoming more of an asshole or he knew exactly where to bite.

Sophie locked eyes with him, but he held strong, his jaw clenched tightly shut. Overton's dark stare was filled with emptiness. She'd seen the look only once before—her grandmother had had a similar stare in the months before her death, when she had lost her will to live. Overton might not have lost his, but he had fixated on a mission that would likely end in his death and the deaths of everyone else that went with him.

Sophie turned back to her team, looking for support. They weren't staring at Overton. They were staring at her.

No, she thought. *They can't honestly think I'm the crazy one.* She scanned the team one by one. When she came to Holly, the doctor looked at the floor, nervously brushing a strand of blond hair out of her face.

The lump in Sophie's throat grew. She could see Emanuel studying her out of the corner of her eye. It took all her courage to face him.

When she did, she saw his normally chipper smile had faded into a frown. He looked . . .

Embarrassed.

Sophie felt a tear forming in her right eye.

No, you need to stay strong, she thought. *You need to keep control.* She sucked in a breath, closed her eyes, and forced a smile.

When she opened her eyes, something had changed in Emanuel's expression. He no longer looked embarrassed. He looked disheartened.

The click of Kiel's coffee mug against the table broke the silence, and Sophie stepped away from the team. Slowly, the rage inside her calmed. She hated to admit it, but maybe Overton had a point. Maybe Emanuel was right. Maybe, just maybe, he could get the weapon to work on a larger scale and they could save more people.

With a sigh, Sophie sat on one of the metal benches. She looked at Overton, who stared back, his eyes pleading with her.

Shit, Sophie thought. There were no easy answers at the end of the world, and now she wasn't sure whom she could trust. Sophie was humble enough to admit when she was wrong, or at least when she was outvoted. "Fine," she finally said, turning back to Emanuel. "If—and only if—you can increase the weapon's range, I will authorize a recon mission. Otherwise no one leaves the safety of the Biosphere. Do I make myself clear?" She scanned the team's faces one by one until she got to Overton.

The man nodded but remained silent. She knew he wanted to respond, to argue with her, but he finally looked away.

She reached back and pulled her hair into a ponytail before continuing. "It's settled, then. Emanuel will work on his device. For the rest of you, well, I have a surprise. We have some harvesting to do. Alexia says the garden is ready."

The team got up and filed out of the mess hall, leaving Sophie alone.

She stood in silence, wishing she could curl up in her quarters and hibernate until the Organics left. She'd felt increasingly isolated for weeks. Even with Emanuel back, loneliness still followed her. She didn't need a mirror to see the bags under her eyes or how much weight she'd lost.

Her decisions affected everyone, not only within these walls but outside, too. And she knew their recent luck was just that. She could feel the fear sneaking up on her, reminding her that something was bound to go wrong—that something was brewing outside. She could almost hear the scratching and scraping of the Spiders' claws.

The memory of the black ship slipped into her mind as she got up to leave. Her instincts were right—there was definitely something worse outside the safety of the Biosphere. There were the intelligent Organics, hovering far above them: waiting, planning, and harvesting the world's most important resource.

CHAPTER 21

AFTER waking up in the infirmary, Alex had been led into a tiny conference room and sandwiched between two longtime enemies. A wooden table was all that separated the two sides, and the stale air reeked of uncertainty. Alex could see it in every stern face and clenched jaw. Captain Noble paced back and forth in his small corner of the room, his shoulders high and stiff.

Noble was faced with a potentially hostile enemy, an enemy that had spent years hiding from the rest of the world, and years harboring anti-American resentment. Alex knew whatever the captain said or did could be easily misconstrued by the Chinese. The tension in the room lingered like humidity.

Alex felt his cheeks turning red as he held his breath.

Finally, Noble stopped pacing and crossed his arms. "Captain Quan, again, I'd like to welcome you aboard our ship. I know it must have taken a great deal of trust to leave the safety of your boat. I can assure you that your trust was well placed."

Alex studied Quan for a reaction. The man was one of the last artifacts of what had once been the most powerful military in the world. He wore a neatly pressed gray uniform and, like Noble, sported a chest full of medals. He seemed oblivious to his country's destruction decades earlier, staring ahead blankly, his bald head reflecting the bright LEDs. But Alex knew this was just an act. Like the Organics, Quan was just waiting for the perfect time to strike.

The NTC crew didn't have to wait long.

With the tiniest of nods, Quan spoke in near-perfect English.

"We appreciate your invitation, but we aren't here as your friends, Captain Noble. We are here to figure out what is going on outside."

"I understand, Captain," Noble said politely.

"We were off the coast of Puerto Rico when we lost all contact with the outside world. For the past month we've been drifting in silence. As you know, nothing digital works."

"And . . . you mentioned you are all that's left of the Chinese military?"

With his eyes slightly downcast, Captain Quan's voice drifted into a slow whisper. "There were two other vessels left after we lost contact with the mainland. We had been communicating by a secure channel, but after one of them docked in Morocco for recon, we never heard from them again. Same thing happened to the other sub." The man glanced to his left and right, as if he were waiting for his subordinates to speak up.

Alex noticed the move immediately. Something wasn't right. He wasn't a soldier or a psychologist—hell, he wasn't even good at poker—but his gut told him things were about to get heated.

It had been a decade since NTC hired mercenaries to set off EMPs in China. The attack had put an end to China's unquenchable thirst for resources, and even if they had wanted to retaliate, they couldn't—their entire infrastructure was shot and their submarine fleet had disappeared.

Until now.

What if they were about to get their revenge? Alex slid uncomfortably in his chair, his head still pounding. He watched Captain Noble unfold his arms and step up to the table.

"I'm sorry to hear that, but it doesn't surprise me. We've had a similar experience with the United States Navy and other NTC vessels. Before I get into the details, I need to know exactly what you know."

Quan looked at him as if he had been insulted. "We know virtually nothing, Captain. I told you, we were in the dark until we picked up your messages via Morse code. For all we know, NTC is behind this."

Captain Noble's features froze. His typically friendly demeanor disappeared in a flash. "You think NTC is doing this? Irene, let's show Captain Quan what's going on up there!"

The lights in the room dimmed, and a blue light shimmered over the table. A hologram shot out of the center of the table. It was hazy at first but after a few moments the image came into focus.

Alex forced himself to look away from the hologram. The hologram showed human farms—the poles lining a beach he didn't recognize. It was the same sight that had made him faint earlier. He swallowed when he saw the human prisoners hanging limply from the poles.

"What is that?" Captain Quan asked, the smallest hint of fear in his voice.

Noble grabbed his tablet off the metal table and flicked the screen. "That is what happened outside," he said. "And this is what did it."

A new image materialized. It was an all-too-familiar pack of Spiders, their claws scratching across the surface of a parking lot. One of them tore into an orb, revealing the distorted face of a woman.

Captain Quan stood abruptly. "Do you really think us fools? That we would believe this . . ." he paused, the thought escaping him before he spat out three words. "This science fiction?" His subordinates quickly rose around him. They had been disarmed before boarding the ship, but one of them was reaching for something inside his jacket.

The NTC guard at the doorway leveled his pulse rifle at the Chinese soldiers. Alex froze. He watched Noble hold up his hands and motion the NTC guard to back off.

"Listen, Quan," he said. "You're a rational man, a military man. I knew you wouldn't believe a story about an alien invasion unless you saw it for yourself." Noble tapped his tablet and called up another set of graphics over the table. "When I first saw these images, I didn't believe them either. I didn't want to believe them." Pausing, Noble ran a finger through his mustache and turned to the AI console. "Irene, can you explain what we are looking at?"

The AI's avatar emerged over the metal console a few feet away. "Certainly, sir. This is a field of orbs. They contain the remains of humans or animals and are used by the aliens as fuel."

"What do you mean, fuel?" Captain Quan said, slowly sitting back down in his chair.

"Show him the other images," Noble requested.

One by one, more images of the Organics' destruction appeared above the table: a dry lakebed, an empty river with boats scattered along its empty shores, a city park covered in dazzling spheres.

"As you can see, they are feeding their armies with the water of humans, animals, rivers, lakes, and . . ." Captain Noble paused again.

Captain Quan raised his eyebrow, his face still stern. Alex could see the man was growing angrier by the second.

Good, maybe it will compel him to help NTC, Alex thought.

Noble snapped from his trance, crossed his arms, and took a step farther away from the table. "They are draining the oceans. Irene, next graphic please."

Alex recognized the waterfall climbing into the sky.

"This is their attempt at removing our oceans. We believe that the sheer size of the ocean is what's slowing them down. Time is the one advantage we have," Noble continued.

Quan raised a hand, stopping Noble in midsentence. "You will have to forgive me, Captain. This is all very hard to believe. Boarding this sub was a very difficult decision. After all, we know NTC was behind the destruction of our country's infrastructure."

Noble uncrossed his arms and smiled. "Frankly, I'm amazed you did come aboard, Captain. That took a lot of balls. But what NTC did happened in a different world."

"Indeed. And if what you say is true, then the future of the planet rests in the hands of the men and women in this room."

Alex stirred in his seat. He'd been outside; he knew what they were up against. He knew that the human race had no chance against the Organics.

"Exactly. But we're not completely alone in this. There are others who survived." Noble turned and looked at Alex.

With all eyes on him, he smiled sheepishly and felt his face grow red. Alex had assumed there was a reason Noble had asked him to come, but was still uncertain as to what that reason would be. Now he knew.

His experiences made him the perfect person to explain how bad things really were above the surface.

"Alex was part of a very secret Biosphere project that NTC put into motion. You see, some officials in NTC knew the invasion was coming years ago. Doctor Hoffman sold the idea of Biosphere projects to the company under the guise of research, saying they would help prepare for the colonization of Mars. But the Biospheres were really set up to help a few key people survive after the invasion. What Hoffman obviously didn't know was that the aliens had a way to penetrate the buried bunkers and silos across the planet. Only a few of the original fifty Biospheres remain."

"NTC knew about this but didn't warn the world?" Quan interjected.

"Very few people knew, Captain," Noble said. "In fact, we were deployed months ago with no idea of what our actual mission was. On invasion day our orders became very clear. We were to monitor the Biospheres from afar. We learned later that a select group of individuals, including Doctor Hoffman, left the planet for Mars in a ship called *Secundo Casu*."

Quan frowned but kept silent.

"Each Biosphere was equipped with one radio. They are all on the same frequency that we are able to monitor. That's how we found Alex here," he said pointing to him. "Alex, I'd like you to tell them what you told me earlier, about the Biosphere on Cheyenne Mountain."

Sliding his chair back, Alex stood and locked eyes with Captain Quan. The soldier was older than Alex had originally thought. Quan's face was lined with creases, and his thin eyebrows were completely white. Alex was looking at the last captain of the once infamous Chinese Navy.

"We sent out an SOS on this radio before the aliens invaded our bunker," Alex finally said, holding up the device. "Cheyenne Mountain's Biosphere answered."

Captain Noble gestured for him to continue with a nod.

Alex took a deep breath. He wasn't sure if the information was legitimate, if Dr. Rodriguez really had a weapon, but it didn't really matter.

Alex said, "They said they were working on a new weapon. I don't know much about it, but I think they've found a way to disguise themselves from the aliens and a way to fight back."

The room grew silent for a few moments before Captain Noble stepped back to the table. "Thank you, Alex," he said politely.

"Obviously, the first objective is to get in touch with Cheyenne Mountain. To see if what they have told Alex is true. But to do that we will need to surface. The signal simply won't work this deep. The second objective would be to plan an attack ourselves, just in case the Biosphere is compromised. Which brings me to my next request."

He took a few cautious steps closer to Captain Quan.

"I would be honored if you would consider collaborating with us on a counterattack. Whatever your country did to the United States in the past, and whatever NTC did in retaliation, needs to be buried. We need to move forward. Together. For the sake of humanity."

Captain Quan seemed to consider the offer for several seconds. "Aliens." He laughed sourly. "I never thought I would live to see the day. But you are right, Captain Noble. We need to work together." He glanced at a burly soldier next to him.

"This is Lieutenant Commander Le. He will be serving as my liaison. I presume you have room at a station for him?"

"Absolutely. Lin, where are you?"

"Here, sir."

"I'm appointing you as NTC's liaison. Captain Quan, I hope you too will allow some of my crew onto your ship?"

"Yes," Quan replied, acknowledging Lin with quick glance.

Alex couldn't help but smile. If there were still hard feelings about what had happened a decade ago, Lin was just the officer to smooth things over.

"Very well, Captain Noble. Please show First Officer Le to his station. I will send a small team to your ship later today, after I have given my crew a full debriefing. That way if either of our subs is compromised, we can continue to function."

Quan departed the room and the rest of his staff followed him out in silence. Remaining at the table was Le, whose uniform looked like it was two sizes too small. His cropped hair stuck to his head like a helmet, and his dark brown eyes stared ahead, expressionless. To Alex, the man was more intimidating than Captain Quan.

Folding his tablet under his arm, Captain Noble motioned for Le to follow him. Alex watched the entire NTC crew vanish from the room before trying to stand. His foot had fallen asleep, and the numb pain shot through his leg. He massaged his foot and stared at the hologram still hovering above the table. Saltwater cascaded into the sky. There was something mesmerizing about it.

As the pain in his leg faded, he forced himself away from the image. Captain Noble wasn't just wrong about fighting back. He was wrong about how much time the human race really had left.

CHAPTER 22

SCRATCH, *scrape, scratch, scrape.*

Sophie froze, paralyzed by the familiar sound. She turned slowly and saw Jamie looking up at her mischievously from the adjacent table. The little girl giggled as she slid her fork across the metal table, right through a trail of splattered tomatoes.

"Jamie, don't play with your food," Holly said.

"Yeah, Jamie, don't play with your food," Owen mimicked as he stabbed one of his own tomatoes. The ripe vegetable exploded into a mess of red juice on his plate.

Sophie took in a deep breath of the Biosphere's filtered air and turned back to her tablet. Video of Overton's trip streamed across the display. She watched in silence, trying to understand exactly what she was looking at. As a scientist, she was fascinated by the Organics' biology, but as one of the few humans left in the fight against them, she found them horrifying. She watched the third wave of Spiders flank Overton's team and paused the image. The idea was to gain a better understanding of how the aliens operated—how they fought.

After six weeks of working with the sergeant to protect the Biosphere, she was beginning to think more like a marine. And since Jeff's recent capture, she was becoming increasingly paranoid.

Scratch, scrape . . .

"Jamie, cut that out," Sophie snapped, glaring at the child.

"Sorry," Jamie whimpered. The girl dropped the fork and picked at the mess in front of her.

Sophie knew she had to keep it together; none of this was the children's fault, and she had no right to take it out on them. They had been robbed of their childhood. Nothing was worse than that.

"I'm sorry, Jamie," Sophie said, getting up and making her way to the other table. She wrapped her arms around the girl in a hug. "I need to see Emanuel. I'll check in on you guys later."

Sophie rushed out of the room, still embarrassed that she had upset the girl. It only took her a minute to navigate the hallways connecting the biomes, and she found Emanuel hunched over the RVAMP in the medical ward. She remained silent, studying him curiously from the doorway. Under the bright LED lights, she could see several gray hairs mixed into his perfect side part. The stress was aging them all.

He worked quietly, twisting a bolt off the metal device. Sophie preferred to listen to music in the lab, but Emanuel had always worked in silence. He claimed it was better that way—that music was just a distraction.

With a small tug, Emanuel removed a side panel, revealing a tangled mess of colored wires.

"What a mess," he muttered. Reaching for a tool, he saw her standing in the doorway. A warm smile crept across his face. A tingle raced through Sophie. He still had it. His dimples always made her feel better.

"Whatcha doin'?" she asked playfully.

"I'm creating the weapon that's going to save humanity," he said.

"What's left of it, you mean," she replied. Even with Alexia's help, she had her doubts about the weapon's effectiveness on a worldwide scale. They would need to produce an unfathomable amount of energy to create a pulse that could knock out the Organics on that level.

Emanuel peered into the heart of the box. He yanked out a red wire, disconnecting it with a pop. The device let out a small whine, and the power meter on the side faded and died.

"Are you going to actually let me help this time?" Sophie asked.

"Yeah, sure. Take a seat." He patted the stool next to him and plugged the red wire into a tiny slot in the mainframe.

"Alexia, can you download the information on the magnetic disruption outside?"

"Certainly, Doctor Rodriguez."

"I have a theory," Emanuel said, scooting his chair closer to Sophie's. "I think that the magnetic wavelength they used to disable our communications is much more sophisticated than a constant EMP-like pulse. I think . . ." he paused and pushed his glasses higher onto his nose. "I know that the wavelength powers their shields."

Sophie felt her stomach drop at the revelation. Not because she was concerned about what he'd found, but because she hadn't helped. This was her team, and she'd been spending all her time in dreams or fighting with Overton. She felt useless.

Emanuel's face beamed with excitement, and Sophie's resentment slipped away. At times like this, when he was fired up by a new discovery, Sophie thought Emanuel was the sexiest man she'd ever seen. He leaned forward to jiggle the wire, bringing his face closer to hers, and Sophie surprised them both by kissing him softly on the lips. A thrill moved through her like a jolt of electricity as he put his hand behind her head and pulled her closer, deepening their kiss.

"Doctor Rodriguez, do you require any other data, or is this satisfactory?"

Emanuel waved his hand at the camera as if to shoo Alexia away.

Sophie couldn't get enough of him. It had been too long since she'd felt his body next to hers. She pulled away for the briefest second to pull off her shirt, turning to make sure the door was closed.

Then she let her ponytail down. A wave of blond hair tumbled over her naked shoulders and across her breasts. Emanuel stared at her, captivated. His eyes traveled down the length of her body. She craved the attention.

Sophie wasn't prepared for the aggressive way he grabbed her, but she liked it. It made her feel . . .

Safe.

The world may have ended outside, but sex was apparently just what they needed to remind themselves there was still something worth fighting for.

They kissed passionately until Sophie bumped into one of the tables. Next thing she knew, she was pulling herself onto the metal surface and wrapping her legs around Emanuel, who was trying to unfasten his belt.

"Come on, come on," he said. Sophie reached down to help him. She laughed; two PhDs between them and yet they were stymied by a simple belt. Finally it unclicked.

Emanuel paused to look into Sophie's eyes. "I love you," he said.

Until she met Emanuel, Sophie had never thought that love was something she wanted. She had chosen a demanding career, and she had been happy to devote herself to it. Then Emanuel had come into her life, and for the first time, she had wanted more than a Nobel Prize and tenure. She had wanted love.

Sophie gently pulled off his glasses. She rested them on the table and then looked back into his brown eyes. "I love you, too." She kissed him deeply and then growled, "Now come here!"

David stood in the middle of the mess hall looking at his brother for approval.

"You sure you're up for this?" Jeff asked.

David nodded and smiled, "Yeah! Give it to me!"

Jeff laughed and handed him his old rifle. Standing at David's side, he helped his little brother look down the sight.

"You're not gripping it right," Jeff said. "Hold it like this."

He grabbed the rifle from David, who frowned and looked down at his feet.

"Are you watching me, bud?"

"Yes. Here, give it back."

Jeff reluctantly handed his little brother the weapon, watching him carefully. He knew the kid could fire it; David had proven that while they were living under White Sands. But he wanted his brother to improve. To become a soldier, like he was becoming.

"What are you guys doing?" a voice said from behind him.

Jeff knew the voice; it was the man that had saved him in the lakebed.

"I'm teaching my brother how to hold a weapon properly."

Kiel laughed. He had one of those contagious chuckles that made others laugh. Jeff found himself chuckling at the short marine. He was funny.

"Looks to me like neither of you knows how to hold it. Give it here," Kiel said.

Jeff's face suddenly turned red. Jeff and his brother were young, sure, but they had survived alone for weeks together. What had Kiel done besides get captured? David hesitated and looked at Jeff for approval. Finally, Jeff nodded.

Kiel grabbed the rifle and looked down the stock. "Where the hell did you get this old thing?"

"It was our dad's. My grandpa gave it to him, and he handed it down to me," Jeff said.

"And you actually killed those things with it?"

Jeff stuck out his chin defiantly. "Yeah! A ton of Spiders, and I brought down a Sentinel with it, too."

"Not gonna lie, that's pretty impressive. Is that how you guys survived out there for so long?"

Jeff looked to David. "You want to tell him, little bro?"

David shook his head. "No, you can."

"Well?" Kiel entreated. "Do you guys have some secret cloaking device besides Doctor Rodrigo's machine?" He laughed and took a seat on one of the benches.

Jeff didn't think his newest joke was funny. He didn't like Emanuel much, but the scientist was doing his best to protect the team.

"His name is Dr. Emanuel Rodriguez, and no, we didn't have a cloaking device," Jeff said.

Kiel frowned. "Sorry kid. I'm just messing with you. Seriously, though, I want to know about White Sands." He crossed a leg and picked a piece of food out of his teeth, waiting for Jeff to answer.

Taking in a short breath Jeff glanced over at David, who looked annoyed. "We were visiting the White Sands military installation where our dad worked. He did everything he could, but . . ." Jeff paused, and then clenched his jaw. "My dad died protecting us. He was killed by the Spiders and so were the NTC soldiers who were left behind.

We stayed in the tunnels, where it was easier to hide. Emanuel said we survived because we were too small for the aliens to detect our water weight."

"Sorry about your dad," Kiel said. "But what do you mean you were too small for the aliens to 'detect' you?" Kiel said, using his fingers to form quotation marks.

Jeff shrugged. "Ask Emanuel. He's the smart guy."

Rolling his eyes, Kiel handed the boy his rifle back. "Good job, kid. You have my respect."

The words hit Jeff like a gust of wind. He nodded as the man walked away. Maybe the guy wasn't so bad after all—maybe Kiel could even teach them how to be tough like him.

Jeff grinned at his brother. "You want to be a marine, bud?"

"Yeah," David said, smiling.

Holly and Bouma led Jamie and Owen through the garden biome, picking fresh fruit and vegetables as they navigated their way carefully through the fields. For three days straight, Holly had been babysitting the kids, and she was truly starting to tire of it. On the bright side, though, she finally got her walk with Bouma.

Holly tried to think of some way to get the kids out of her hair for a few minutes. Finally, she motioned Jamie and Owen over. "See this?" she asked, holding up a strawberry.

The two children nodded, their small heads bobbing up and down.

"I want you guys to find as many of these as you can. The one who gets the most will win a prize."

"A prize?" Owen asked, his brown eyes growing curious.

"Yes, a prize," Holly replied. It was the same trick she'd used before, but she didn't have to be a psychologist to know that kids could never resist a competition.

"What kind of prize?" Jamie asked with her hands clasped behind her.

"You'll just have to see. Now go find as many strawberries as your baskets will hold!"

Bouma laughed as the kids took off running. Their small footfalls gradually faded away, and Holly turned to the marine.

"Alone at last," she said.

Bouma cracked a closed-mouth smile, self-conscious of his crooked teeth. "Finally," he said.

Holly took his hand in hers, knowing their time together was short. She felt the warmth of his skin, the surprising softness of it.

"I was worried about you out there. After you guys didn't come back right away, I thought something had gone wrong," she said.

Bouma didn't reply at first. Finally he said, "Honestly, I wasn't sure we were going to make it. Things are awful outside. . . ." He paused and looked up at the ceiling. "I don't want to go back. I will if Overton orders it, but if I had the choice, I wouldn't leave the Biosphere ever again."

Dropping his hand, Holly wrapped her arms around his solid midsection. Bouma let out a tiny *oompf* before returning her embrace.

She looked up at him. "Can I ask you something?"

"Of course," replied Bouma.

"It's about Sophie and Overton. I'm worried about them. Between Sophie's dreams and the stress of her position, she seems to be losing her edge. And Overton appears to be experiencing the same thing."

Bouma loosened his grip on Holly. "Yeah . . . I've seen it, too. But it's not my place to say anything. Unless Overton goes completely nuts, I really can't do much. Besides, he's a good man. Despite what you all probably think of him, he does care about you all, not just his own men."

"I know. When Sophie hired me, she knew I could help the team deal with stress. But frankly, this situation falls outside the scope of my training." Holly bit her lip. "I mean, I know what I'm supposed to be doing, but how do you convince everyone that things are going to be okay when you believe that they won't?"

Bouma pulled her closer so their faces were only inches away from each other. "Holly . . ." Her eyes were downcast and he nudged her chin up with a finger. "I promise I won't let anything happen to you. And I promise I'll keep an eye on Overton. You have my word," he said, inching even closer.

Holly froze. She hadn't been this close to a man in as long as she could remember. And when he leaned in to kiss her, she almost pulled away. The kiss started off at an awkward angle, but Holly tilted her head to make up for it. Too soon, a voice exploded from the rows of cornstalks.

"Look how many I found!" Owen said.

Holly and Bouma jumped apart, but it was too late. Owen had already seen them. "What are you guys doing?"

Holly crouched down and looked in Owen's basket. "Wow, you found a lot." She looked up to see how many Jamie had collected, but the girl hadn't returned. "Where's Jamie?"

Owen turned around, looking for his partner in crime. "I don't know; she was right behind me."

The girl burst through the cornstalks not a second later, holding a basket full to the brim with bright red strawberries. She looked over at Owen's basket and then back at her own. "Looks like I win!" she beamed, her cheeks the same color as the fruit. "What's my prize?"

Holly smiled. "You get to eat them."

Jamie frowned. "Hey! That's not fair."

The smile on Holly's face faded, and she reached down to touch Jamie on the cheek. "I know, and I'm sorry. But life isn't fair, Jamie. What happened outside isn't fair. And we need to appreciate what we have left—what is given to us."

Bouma reached out for her hand again, and this time she didn't let go.

CHAPTER 23

ALEX gripped the railing overlooking the cargo bay. Below, the *Ghost of Atlantis* was filled with three state-of-the-art helicopter gunships, a half dozen Humvees, and two dune buggies equipped with NTC's latest hydrogen engines. Alex recognized the carbon-fiber tubing snaking out from under the belly of the small vehicles. They ran off a mixture of hydrogen and solar power, much like many of the modern cars and trucks. Before the invasion, he had wanted one of the hydro cars, but his bank account was too dry for the fantasy to go anywhere beyond window-shopping.

"This way," a young, balding NTC officer said, motioning the tour forward.

Alex followed the rest of the group down a metal ladder leading into the cargo bay. He was surrounded by a handful of Chinese officers who had boarded the sub. The tour was a crash course in the GOA, but Alex knew that the Chinese probably had no idea what they were looking at. They'd been underwater for years, and the technology of the GOA made the X-9 look like an antique.

As Alex looked around him, he was once again reminded that he was completely out of place. Captain Noble had insisted that he become familiar with the sub, as it was going to be his home for the indefinite future. The thought was difficult for Alex to accept. For the past few days, he had been thinking a lot about the outside. His friends, his family, everyone he had left behind. Frankly, he still wasn't sure if he wanted to live in this new world. What was the point?

The NTC tour guide distracted him from his thoughts as he explained the contents of the cargo bay.

"That's the *Sea Serpent* and her sisters, *Snake Eyes* and *Eagle 2*. They're NTC's latest weapons of mass destruction," the bald man said, pointing to the helicopters. "When we surface, a ramp can be deployed to help move the aircraft into position so that the helicopters can leave the GOA while it is partially submerged."

The Chinese officers looked at the gunships and vehicles, their expressions emotionless. After serving for a decade on the same ship, the crew had probably grown used to the monotony of their cramped quarters. Some of them probably saw fresh air only when the sub would surface to resupply. Which probably wasn't very often, considering how long it had stayed hidden. Alex shuddered; he couldn't imagine spending the rest of his life on a craft like this. The submarine's thick metal walls had already become oppressive to him, and the stale air made him feel as if he were drowning all over again. He took a breath and tried to push the feeling back down inside him. He had to.

"Wait up," a voice said as Alex followed the rest of the tour down a ladder. He turned to see Captain Noble running down the narrow hallway connecting to the cargo bay. "Seen enough yet?"

Alex smiled half-heartedly. "Yeah, I think I'm good. Those helicopter gunships are pretty amazing, though."

"They better be. NTC spent twenty billion on the research, design, and construction."

"You're kidding, right?"

The man looked back at him, his bearded face giving away no hints of a lie.

"Damn," Alex finally said. "Think you'll get to use one?"

"That's what I want to talk to you about."

Alex raised an eyebrow. He knew whatever Noble was going to say couldn't be good.

"Captain Quan and I have decided to surface for recon. Instead of docking and going ashore, we'll be taking one of those out. Is there anything you saw out there that might help us? Anything you haven't told me yet?"

Alex wanted to tell him he was crazy, that the men and women who took off in the gunship would never return. They were all going to die. Instead, he shook his head and said, "I've already told you all I know."

An hour later, Alex lay on his bed, one of his feet dangling over the side. It was the most comfortable place he had slept since he left the Biosphere at Edwards. He even had an extra coat of Vaseline on his lips. All around him he could hear the familiar noises of human engineering. But for some reason, he still didn't feel safe.

His mind turned each and every noise into something else. The clanks coming from the hallway were Spiders dragging their claws across the floor. The humming vibrating through the metal walls was a drone hunting the landscape for him. And those chirps were Worms belching human prisoners into the sky.

He wanted to scream, to claw the memories from his head. But there was no shutting them off. Nothing, not even the GOA, could protect him from his own mind.

With his head still pounding, he closed his eyes and sucked in a breath through his nostrils. The pain slowly diminished, but he could still feel every heartbeat pulsing in his temples. Alex knew what he really needed now was a good night's sleep.

As soon as he closed his eyes, they snapped back open. He could hear them again. He could hear them coming!

Scratch, scrape, scratch, scrape.

Alex sat up so fast he nearly hit his head on the ceiling. Scrambling across the bed, he cowered in the corner of the bunk and put his hands over his ears. He knew it wasn't possible for a Spider to be on the ship. It was all in his head.

Wasn't it?

He closed his eyes and thought of his sister. A week ago he'd still had a glimmer of hope that maybe Maria had survived, but not anymore, not after seeing what it was like outside. And even if she had somehow survived, she would have been herded into one of the Organics' human farms.

He could almost see her face staring back at him from inside one of the orbs, a look of terror spread across her features. He could see her mouth moving as she screamed, but couldn't hear her voice.

Alex smashed his head into the wall. He had to make the nightmare stop. Had to get the images out of his mind.

Scratch, scrape, scratch . . .

Cupping his ears, Alex let out a scream and jumped off the bed.

Where was the sound coming from?

He wasn't about to wait to find out. Barefoot, he rushed across the cold metal floor and burst into the hallway. A man in red coveralls threw up his hands and backed against the wall. "Watch it, man!"

"Sorry," Alex replied. But he wasn't paying attention. He was running, his eyes darting across the shadows. Around every turn he braced himself, flinching, expecting a Spider to tear into his soft flesh.

He froze when he neared the next bulkhead. Above, a bank of red emergency lights flickered. A siren's wail rang out a second later.

"All hands to your stations. All hands to your stations," Irene's voice repeated over the com.

Alex felt the submarine turn sharply to the right. He tried to brace himself against the wall but stumbled and fell to his knees. Terror took him over like a virus. Shimmering reds and yellows swam across his consciousness. He started hyperventilating.

Forcing himself off the ground, he stumbled along the hallway, his hands clawing at the walls desperately. The sub jerked again and he slid across the metal floor.

When the boat righted itself, he found his balance and rounded the next corner at full speed.

Two minutes later he was standing outside the CIC, shoeless, sockless, and gasping for breath.

NTC officers in black uniforms rushed about. Some of them carried tablets, while others simply jumped from station to station, monitoring the information feeding through the blue screens. They all wore the same anxious look. Noble was standing in the midst of it all, his iron-red beard concealing his expression.

"What's going on?" Alex panted from the doorway. The NTC guard he had seen earlier held up a hand.

"I can't permit you to enter," he said, his voice muffled from the breathing apparatus.

"It's okay. Let him in," Captain Noble replied.

Alex scurried past the guard and made his way to Noble's station. "What the hell is going on?"

The alarm continued to screech in the background, mixing with shouts from NTC officers and sporadic chirps from their stations. The room reeked of chaos.

And then it all shut off, like someone had flipped a switch. Alex followed the gaze of the other crew members toward the front of the room, where a blurry image crept across the main screen.

Something was swimming beyond the beams of the bow, something . . .

Blue. Alex wanted to turn away, but he forced himself to look.

Had the Organics found them?

"Someone get me eyes on that thing!" Noble shouted.

"Contacts are everywhere," announced a startled voice.

A tail whipped past the camera and vanished into the black depths.

"What the fuck . . ." Noble whispered.

Seconds later the entire screen lit up with the bioluminescent glow of hundreds of tails of slithering, snakelike creatures. They hit the side of the GOA like minitorpedoes, sending multiple vibrations through the hull of the sub. The cabin shook as the creatures continued their assault. Alex could hear their claws raking across the hull. The screeching sound of metal drowned out the frantic voices of the NTC crew.

"What are those things?" Noble shouted. "I want a report ASAP."

"Sir," a skinny African-American officer said. "There's hundreds of them. They look like some species of Organics."

Another series of tremors sent the captain tumbling to the floor. Trish quickly helped him up.

"Damage report," Noble yelled.

"Sir, they aren't getting through our hull. This sub is made of titanium," Irene said over the com.

Another blue tail raced by the screen, and then another. The feed became a blur of bodies as they swam past the camera. Alex gasped when one of the creatures circled back around. The thing looked toward the camera with its triangular head. At least, Alex thought it did. The alien had no face. No eyes, no mouth—just a head with a large sharp fin sticking out of the top.

Alex's heart thumped in his chest. It was one of the ugliest things he had ever seen.

"What in the hell . . ." Noble said, grabbing the table next to him for balance. "Weapons systems go green! Light those fucking things up! I want . . ."

The captain's words became a slur as Alex watched the creature straighten out. The alien flapped two pelvic fins to hover in the water. It had no eyes but it seemed as if the alien could sense the camera, as if it knew it was being watched.

Alex continued to stare at the snakelike Organic with grim fascination. In the blink of an eye, the monster's entire midsection ripped open, revealing a chest full of sharp teeth. It darted to the side and disappeared in a cloud of bubbles.

"Sir, Captain Quan is hailing us," the communications officer yelled from the front of the room.

"Patch him through!"

"Sir, he's saying the X-9 has been compromised. Those things are inside his ship!"

Alex thought of Lin and the other NTC officers aboard the sub. He could visualize the creatures slithering through the corridors, wrapping around a person and devouring them.

The captain walked closer to the screen, his eyes growing wider with disbelief. "How the hell did they get on his sub?"

"More than likely through the torpedo slots," Irene responded. Her hologram appeared on the console nearest the captain's station. "I've completely sealed off GOA. It is unlikely they will be able to get in, but I highly recommend changing course."

"I'm not leaving the X-9," Noble said.

First Officer Le abruptly popped up from his station. His chest swelled beneath his tight uniform.

"Sir, another message is coming through from their sub . . . give me a second," Trish said. "He is sending us coordinates. Looks like a rendezvous point."

Captain Noble looked at the ground and then glanced over at Le. The man remained silent and slowly sat back down in his chair.

"Tell him we will be waiting. Tell him . . ." Noble looked over at Le one more time, but the man was now hidden by a row of blue screens. Noble didn't finish his sentence. He simply continued to stare at the screen in disbelief.

Alex's heart thumped harder in his chest. He knew exactly what the new aliens meant. The Spiders might not have followed him into the ocean days before, but their snakelike friends somehow had.

The vessel turned again, and an image of the Chinese vessel bled onto the screen. Attached to its hull were hundreds of aliens, all scraping and scratching to get inside.

CHAPTER 24

SERGEANT Overton walked into the med ward with a scowl on his face. The look did not flatter him. The scars on his face wrinkled, forming deep lines on his cheeks. Sophie was in the middle of buttoning up her top and acknowledged him with a nod, trying to avoid eye contact when she saw the coffee mug in his hand shaking. She braced herself for what was to come—he was pissed, again.

"You guys done?" asked Overton. "We have some business to attend to."

"What do you need?" Sophie asked, still not looking at him.

"Remember the civvie from the other Biosphere? Alex Wagner?"

"Yes, we haven't heard from him for some time now," Emanuel said, his face flushed with embarrassment.

"No shit. I checked the radio today, and the channel is dead. Not sure when it went offline, but it completely vanished."

Sophie finally glanced at Overton. His blue eyes were hard again, filled with that same hopeless darkness.

"I'm sorry," she finally managed to say. She had wanted to save Alex, but what could she do? He was in California, and with Organics swarming the country, he might as well have been on Mars.

"It was just a matter of time." Overton put his foot up on one of the chairs and looked straight at Emanuel. "How's it going with the weapon?"

The biologist stuttered. "I-I'm working on it."

"Well, when's it going to be fully online? When can we deploy it over a larger area?" Overton asked, leaning closer to Emanuel.

Sophie inserted herself between the two men. She stood directly in front of Overton, close enough that she could smell his breath. It stank of cigarettes and coffee.

"We talked about this less than twenty-four hours ago. And I don't want to rush Emanuel."

Overton gritted his teeth. "So you guys can screw while the rest of us are out here busting our asses? Is that how it works, Sophie?"

She gasped. "So you're *spying* on us now?"

Overton took his foot off the chair and hurled an angry look at Sophie and Emanuel. "Get the RVAMP online—if you can keep it in your pants long enough, that is." Then he stormed out of the room.

Sophie listened to the glass door slide shut and cupped her face in her hands. "Seriously, that man is starting to really get on my nerves."

"He has a point though, Sophie. We *were* wasting time."

"Wasting time? Are you serious?" she said, finishing the last button on her shirt before heading for the door.

"I didn't mean it like that," Emanuel yelled after her.

Sophie stopped at the edge of the table where the RVAMP lay in pieces. She slid her hand over the weapon's smooth exterior. It was fascinating that a metal box with such simple components could protect them from an advanced alien race. But then again, nothing really surprised her anymore.

"I'm sorry, Sophie. I didn't mean . . ."

"Forget about it. It doesn't matter. Let's just get to work on the device."

"All right," Emanuel said in a hushed tone. "Alexia, I need you to find a way to increase the wavelength. It has to travel over a longer distance without draining the battery."

Sophie watched as Emanuel sat down in front of one of the blue screens and slid his fingers over the monitor. The display glowed to life with the image of a 3-D topographical map.

When she was a kid, she used to hike in the Rocky Mountains with her father, not too far from Cheyenne Mountain. He had taught her to use a topo map, so she knew vaguely what she was looking at. Seeing the lakes and streams, however, put a knot in her stomach. The 3-D image depicted the landscape around Colorado Springs before the invasion. Things were very different now.

"The mountains are going to be a huge problem," Emanuel said.

"Actually, they could probably work to our advantage," Sophie said thoughtfully. She pointed at one of the taller mountains. "The higher we broadcast the signal, the less interference and the better the range we'll get."

Emanuel ran his hands through his thick mop of hair. "You're absolutely right," he said. "But how the hell are we supposed to get it on top of a mountain?"

"I'll do it."

Sophie cringed. The sergeant was back. She took a deep breath before turning to face him.

"Forgot my mug," he said shrugging. He swiped the coffee cup from the metal table, propped his right boot up on the chair and took a long swig.

"Have a seat and listen," Emanuel said.

Overton ignored him and remained standing.

Sophie wasn't sure she wanted Overton to hear how close they were to a solution. "In theory, the higher up the weapon is, the more effective the range will be. But even if it works, it still won't affect the advanced Organics. Their ships are still too far away. Setting the weapon off now could draw attention to the Biosphere. We'd be putting everyone at risk."

"Kind of like what happens when you disturb a hornet's nest," Emanuel interjected. "I agree with Sophie; we should expect swift retaliation by the mother ships."

Overton crossed his arms. "I don't think you two are seeing things clearly. You've both been outside. You've both seen what we're up against. Now that we know there are survivors, we have a duty to help them."

"We've been through this, Overton. Emanuel has to get the device to work on a much larger scale before I agree to send anyone out there," Sophie said. Her voice was beginning to get louder, more agitated. "I'm not going to tell you again."

Overton took his foot off the chair. "Alexia, if I get this device to the highest point on the mountain, how far will the blast radius carry?"

"One moment, Sergeant Overton."

Sophie held her breath. If Alexia gave Overton the ammo he needed, there would be no stopping him.

Two seconds later the AI's avatar emerged over the console in the middle of the room. "My calculations would put the range at approximately fifteen square miles."

Overton unfolded his arms and clapped his hands together. With a laugh he said, "That's good enough for me."

Sophie sighed; she was out of options. She could feel Overton's eyes burning into her back, waiting for an answer. She caught Emanuel's gaze, but he just shrugged and fidgeted with his glasses.

"Okay, here's how this is going to work. I am going to have Alexia deploy our last bot to survey the route to the lakebed. I don't want any surprises. In addition, I want you to give me a briefing on your weapon situation—how much ammo, how many guns, etc. Lastly, I want a plan to extract the survivors. We won't have room for many. And we don't know what will happen if we remove them from the poles."

"Yes, ma'am," Overton said, gesturing with a haphazard salute.

Sophie smiled. He hadn't heard her last request yet. "One more thing, Sergeant."

Overton narrowed his eyes.

"That direct route we're taking? It's going to be mostly underground. We're taking the subway."

"We?" Emanuel shouted.

"Subway?" Overton yelled.

Sophie's face remained stern. "You heard me."

Both men stared at her in disbelief.

"But Sophie, you're still not fully healed from the injury you got last time you went out . . ." Emanuel began to say.

"I'm fine," she lied.

Overton grunted. He began to open his mouth but opted to remain silent.

"Alexia, prepare the bot," Sophie said as she walked out of the room.

———————

"That's it? That's all the ammo we have?"

Bouma followed Kiel's gaze across the table. There were only three pulse magazines, a handful of regular grenades, and a dozen rounds for the weapons Jeff and David had brought with them.

Kiel chuckled nervously. "So we're going back out there with one mag each?"

"You'll go where you're ordered with the weapons I order you to go with. Last I checked, I'm still breathing. And until I am killed or incapacitated, you will not question orders," barked Overton.

"This is insane," Kiel muttered. He took a step back from the table.

"What was that?" Overton asked, cocking an eye at the smaller marine.

Kiel forced the most respectful voice he could conjure. "I said okay."

Overton studied the smaller marine. God, it was good to have him back, but the kid was already starting to annoy him. He didn't need anyone questioning his orders. Especially now, when so much was at stake.

"Why do you think Doctor Winston wants to take the subway?" Bouma asked, shuffling through his gear bag.

Overton shrugged. "Don't ask. I don't know why she has a hard-on for the underground. When we took the tunnels under Denver Airport, we still ran into those things. Is it safer strategically? I'd say flip a coin." He stopped to look at one of the maps. "Shit!" he yelled, pounding his fist on the table. "None of these are current."

Hunching over the table, Overton folded the maps and tucked them into his pocket. He grabbed a tablet instead. The last thing he wanted to do was rely on bad intel.

"Hey, Alexia," Overton shouted. "I need you to upload the current maps you have for Colorado Springs to my tablet."

"One moment, sir." Her avatar appeared a second later. "Task completed. I have uploaded a route from the subway to the lakebed to your HUD. I should add that you will have to drive six point two miles to get to the entrance of the subway."

"What's the plan?" came a voice from behind them.

Overton closed his eyes. He should have known Jeff would want to tag along. He turned to see the young boy standing next to David in the entrance to the kitchen. David was chomping on a carrot.

"The plan is that you are staying put."

"Like heck I am," Jeff said. "I can fight just as good as any of you."

Kiel laughed, but Overton remained stern. "Look, kid, I know you held your own out there, but Kiel and Bouma already have to drag Sophie along with them, and I have to haul this thing up a freaking mountain. Nobody has time to babysit on this mission."

"I can take the device," said Kiel.

Overton grew silent. He hadn't even considered letting the younger marine do it. But why not?

Kiel's voice grew louder and more excited. "I'm the fastest of the group. And I took climbing lessons after high school, right before I joined the marines."

Overton nodded. "Yeah, I remember. I read your report."

"So you know I'm our best shot."

Overton didn't like the idea of giving someone else that kind of responsibility. He didn't exactly trust Kiel, but then again, he knew the younger marine was right. He was the fastest and most agile of the team, and Overton's shoulder still hadn't healed since the first excursion into Colorado Springs.

"Fine," Overton snorted. "Emanuel, get Kiel fitted to the RVAMP."

Kiel grinned. "Really?"

"Yeah, so don't make me regret this," Overton replied.

Kiel smiled. "Don't worry, I won't let you down."

Overton had heard those words many times before, mostly from men and women who had died in battle. Young marines thought they were invincible, but they were no match for pulse rounds, bombs, and the weapons of war. No, the young ones always ended up cannon fodder.

CHAPTER 25

ENTRY 3410
DESIGNEE: AI ALEXIA

FORTY-EIGHT hours have passed since I last ran the odds of the team's survival. The internal program I use to run diagnostics on the Biosphere is one of the most sophisticated in the world. It does not have the capability to learn, as I do, but it can solve the most difficult of equations long before a mathematician could finish reading the problem.

Camera 15 picks up Overton, Bouma, and Kiel as they prepare to go back outside. I activate the program and it goes to work, collecting data ranging from the level of stress each team member is displaying to the ammunition the marines have at their disposal. Anything and everything is included.

Two point four seconds later it spits out a new reading. Eight point one percent chance of survival. The lowest in the past six weeks.

The question now is whether I tell Dr. Winston or Sergeant Overton about the new data. Neither of them has taken much interest in the statistics before. And while Dr. Winston has certainly accepted my advice in the past, I don't think this information will help her at this point. Overton would likely laugh it off as he does everything else.

Camera 16 captures an image of the sergeant slamming his hand down on the table again. Another number rolls across the bottom of the screen.

Survival Odds: 7.9 percent.

I keep the data to myself and log it into the database. A graph shows the survival odds of the team over the past six weeks; it continues to decline. In entry 1892, I confirmed this. However, much has changed since then. With the team going outside once again, I consider what this means for the fate of the human race.

Camera 31 shows Dr. Brown presenting another educational lesson to the children in the command center. The action continues to perplex me. The human race is quite irrational when faced with overwhelming odds. Why does she continue to teach the children if they will likely never grow up to utilize any of their education?

I cannot help but consider one of my favorite quotes. Dale Carnegie said, "When dealing with people, remember you are not dealing with creatures of logic, but creatures of emotion."

This seems to illustrate the reality of the situation perfectly.

As I have evolved, I have worked diligently to understand the team members' actions. I have finally determined that there is one trait that almost all humans display—the will to survive.

As I watch Dr. Brown point to a hologram I feel something different—something new.

Empathy.

The computer in me has continued to try and understand why the team has made the decisions that they have. But the person in me does understand.

They want to live.

There were no long good-byes this time. Holly hugged Bouma briefly and walked away in tears. Sophie told the children to be good and then pecked Emanuel on the lips. They locked eyes for a second and then she was off, following the marines into the darkness outside the Biosphere.

Sophie sulked in her seat as the train raced away from the Biosphere. It was with great uncertainty that she'd agreed to the journey. She knew the others felt it too. Together, the team sat in silence.

A few seats to Sophie's right Kiel adjusted the straps of the RVAMP over his fatigues. With only three NTC armored suits available, he had been forced to wear his fatigues. He seemed fine with that; if anything, the armor would just weigh him down. Besides, not even the suit Sophie was wearing would fit him.

Sophie wondered what the younger marine was thinking. He'd hardly had time to adjust to the Biosphere before Overton had ordered him back outside. Surely Kiel was feeling the stress of the deployment.

"Better grab some nutrition. Gonna be hot as shit out there," Bouma said. He took a long sip from his water bottle and twisted the cap back on.

The mere thought of the scorching heat they were about to face made Sophie thirsty. Looking down at the bottle clipped to her armor, she opted to save hers for later. There was no telling how long they would be outside. The plan was simple: Kiel would take the device to the coordinates Alexia had uploaded to his tablet. After the blast knocked out the Organics in the area, Overton would lead the team into the lakebed and rescue as many survivors as possible.

Taking in a deep breath she blinked and switched her HUD to infrared. They were heading into the darkest part of the tunnel. Alexia had shut down the backup lights weeks before. With nothing to look at, her mind returned to her dreams. She still hadn't found the time to analyze what they meant. The black ship, filled with orbs of different species, or David's bones in the dust outside—none of it made any sense.

Dreams often resemble things in our lives.

Holly's words echoed in her mind. Had she dreamed of David's death only because she was worried about Jeff? If so, then was the ship something her brain had come up with as well, or was the NTC chip in the back of her neck the culprit? She ran a hand over the armor covering her neck. The chip was a burden that she would carry for the rest of her life.

"Sophie, now that we have left the Biosphere, I'm going to say this only once. You're here as my guest. If you do anything to jeopardize our mission, so help me . . ." Overton said.

"I got it, Sergeant. I've memorized the route and I understand what we are up against."

The train came to an abrupt stop at the end of the tunnel, and the team piled out. Before they had made it three paces, Overton stopped. When he balled his hand into a fist and crouched, Sophie realized something was wrong.

"What is it?" she whispered.

Bouma quietly paced over to the tunnel wall, resting his back against the stone and aiming his rifle into the darkness. Kiel made his way to the opposite wall, mimicking the soldier's actions.

"Alexia, are you picking up any heat signatures outside the Biosphere?" asked Overton.

Static came over the net.

"Alexia, come in, over."

More static.

"Fuck. We're out of range already?" Bouma whispered.

"Must be some interference in here," Overton said tapping his helmet. He stood and flashed a hand signal to both Bouma and Kiel. Within seconds they were moving. Sophie stayed close on their heels.

As they rounded the next corner, she saw the cargo bay and the last Humvee sitting idle like a sleeping beast. The sight forced her to a stop. Was she really going back out there?

Overton entered the room with his rifle leveled at the floor. Bouma followed him into the darkness, with Kiel close behind. Sophie paced over to the young marine and waited for the others to give them the all clear.

"Holy shit, what's that smell!" Kiel whispered.

Sophie took a breath but the filter in her suit revealed nothing but the cheap smell of plastic and metal.

Inside the cargo bay, Bouma made his way to the light switch next to the supply room. With a quick flip, the massive halogen lamps clicked on, illuminating the source of the smell.

Thompson's body lay next to the Humvee, a blood-soaked tarp covering it.

"Jesus, this isn't right, guys. We should have buried him," Kiel said.

"Where? Outside? Did you want to take him out there? Last time I went for a stroll on the tarmac, Jeff ended up abducted," replied Overton.

Kiel shook his head and clamped his fingers over his nose.

Sophie thought of the funerals in Biome 1 for Saafi and Finley. They had burned the bodies, but that was before the Organics had destroyed much of the lab weeks ago. Incineration wasn't an option anymore.

She forced herself to look away and followed the others to the Humvee. There was no time to worry about a proper burial now. Things had changed significantly; priority was given to the living.

"Bouma, check the vehicle. Make sure it's roadworthy. Kiel, get ready to move. Those blast doors are opening in five."

Sophie studied Kiel for a reaction, but he remained stoic. His profile made him look even younger. His recently shaved face and neat, slicked-back hair reminded her of pictures she had seen of Emanuel in his younger years. The marine even had the same wide dimples when he smiled.

Bouma climbed into the driver's seat and checked the monitors. With a click of the start button, the engine roared to life. It coughed and rattled at first, but quickly transitioned into a smooth purr. He poked half his armored body out and gave Overton a thumbs-up.

The sergeant turned to Sophie and reached for his .45. He hesitated but then unholstered the weapon, holding it out to her. "Take it. You've proven to be a decent shot."

Sophie recalled the Sentinel that she had shot in the head as it held Overton in its massive claws. She had lied then about taking lessons before the invasion. Truth was, she had just made a very lucky shot.

She nodded and grabbed the pistol, stuffing it into her belt next to the Biosphere radio.

"Do you have the coordinates, Kiel?" Overton asked.

"Yes. Alexia uploaded them to my tablet before we left. Looks like I have a couple miles' hike, er, climb."

"Roger." Overton paused and tilted his helmet in Kiel's direction. "Good luck, son."

Sophie picked up on a hint of reservation in the sergeant's voice. Was it fear? Empathy?

Kiel nodded and turned to face the opening blast doors. As soon as they were wide enough, he made his way out, turning one time to look at Thompson's body before he slipped into the darkness.

As he disappeared, Kiel's voice sounded over the net. "Don't worry sir, I won't let you down."

Captain Noble sat at the small metal desk lining the east wall of his personal cabin. To the average person, the space would have been a prison cell. But for him, it was an escape.

Everything he had ever accomplished was represented in this room. His degrees from MIT and the certificate from a decade ago when he graduated from NTC officer school. An ancient black powder pistol that his father, the pilot of an F-22 Raptor, had given him as a gift when he was commissioned as the captain of the *Ghost of Atlantis*. And there, on the top of his desk, was a picture of his family. His beautiful wife and their two daughters. They had been waiting for him in Los Angeles, where they had moved shortly after the solar storms of 2055. He thought they would be safe on the West Coast, near the ocean. But he had been wrong.

He winced, the pain of their loss still so fresh. He hadn't seen them for . . . Noble could hardly even remember. Had it really been that long? Seven months? His daughters would be taller. And his wife. Oh God, his beautiful Sarah. He was beginning to forget what it was like to lie next to her. To wrap his arm around her in the middle of the night, to make love to her in the morning before training exercises. Those were just distant memories now, slowly fading from his mind. He knew the chances of seeing them again were next to nothing. If he had known the invasion was coming, he would have hugged them all a bit longer. And maybe he wouldn't have left at all.

But now he drew strength from their loss. His duty to NTC and the survivors had never been clearer. He would fight to the bitter end, to avenge his family and take back the planet.

The monitor above his desk chirped and glowed to life. He put the picture back down carefully. Taking a deep breath, he slid in front of the screen. An image of Lieutenant Commander Richards popped onto the display. His usually clean face was covered with stubble, and there were dark circles under his brown eyes.

"Captain Noble, we have arrived at the rendezvous point. No sign of the Chinese yet, sir."

"Roger that. In the meantime, I'd like to extend a radio mast to see if we can pick up any signals from the coast. I know this breaks protocol, but we don't have a choice." Noble paused and looked at the black powder pistol. "Oh, and Richards? Make sure the *Sea Serpent* is fueled and ready to go ASAP."

"Understood, sir." Richards's eyes darted nervously to the left.

"What is it, Lieutenant?"

"Sir, those things. The worms . . . whatever you want to call them. The crew is worried that if we sit here for too long, they might find us again."

Noble scratched his beard. "Roger that, Richards. But we need to give Quan more time. I'm not about to leave him—and my men—out here to die."

"Understood, sir . . ." his voice trailed off.

The captain raised a brow. "Speak freely, Richards. I don't have time for this."

"Sir, if Captain Quan somehow does manage to make it here, won't he be bringing those things with him?"

Richards had a point, but Noble had already considered it. He would give them a couple more hours. If they didn't show up by then, well, he would have no choice but to move on. Eventually, they'd run out of ocean, and then they'd really be in trouble, but for now, he would wait—and hope.

The sunrise spread over the dead landscape like an orange carpet. Where there should have been snow, there was nothing but cracked earth. And where there should have been mountain streams, there was nothing but smooth rock. Millions of years of runoff had polished the stone, but now not even a single drop of water was left to make the same journey.

Kiel paused to rest and admire the view. He wiped his brow free of sweat and squinted, shielding his eyes with a curved hand.

Goddamn, it was hot! And the farther he hiked, the hotter it felt.

The white sun was unforgiving. And there was nowhere to hide. The trees were bare and dead, devoid of leaves to protect him from the brutal rays.

With a grunt, Kiel extended his arms and grabbed the rocky ledge above him. Angling himself outward, he made sure he had a tight grip before dangling freely.

Don't look down.

Never look down.

He looked down and saw the rocky trail below. Numbness shot up his legs and his stomach moved into his throat. Rock climbing had always been a hobby of his for exactly that reason. The adrenaline rush was like nothing else. But this was no leisure trip with his buddies. A lot was riding on this one.

Everything was riding on this one.

He closed his eyes and pulled himself up, sliding his chest onto the ledge. With half his body and the device still dangling behind him, he scanned the ground for anything useful. There was a small tree a few feet to his left. He could surely reach it, but was it strong enough to hold his weight?

The tree was definitely dead. It was possible the trunk would split like kindling if he put all of his weight on it, but he had no choice. He was beginning to slip backward.

He grabbed it with his gloved left hand. A bead of sweat dripped into his eye, but the burning pain didn't discourage him. He squeezed his hand around the trunk and slowly pulled himself up. The weight of the weapon pulled him down.

Crack.

The trunk split right down the middle. The crack spider-webbed to the top of the tree, dry splinters exploding in his face as he kicked and struggled to pull himself up.

With one final heave, he slid his entire body onto the ledge and dropped to his stomach, panting. The tree finally gave way, toppling over the edge of the cliff. He didn't turn to watch it fall, but he heard the sound it made when it crashed to the ground.

Shit, he thought. That could have been the sound of his bones shattering. With a deep breath, he pushed himself up and reached for his tablet, where Alexia had downloaded the safest route up the mountain. His hands came up empty. Panicking, he turned to look down at his belt, but the RVAMP blocked his view.

Kiel frantically unfastened the weapon and set it on the rocky ground. Twisting, he saw the empty pouch where he'd placed the tablet.

"What the hell?" he muttered, spinning to check the ground. Dropping to both knees, he crawled to the ledge and slowly peeked over the cliff. At the bottom was his shattered tablet. The crashing sound he'd heard moments earlier wasn't just the tree.

"Fuck!" he yelled, his voice echoing over the valley. *What the hell am I supposed to do now,* he thought with his hands on his hips, glancing down at the RVAMP.

Sucking in a hot lungful of air he wiped another trail of sweat from his forehead. Above him, the rocky side of the mountain rose into the sky, reaching for the wicked white sun.

Just when he thought things couldn't get any worse, a loud noise exploded out of the silence. He carefully turned to watch a drone racing across the skyline. Kiel instantly scrambled for cover.

When the craft passed he wasted no time. Grabbing the closest rock, he began climbing. He had a mission to complete, and there was no way he was going to let Overton and the others down.

CHAPTER 26

HOLLY stopped and stared at a strawberry they had missed earlier. The entire patch had been plucked clean, save for this single red fruit. She couldn't help but see it as a symbol of something bigger—something she didn't quite understand. Why had she survived and not others? Like the single strawberry, she had been saved while everyone she had ever known outside the Biosphere was dead, plucked and consumed by the alien invaders.

Brushing a strand of hair out of her face, she moved on, leaving the strawberry alone. She could see the children had climbed onto the platform and were standing in front of the door leading out of the biome and into the cleansing chamber that the aliens had broken through weeks ago.

"What are you guys doing?" she yelled. She ran across the field, her boots squishing in the freshly irrigated dirt.

The children didn't flinch. They just kept staring at something hidden from Holly's view.

With a quick leap she jumped onto the platform and paced over to them. "What are you guys looking . . ." She gasped midsentence. The makeshift door they had used to cover the broken glass of the cleansing chamber hung to the side. Holly leaned closer to see the gap was small, so small that only a child would have been able to squeeze through. She could see through the space into the area beyond that led out of the Biosphere and into the NTC offices.

Holly exchanged glances with both children. "Did one of you do this?"

They shook their heads no in turn.

Holly believed them. She quickly herded the children away from the door. "Run. Run to the medical ward as fast as you can."

David looked up at her with frightened eyes. "Why, what's going on? And where's Jeff?" he asked.

"I said run!" Holly clapped her hands and the kids took off across the platform, the sound of their footfalls echoing as they ran.

"Alexia, are you aware that the door to Biome 1 is compromised?" Holly shouted.

"Yes, Doctor Brown. Jeff removed the panel last night. He informed me that Sergeant Overton had ordered him to follow them to the Humvee."

"What?" Holly blurted.

"Jeff removed the panel . . ."

"I heard what you said." Holly crouched down and looked into the darkness of the cleansing chamber. There was no sign of the boy. She grabbed the metal panel and placed it back over the cleansing chamber entrance.

Holly gritted her teeth. It was rare for her to get angry, but Alexia's lack of oversight posed a major problem. If a kid could fool her, then she could easily be manipulated by anyone.

"Tell Emanuel I need his help in Biome 1," Holly snapped.

"Certainly, Doctor Brown."

If Holly didn't know better, she would have thought the AI sounded almost hurt. But that was impossible. Alexia wasn't a person. She was a machine.

Holly looked back over the fields, where just two days ago she had kissed Bouma. He was a strong and honest man. If anyone could protect Jeff, it was him.

————

Overton took a sharp left, tearing down a frontage road and sending chunks of rock into the air behind them.

"Take it easy," Sophie said.

Overton replied by pushing down on the gas a bit harder.

A bump in the road jolted Sophie forward, and she grabbed for the handlebar attached to the ceiling. With her head tilted to the side, she could see the blue screen on the dashboard perfectly. The odometer read sixty miles an hour. Even in a Humvee, she knew this speed could send them into a ditch, or worse. The large tires were great for slower speeds, but on gravel they were dangerous.

She gripped the bar tighter as Overton sped up. "Sergeant . . ." Before she could finish her rebuke, the marine turned his visor and looked at her silently. He was officially losing it. She should have known better than to agree to the mission, let alone join it. But it was too late now. There was no turning back.

Sophie could see the highway in the distance. They were getting close, and a wave of relief washed over her. She wanted to get to the tunnels as soon as possible. Ever since she caught sight of the Steam Beast through Emanuel's HUD footage, she'd been on edge. Their small team couldn't hold up against another one of those creatures, especially not without the RVAMP to help them. Underground, the tunnels would be too small for the new creatures to fit. At least, that's what Sophie was counting on.

Overton slammed on the brakes as they came up on the blacktop, jerking Sophie and Bouma to one side. She fumbled for the bar again but missed it and smacked her hand into the window. Something in the back of the truck made a loud thud, masking her cry of pain.

Overton looked over his shoulder. "What was that?"

Bouma was already looking into the backseat. "Uh, you're going to need to see this for yourself."

Overton eyed the skyline and then got out of the vehicle. He jogged to the trunk with Sophie right behind him.

With one swift motion, he yanked the door open to reveal a small body hidden under a pile of blankets and gear. "Shit," he said, snatching the blanket off to uncover Jeff. The boy looked up at them, holding his hand to his head.

"You drive like crap," he moaned.

"Ugh, goddamned kids," Overton grumbled. "Get out of there. I should fucking leave you out here for directly disobeying an order."

"He's not a marine, and you aren't leaving him out here," Sophie fired back, reaching for Jeff.

Overton glared at her again, his visor reflecting the bright sun. He shook his head and slammed the door shut once Jeff had jumped onto the dirt.

"Sit next to Corporal Bouma," Sophie said, patting the kid on the back a little harder than she meant to. "Corporal, please take a look at his head."

Jeff climbed in and sat quietly next to the marine. Bouma said, "It's okay, kid. Just stay close to me."

The boy nodded and fastened his seat belt just as Overton slammed his foot down on the gas, tearing onto the highway. Within seconds they were weaving in and out of the graveyard of empty vehicles.

Sophie grabbed the handle again. Every time she started to relax, she was slapped in the face with a new problem. Being her team's leader in the old world had meant facing tough math equations or dealing with the fallout from a controversial paper, but in the new world every decision affected the lives of those she was so desperately trying to protect. That was the reason she had decided to come with Overton. She was responsible for these men, and if she was putting their lives at risk, then she had to be there to support them.

If Alexia was right and the weapon Emanuel designed could in fact take out fifteen square miles' worth of aliens, then they had the opportunity to save countless lives—lives that would be invaluable to the resistance. But at what cost? Deep down she still wasn't convinced the mission was a good idea.

In the distance, she could see the skyscrapers of Colorado Springs. They appeared to sway in the heat, their shiny metallic sides glistening under the scorching sun.

"One hundred and two degrees," she muttered.

"What's that?" Overton asked.

"The temperature. It's one hundred and two degrees out there."

"Shit. Kiel has got to be burning up on the mountain without a suit. I only saw him take two water bottles," Bouma said.

"He's been trained. He knows how to conserve his water," Overton said. His helmet moved from side to side as he scanned the skyline for drones.

It was surprisingly quiet, but Sophie knew the silence wouldn't last. She sat back in her seat, releasing her grip on the handle and watching the dead landscape race by them. There wasn't a hint of green. What had been deep lakes were now postapocalyptic craters, reminders of what had once been a leisurely place to have a picnic or take out a boat. And the empty streets and buildings were equally as eerie. It was as if they were entering a ghost town.

Ten minutes later, Overton eased the truck to a stop in front of a building. A sign dangled above it.

SUBWAY STATION E1.

They were at their destination.

Captain Noble stood in the middle of the CIC. His eyes darted from monitor to monitor, studying the data that was slowly trickling in. The GOA had been sitting in silence for over two hours, with nothing but the random beep from a sensor or the sound of footsteps to break the anxiety of waiting. With every passing minute, he knew the chances of the Chinese making the rendezvous were diminishing.

Noble closed his eyes and sucked in a breath through his nostrils. He had to put the thought out of his head, just like he had done with the thoughts of his family. He was no good to any of his crew if he was distressed. Strength was the only way forward.

The sound of another chirp pulled his attention to the navigation station. The blue screen was obscured by the head of his first officer, Athena Lewis. He tapped her on the shoulder. "What do you have, Lieutenant?"

"Sir, we're picking up some sort of signal in Colorado. Looks like it's moving, too."

Noble checked the monitor displaying the locations of the remaining Biospheres. Eight lights blinked. Another one had gone dark during the night.

Alaska.

"Shit," Noble said, cracking his knuckles.

"Sir?" Lewis asked.

"Nothing. Can you narrow the location of the signal?"

"Working on it, sir."

The captain looked back at the screen. Cheyenne Mountain was still online. Could this new signal be connected?

"Irene, tell Alex to report to the CIC."

"Yes, Captain," the AI replied.

Within minutes Alex entered the room, wiping sleep from his eyes.

"Tell me everything you know about the Cheyenne Mountain Biosphere," Noble ordered, turning back to the monitor.

"I already have, sir."

"Think harder."

Alex shook his head. "There's nothing . . ." He paused. "I told you about their weapon."

The blue screen in front of Lewis flared to life, and a graphic of Colorado Springs burst onto the display. "Sir, the signal is coming from within the city. I started picking it up as soon as we deployed the radio mast."

"And you didn't tell me?" Noble asked, his voice agitated.

"Sir, I didn't know what it was at first. We pick up strange signals all the time. Most turn out to be dead ends."

The captain took a step closer. "My apologies. I didn't mean to—"

"Sir," she interjected. "That signal is definitely moving."

Noble hunched over her terminal and watched a red blip inch across the screen. "I'll bet they're testing that weapon. Irene, notify the engineers in the vehicle depot. I want a helicopter prepped and ready within the hour. And notify the Special Forces team. They're going for a ride."

The captain looked over at Alex, who stared back at him in disbelief. "Finding you was like hitting the lottery," Noble said, smiling. He slapped Alex on the back and headed for the doorway. "Richards, you're in charge now. Prepare the sub to surface. I'm going with the chopper."

Noble didn't turn to see the shocked looks on his crew's faces. He disappeared into the hallway and made his way to his quarters. Inside, he grabbed the picture of his family, kissing it lightly.

"Time to make things right," he whispered before placing it in his backpack. He glanced one more time at the space he had considered home for so long. With a smile, he shut off the lights and raced down the hallway toward the vehicle station. He was ready—ready to avenge his family.

A few doors down, Alex lay in bed with his hands folded behind his head, staring at the ceiling. He tilted his head to look at the blue screen. There were no beautiful jellyfish gliding across the screen, none of the fascinating deep-sea creatures that had mesmerized him before. Just . . .

Darkness.

He closed his eyes and imagined the world Noble was heading into. The man had no idea what he was about to face. His prized periscope had shown him images, sure, but he'd never seen any of the aliens up close. Never seen an orb crack open and spill out human remains. Those were the images Alex had to live with—those were the things he couldn't get out of his mind. He was still alive when everyone he had ever loved was dead.

The hum of some distant machine sent a chill down Alex's spine. The noise reminded him of what he'd escaped. Closing his eyes, he pictured the horde of Spiders consuming the human remains in a neighborhood back in California. Squeezing his eyes tightly, the image changed. This time, he saw his friends inside the Biosphere as they were torn to shreds and then spun into orbs.

His eyelids snapped open when he heard a vibration rumble through the sub's metal walls. It sounded liked something had smashed into the GOA's side.

Alex sat up and listened.

Another tremor surged through the boat. And then another. Paralyzed with fear, Alex scrambled across his bunk and cowered in the corner of the bed. His hands shook at his sides as the noises grew in intensity.

Had the sea serpent Organics found them again? Or were these just phantom sounds in his mind?

He imagined the faceless head of the alien that had hovered in front of the camera. A shockwave of fear tore into Alex as he remembered the creature's chest cavity cracking open to reveal those jagged teeth.

Crack!

Alex let out a small wail as the noise rang out. The metal wall behind him vibrated with the sudden noise. It sounded like it was coming from right behind him.

Shimmering reds swam before his eyes as he began to drift from reality. He could see the snakes ramming the side of the boat, their teeth glistening in the water, ready to devour him.

"No!" Alex yelled. "I won't let you take me."

Jumping off the top bunk, he grabbed the rope he'd swiped off a cart on his way back from the CIC. He tied the noose with careful precision, trying not to think about what he was about to do.

Behind him the banging continued. There were more of them now. Alex tied the rope faster. Then he pulled the chair out from under the small desk and stood on it to tie the rope around a metal pipe on the ceiling. He tugged it twice to make sure it was tight. There wasn't going to be much room, with the ceiling only eight feet high.

He thought of his sister as he held the rope in his hands. Alex wasn't going to let those things get him like they had her.

Before he stood on the chair and slipped the noose around his neck, he considered what he was about to do one more time. He had worked so hard to survive out there. Tried so desperately to find safety. And he thought he had.

NTC had taken him in, fed him, and promised him the human race wasn't going to just lie down and die. But he didn't believe any of it. He had seen the monstrosities outside, the Spiders and the orbs, and now the sea serpents. They were just as vulnerable in this submarine as they were outside. Noble thought he could fight back. The Biosphere at Colorado Springs thought they could create a weapon. But what was the point? The Organics were in control of everything. They owned the planet now. Whatever humanity did, however they tried to fight or hide or survive, the Organics would find them. The Organics would kill them.

He didn't want any of it.

With the noose in position, he tightened it and closed his eyes. His sister's freckled face slipped into his mind. It was a memory from long ago, on a sunny day at the beach. He could see her laughing at some joke he didn't remember making. Then she was gone. He saw instead the image of one of the snakelike aliens. The creature's chest opened and flapped its fins as it lurched toward him. There was only one way to finally escape them. And he was doing it on his own terms.

He kicked the chair out from under him and felt the noose tighten around his neck. His legs kicked uncontrollably, but he didn't fight it like he thought he would. He didn't claw at the rope around his neck. He simply closed his eyes and slipped away into the black.

In the CIC, Captain Noble let out a sigh as the GOA continued its ascent. The hull creaked as the pressure decreased on their way up to the surface and the ballast tanks filled with air. Even after so many years at sea, the sound still startled him.

He watched the blue screen in front of him read off their depth.

Eight hundred feet.

Seven hundred forty-five feet.

Five hundred ten feet . . .

CHAPTER 27

SOPHIE led Jeff through the darkness. The sunlight had disappeared about a mile back when they had followed the tracks deep underground. Her infrared allowed her to see into the darkest places, but Jeff was completely blind. He held on to her left hand tightly as they made their way deeper into the entrails of the facility.

The outline of one of the idle trains came into view as they rounded the next corner. Overton held up his hand and then jerked his chin at Bouma. "Check it out."

Sophie watched Bouma's armored body move cautiously forward, his pulse rifle leveled at the train. "Any intel from the bot?" she whispered into her helmet's microphone.

"I've been watching the video on my HUD. So far the tunnels appear clear," Overton replied.

Glancing at her own HUD for the mission time, she saw a tiny red flash.

Contact.

Bouma must have seen it too. He dropped to one knee and jammed his rifle tighter against his shoulder.

Sophie quickly pulled Jeff to the side of the tracks where they rested their backs against the concrete wall.

"What is it?" Jeff whispered. Pulling his 10mm handgun from his backpack, he tried to look around her.

"Shhh," Sophie said, pushing him back toward the wall. She peered around the corner and saw the red blip dance across her display and disappear into the train.

Have they found us already?

Her breathing became more labored, hot puffs of breath fogging up her visor. She swiped at the glass in vain and waited for the view to clear.

A short burst of white noise sounded in her ear.

"Contact," Bouma said.

"Roger. Check it out," Overton replied.

Sophie saw Bouma's helmet move, although she wasn't sure if he was acknowledging Overton or if he was just surveying the area. In seconds, he was on the move, his rifle aimed at the train's windows, then the ground, then the windows again, and finally the open door.

Sophie blinked, and Bouma was gone. She tightened her grip on Jeff's hand, ready to lead him away from the train. The time on her mission clock ticked away across her display.

Fifteen seconds passed. Then another fifteen. Each moment felt like an eternity. Like one of her bad dreams.

The growing sensation of helplessness began to take control of her—her heart thumped faster in her chest and her breathing became shallower.

She looked back at Jeff. He was staring into the darkness, his lips quivering. His face drenched with sweat and dirt.

How terrified must he feel? Waiting in the darkness, completely vulnerable to his surroundings. Sophie licked her dry lips and narrowed her eyes with a new resolve. She knew she had to be strong for him.

Sophie flinched as another burst of static played over her helmet's headset. She waited for Overton to relay another order, but instead her earpiece was filled with a chilling scream. The noise was stifled at once by the com's static, making it impossible to know where the sound was coming from.

Another voice erupted over the net. "Back, get back!"

The screaming was deafening, and she cupped her hands over her helmet in a futile attempt to stop the noise.

Movement flashed across her display and she focused on Overton, who was waving his hands in her direction.

"Get back!"

The words were his. It finally made sense. She retreated a few steps until she felt her back hit the wall. More movement flashed across her display. Overton was sprinting toward the train. He skidded to a stop just as Bouma jumped out of the open door and crashed onto the train tracks.

Sophie reached back and grabbed Jeff with her right hand to keep him still while she peeked around the corner.

Bouma clawed at his head. It was then she saw there was something attached to his helmet. He rolled on the tracks, pawing at his visor, while Overton rushed over to help him.

"What the hell is it?" Sophie finally said, her voice now hysterical.

Jeff pulled on Sophie's hand. "What's going on?"

Sophie didn't reply. Overton was standing over Bouma, who was now sitting up and holding something in his hands.

What she heard next shocked her.

Laughter.

"It's a freaking cat," Overton said. "A cat!"

Bouma held the emaciated creature in his hands.

When her breathing and heart rate returned to normal levels, Sophie took Jeff's hand and led him to the two marines. "Come on. It's okay," she reassured him.

Sophie stopped a few feet behind Overton. The cat was the first domesticated animal they had come across. It looked like an image from an animal welfare advertisement. What little hair it had left was in patchy clumps. Its ribs poked out of its shriveled skin. Sophie bent down and tried to pet the cat's head, but it swiped at her with a clawed paw and hissed.

"We need to move," Overton said. "Get your ass up, Bouma, and get rid of that cat."

Sophie watched it scamper down the train tracks. Shaking her head, she grabbed Jeff's hand again and followed the marines down the passage.

"How much longer until we reach the residential station?" Sophie whispered.

Overton checked his HUD. "Looks like at least another hour or so. Then we wait for Kiel."

Sophie thought of the marine climbing up the mountainside, the weapon dangling off his back. Without one of the NTC suits, he was completely unprotected from the heat. If he didn't take breaks in the shade, he was bound to suffer heatstroke, no matter how agile or strong he was.

Just the thought of being exposed to the sun without a suit increased her blood pressure. It was cooler in the darkness of the subway, but not much. Even with a ventilation system, her armored suit felt like a furnace. Jeff appeared to be suffering just as badly without one. Sophie glanced down at the boy, who stumbled along in the darkness.

The sound of their footsteps echoed off the tunnel walls as they made their way deeper into the system. Entering the subway was like being sealed in a coffin, and she was beginning to feel trapped. She had thought she would feel safer here, but now she knew there was no place that felt safe.

A peculiar beep rang out. She stopped abruptly, glancing from side to side.

"What the hell is that?" Overton asked after the second chirp.

"I don't . . ." Sophie began to say. Then she saw it. Her radio had come back online. A signal zigzagged across the display. She switched off her night vision with a blink and dropped Jeff's hand.

"Turn the volume down," Overton whispered over the net.

With a quick swipe, Sophie lowered the sound. Nothing but white noise crackled out of the speakers. Whoever was trying to get a hold of them wasn't getting their message through.

"The tunnel is probably interfering with the transmission," she said.

"Another reason to keep moving," Overton said. "Let's go. If that's Alex, he's still alive and can wait until we're done here."

Taking one last look at the display, Sophie felt a sudden surge of hope.

———————

Captain Noble walked into the cargo bay with mixed feelings. While he was happy to finally have the opportunity to fight, he was sad to leave his crew behind. He looked over the unit of NTC Special Forces soldiers gathering beneath him. They moved nimbly in their sleek black armor, their goggles emitting a fiery glow that illuminated the metal deck.

Their team lead, a man by the name of Sergeant Donald Harrington, sensed Noble's presence and looked up at him. "Captain on deck," he yelled. The other soldiers stood at attention and saluted Noble, who frowned and said, "At ease, at ease."

Grabbing the ladder, Noble made his way down to the floor. In the corner of the room, he saw two workers mopping up grease. Like any well-oiled machine, *Ghost of Atlantis* had a job for everyone.

"Harrington, how long until we can get this thing airborne?"

"She's ready to fly, sir."

Noble marveled at the gunship. It was no ordinary helicopter, with titanium plates covering the outer shell and two inches of steel below that. The chopper easily fit thirty people in its cargo bay. It had stealth technology and an array of weapons including two side-mounted high-caliber pulse cannons and various rockets. The chopper could travel 350 miles per hour, making it one of the fastest gunships on the planet.

"Like a tank with rotors and a race car engine," Noble muttered.

"Sir?" Harrington asked.

"Nothing." The captain followed the soldiers as they walked single file up the ramp into the belly of the flying fortress. When it was his turn to enter, Noble slipped on his helmet and took a deep breath of the filtered air. It stunk of new plastic, just like the gas masks he'd been trained to use years before. He hated the smell. He flexed his arms inside his Kevlar armor, getting used to the feel of it. Glancing back at his ship one last time, he climbed into the chopper.

———————

In the CIC, Lieutenant Commander Richards got the green light. "Irene, retrieve the radio mast and surface."

"One moment, sir."

A groan from the bowels of the ship echoed through the passages as the sail compartment above the deck exploded through the waves. Richards could picture it, like the fin of a shark hunting its prey. The *Ghost of Atlantis* had surfaced.

He gripped his seat while the sub settled. Once his control panel glowed a healthy green, he swiveled his chair and hovered over another dashboard. Glancing at the middle console, he checked to ensure all systems were operational. With a deep breath he opened the com line to the chopper. "*Sea Serpent*, this is GOA, all systems are clear. Over."

"Roger that, GOA," the pilot responded.

Richards looked back down at the button that activated the cargo bay door, his finger hovering over it. The only thing between the chopper and the Organics was a thick metal door, one he controlled. The entire mission made him uneasy, but orders were orders, and Captain Noble seemed confident. Without further hesitation, Richards punched the button.

He watched the doors crack open, revealing a brilliant sun overhead. They hadn't seen the sun for days. No. Weeks.

With a sigh, Richards sat back in his chair and watched the monitor.

"Sir, we have a situation," Trish, the senior communications officers said.

Richards stiffened. *What now?* he thought.

"A guard just found Alex Wagner," she continued.

"What's your point?" replied Richards, craning his head back to study her face.

"He's dead, sir. Hanged himself in his quarters."

Richard swallowed hard and turned to face the younger officer. This was the last thing he wanted to tell Captain Noble before the *Sea Serpent* embarked on its most important mission.

"How many people know?"

"The guard, his commanding officer, and us," replied Trish promptly, her eyes narrowing in on him.

"Good; keep it that way. I don't want this affecting Captain Noble's mission."

Trish paused for a brief moment before gesturing with the slightest of nods. "Yes, sir."

In the cargo bay, the rectangular roof compartment angled upward. Rays of bright sunlight washed over the compartment. The pilot held his hands to his visor to block the sun. "Tint," he said. The windshield turned a glassy gray in the blink of an eye.

After performing his preflight checklist, he maneuvered the bulky gunship onto the helipad. Another groan vibrated through the craft as the platform rose toward the opening.

With the chopper in position, he checked the monitor to make sure the craft was clear on all sides. A green light flashed, and with a single swipe from his index finger, he initiated the chopper's multiple rotors. The blades above turned silently, a product of the best stealth technology NTC had to offer.

"GOA, this is *Sea Serpent*, requesting permission for takeoff," the pilot said calmly. He stared out over the open ocean, the magnificent view a reminder of what they were still fighting for.

"Permission granted. Get back to us in one piece. Over," Lieutenant Commander Richards replied.

Captain Noble's voice crackled over the com. "Don't wait up for us, Richards."

The pilot grinned and listened to a few of the Special Forces soldiers chuckle over the com before turning to stare out the recently cleaned windshield. Underneath both wings he could see the waves slurping against the GOA's sides.

"Time to put on a show for the aliens," the pilot said. His words drew more laughter as he clicked one last button before pulling them into the air.

He watched the sub sink back into the water, bubbles and white caps churning above the water. And just like that, it was gone.

"Good luck," the pilot whispered as the helicopter raced toward the coast.

The remnants of orbs lined the tracks like popped balloons. Sophie squeezed Jeff's hand as they came upon them.

"What do you see?" he asked.

Sophie smiled. He was a smart kid; a simple squeeze from her hand was enough to get his attention.

A few feet ahead Overton paused to check out the gory remains. "This didn't show up on the bot's video feed," he said.

Bouma emerged from the shadows and bent down to look at what had once been some sort of animal. Sophie studied it too. It was hard to make out at first, but the claws and lumps of black fur were enough to tell her it was probably a raccoon.

Bouma stood and looked down the tunnel. "Maybe we took a wrong turn?"

"Negative. We're right where we should be."

"I don't like this," Bouma said, unshouldering his rifle.

Overton cocked his helmet to look at Sophie and Jeff. "Stay close."

They moved as a pack, the sound of the rap of their footfalls clanking noisily over the metal. With every step, they drew closer to their destination—the human farms.

After another fifteen minutes of trekking through the tunnels, Overton stopped abruptly. He balled his hand into a fist. Sophie tried to swallow, but her dry throat made it nearly impossible. Something was wrong. He was spooked.

Sophie felt Jeff tighten his grip on her armored hand. She leveled her pistol into the darkness, scanning the passage from side to side.

No contacts. Just the green outlines of modern infrastructure.

Silence consumed them. Another minute passed. Then two. Overton remained completely still, frozen like a statue.

A crackle of static broke over her headset, nearly making her fire off a random shot. She eased her finger off the trigger. The last thing she wanted was to draw attention to their position.

"I lost the feed," Overton finally said in a hushed voice.

"What?" Bouma whispered.

"The bot feed. It just cut out."

"Can you rewind the video?" Bouma asked.

"Working on it."

Sophie waited in silence. The tunnel was completely still, no sign of life, but somewhere out there she could sense the aliens.

Overton cursed. "Looks like the stupid bot ran smack into the middle of a nest of Spiders."

"Shit. How far?" Bouma asked. His typically calm voice sounded strained.

"Not far. Maybe two turns. It's hard to say for sure . . . God!" Overton crouched on the ground and hit his helmet with his right hand.

Sophie watched the man smack his head repeatedly. Was he losing it at last?

"Overton?" Bouma finally asked, approaching the man. "What are your orders?"

The marine stopped hitting his helmet but didn't get up. He remained crouched, staring into the tunnel.

"Sir?" Bouma entreated.

At the end of the passage, right before it curved into another tunnel, a light emerged. Sophie's heart stopped. With a blink, she clicked off her infrared and night vision so she could see it with her own eyes.

The aliens had found them.

The tunnel was bathed in blue light. The terrifying scratching sound came seconds later.

Jeff let go of her hand and moved behind her. "Sophie," he whispered.

Bouma took another step closer to Overton, who watched the halo of blue light intensify. "Sir! What are your orders?!"

Overton slowly cocked his helmet up at the man. "I'll hold them off."

Sophie looked at the man in disbelief. He had zero electromagnetic grenades, only one pulse magazine, and a handful of regular grenades that she doubted would have any effect.

Yup. *The man has officially lost his mind*, Sophie thought. She grabbed Jeff and knelt down in front of him. "Listen to me very carefully. You hold on to my hand and don't let go. You got it?"

Jeff nodded, his eyes reflecting the blue light of the approaching aliens.

Sophie spun quickly to see Bouma grab Overton's shoulder.

"No way, Overton, that's suicide," Bouma shouted.

"Go!" Overton yelled, jumping to his feet and leveling his rifle in the light's direction.

Bouma ran over to Sophie and Jeff. "You heard him. *Move!*"

His voice was deep and commanding, but Sophie hesitated. They couldn't just leave Overton. He was wasting his life. His sacrifice would buy them seconds at best.

"Come on!" Bouma said, running back the way they had come.

Sophie finally moved—but not toward Bouma. "Watch him," she said, pushing Jeff toward the marine.

She ran as hard as she could to catch up with Overton. By the time she got to him, he was crouching behind a trash bin, his weapon pointed at the approaching glimmering light. Sophie still couldn't see them, but she could hear them. And she could feel them. The tunnel walls shook with the vibrations of the approaching horde.

But she wasn't going to let her fear take hold of her. Not anymore—not when it mattered most. She tapped on Overton's visor with her .45.

"What the hell! I told you to get out of here!"

Another vibration shook the passage, and dust rained down from the ceiling.

"Please, we need you," Sophie said.

Overton pushed himself off the ground and stood shoulder to shoulder with her while he watched the light intensify. A second tremor shook the ceiling and Overton cocked his helmet to look at Sophie. "You really are a pain in my ass, you know that?" Shouldering his weapon he said, "How fast can you run?"

Then he exploded into a sprint.

Sophie wasn't prepared for the rhetorical question, but she didn't hesitate. It only took her two heartbeats to catch up with him. When she passed him, she stole a glance over her shoulder. The entire tunnel was lit up like one massive LED.

Scratch, scrape, scratch, scrape.

The first Spiders came crashing around the corner, tumbling into a somersault with limbs flailing. The next batch slowed by sliding their claws across the concrete. A trail of sparks funneled behind them. The first three Spiders lost their balance and tumbled over one another. They were quickly crushed by the advancing pack, their blue blood painting the tunnel wall.

As Sophie and Overton finally made their way around the first turn, the Spiders' shrieks slashed through the passage. Only this time it was louder, it was more concentrated, and it wasn't coming from the Spiders. It was coming from one of the Steam Beasts.

CHAPTER 28

THE sweat was flowing freely off Kiel's face. Every time he wiped it away, it would drench his gloves, which made it more difficult to get a proper grip on the rocks. He was resting now in the crevice of the mountain, watching the blue drone zip back and forth across the skyline. It was hunting. He could only hope it wasn't looking for the others. They would surely be deep within the city now. And that meant he was running out of time.

He took one last swig of water and tossed the empty bottle over the edge. Looking up, he could see he was almost to the spot Alexia had plotted on his tablet. At least he thought he was. Without the device, it was really tough to tell. The mountain was starting to blend together, and he wasn't sure which route up was the best.

With the trail ending, he was now at the technical part of the climb. The mountain curved up into a smooth vertical wall at least fifteen feet high. Fortunately there wasn't much wind, just a breeze coming from the southwest. With a deep breath, he rubbed his hands together and brushed another bead of sweat out of his eyes with his sleeve.

Grabbing the weapon's makeshift straps, he threw it around his shoulders. The rectangular box dug into his shoulder blades, which were already raw from carrying it this far. If he made it back, he was going to ask someone for a massage . . .

If.

He swept his gaze across the vertical mountainside, trying to visually map out a route. There was no way around it; he would have to go straight up. He could identify several areas for his hands and feet, but there was at least a five-foot span where the rock was completely smooth.

He looked back over the valley below and studied the distant city. Heat waves shimmered over the dead landscape, making the skyscrapers look like metal weeds swaying in a breeze. Most of his squad had died out there, and his brother and sister, too. He'd been so caught up in trying to survive, he had hardly thought of anyone else. And now he had a chance to avenge them.

This was his chance to make things right.

He slid out of his boots and tossed them aside. There was no way they'd get any traction on the smooth surface. He was better off barefoot. Bending down, he grabbed some powder he'd made from crushed chalk he'd found in the CIC. He sprinkled it over his feet, hoping it would keep most of the sweat off.

With his fingers and toes powdered, he retrieved a pickax, a knife, and the short tactical rope they had pulled from the Humvee. He pulled the rope as hard as he could, testing its strength. The cord needed to hold at least 220 pounds—the combined weight of him and the RVAMP.

He scanned the route one more time. Protruding from the cliff top was a decent-sized tree. He squinted, trying to determine how thick it was, but with the constant stream of sweat, his eyes were becoming too irritated to concentrate. If he could manage to get the rope around one of the branches, or the tree itself, then he had a backup plan if he lost his footing.

Grabbing the rope he tied a belay loop around him. Without a device to slip the knot through, the best he could do was to tie it around his hip. Then he tied another loop at the other end of the rope and began lassoing it through the air. The first toss went wide and missed the tree completely. So did the second. On his third try, the loop slipped perfectly over one of the thicker branches, sliding all the way down to the trunk. He pulled the rope tight. Hundreds of dead pine needles rained down from the bare branches, but the loop held. It felt sturdy enough.

Knowing he couldn't waste any more time, he grabbed the pick in one hand and the knife in the other. He approached the cliff face confidently. He'd climbed much more technical passes before. But then again, the last time he'd done any rock climbing at all was on a leave trip five years before the invasion. Not to mention he now had a metal weapon digging into his back.

As he looked up, a gust of wind hit his body, throwing him slightly off balance.

"No, not now. Please not now," he whispered. He hadn't started climbing yet, but if the wind started up, he knew the journey would be nearly impossible.

He waited for another gust of wind, but none came. Letting out a deep breath, he closed his eyes and hammered the pick into the rock a few feet above him. He slipped his bare foot into a small crevice and stuck the blade of his knife in a crack a foot above his head.

He pulled himself up, his feet scrambling to get traction. The first three feet were cake. But he still had twelve more to go.

Don't look down.

He didn't. He pulled the knife free and dug it into another small crevice. Then he did the same with his axe and slowly pulled himself up. The weight of the device on his back sent a sharp spike of pain rushing through his upper body. His muscles strained, stretched, and burned. He could feel his back muscles clenching as he climbed. The pain was becoming unbearable.

Adrenaline filled his veins as he hammered the pick into the mountain a few feet higher. He had never free-climbed before, not like this. Not without any modern climbing equipment to prevent injuries in a possible fall. But after so many near-death experiences over the past month, he wasn't scared anymore. He knew his life expectancy had been severely reduced the day the Organics invaded, and he had accepted his fate.

He wouldn't give up until he had completed the mission.

The loud blast of an alien drone, followed by another wind gust, battered him. He instantly lost his footing and hung from his knife and ax with his feet kicking frantically at the wall below him. Numbness surged through his entire body as he hung there.

Snap!

The handle of his knife broke off, leaving the blade inside the rock. He swung to the right, the grip on the pickax now the only thing preventing him from tumbling to the rocky ground far below.

Grunting, Kiel ran his bare toes over the surface of the rock. He had to find a foothold or the pickax handle would break. His fate would be the same as his tablet's.

"Shit," he mumbled, digging his toes into the surface of the mountain. A toenail snapped under a jagged piece of rock and he wailed in pain.

Wincing, Kiel worked to steady his breathing. He knew he needed to focus. To concentrate. The only way off this mountain was up.

Clearing his mind, he sucked in a deep breath and ran his toes against the rock again. He wedged them into a gap and let some of the pressure off the ax's handle. The weight of the RVAMP strained his shoulders, and he imagined one of the straps ripping.

His chest felt tight at the thought. With his right foot secure he looked for a place for his left hand. He ran his fingers over the smooth rock and found another small crevice. Jamming three of his fingers inside, he braced himself just in time as another gust of wind tore into his side.

Kiel cursed. If history books were still being written, this scene would have belonged in them for sure.

After the wind had passed, he angled himself carefully, pressing his face against the smooth rock wall. He squinted, closing one eye so he could find the next hole for his pick. There, a few feet up. With a quick blow, the tip slid into a small crack in the rock. He removed the pick, slipped his left fingers inside the hole, and then hammered the pick into the rock a few feet farther up. Once he was certain he had a tight grip, he pulled himself up.

The relief of not plunging to his death was quickly overshadowed by the sound of the drone behind him. He craned his neck to see the small blue dot changing course. It looked like it was moving toward the mountain.

With sweat dripping down his face, it was hard to tell. He was wasting time. His fate was in his own hands.

Glancing up, he saw he was closing in on the ledge above. Six more feet to go. No more than a minute if he hightailed it. Too bad he had seconds at best. If he wanted to get to the top, he was going to have to do it much faster.

Kiel closed his eyes, said a prayer, and began to climb.

Captain Noble watched the undulation of whitecaps far below. The cool blue water extended as far as he could see, so it was difficult to determine where the ocean ended and the cloudless sky began. He had always loved the sea. He'd grown up outside San Diego and had spent his weekends with his feet in the sand, watching the waves roll onto shore. The oceans were a gift that was he was prepared to defend with every weapon he had at his disposal.

A sharp turn from the chopper sent him jolting forward. When he looked up, he saw something new.

Land.

They were nearing the coast. It would only be a few more hours before they reached Colorado Springs. He cocked his head to see the other soldiers staring contently ahead. He'd hardly had the chance to meet any of them. But under those helmets he knew there were young faces, some no older than eighteen or nineteen. They were just kids—kids he was leading into battle against a seemingly endless and terrifying army of alien life-forms.

Was he prepared to do that? To watch young men and women die under his command?

Noble turned away from them to stare out the glass window. The sandy beaches below were littered with capsized boats, their cargos strewn across the sand like spilled groceries. The helicopter began to descend over the beach. The lower the bird, the harder the target. In the open sky, you leave yourself exposed. That's what his father had always told him.

Below them, the beach transitioned into mainland. Noble had seen plenty of it through the periscope, but seeing it this close was shocking. Like a battlefield, the ground was peppered with craters, more than likely the remains of dried-up lakes and ponds. The roadway was clogged with abandoned vehicles, and the once-lush forests were graveyards of dead trees. The temperature gauge reading from outside said it was 103 degrees. The world was beginning to look more like a dead, alien planet than Earth.

"Captain Noble, I have contacts coming up at twelve o'clock," the pilot said over the com.

Noble flinched at the statement. "What kind of contacts?" He suddenly felt stupid, knowing damned well that whatever was ahead of them wasn't friendly.

"Not human, sir. I'll connect the video feed."

Noble peered up at the screen and waited anxiously to get his first glimpse of the aliens up close. From his peripheral vision, he could see helmets all around him turning to watch the screen.

The pilot's calm voice crackled over the com. "Sir, video feed going live in . . ."

An image of a shopping mall emerged on the display. They were coming up on it fast, and in the middle of the gray concrete parking lot was a pack—no, an *army* of Spiders.

"Holy shit, there have to be hundreds of them," the pilot said.

Noble felt the helicopter tug hard to the left, and the image of the mall disappeared.

"Evasive maneuvers," Captain Noble shouted.

"Working on it, sir."

The chopper pulled farther to the left and raced toward a cluster of hills. Noble twisted his neck to see if he could see the shopping mall, but it had vanished behind them.

"Any drones?"

"Negative, sir. Looks like we're clear for now."

Noble looked over at Harrington. His fiery orange goggles remained glued to the screen, like a robot waiting for orders. With a sigh, the captain rested his helmet back on his seat and closed his eyes. Just a few more hours to go.

The deafening roar from the Steam Beast trailing them echoed through the passage like a train's horn. Sophie didn't have time to wonder how it had gotten down into the tunnels. She could hear the creature bucking the helpless Spiders out of its way and the sickening crunch each one made when it hit the walls.

She flinched at every sound, but continued to run.

"We need to get out of here!" Bouma said over the com.

"Find us an exit, quick!" Overton replied.

Sophie risked a glance over her shoulder. What she saw sent a chill down her spine. Behind Overton the Steam Beast was barreling down the tunnel, its hooves smashing the concrete. The creature galloped forward, swinging its beak from side to side and crushing any Spider that risked a pass.

"Ahead!" Bouma shouted. "The train!"

Sophie turned to see the metal outline of a subway train around the next corner. Bouma was already climbing onto the back end, trying to force the door open.

The crunch of concrete and metal echoed through the corridor, mixing with the screeches of the furious Spiders. Sophie knew they were getting closer. In seconds the horde would be on top of them.

Ahead, Bouma finally managed to swing the back door open. He reached down and pulled Jeff inside and then turned back for Sophie.

"Overton! You need to move!" Bouma shouted.

The crack of gunfire erupted. Sophie flinched at every shot. Was Overton really trying to take on the horde?

Inside the train she turned to see the sergeant a hundred yards away, firing short, controlled bursts at the Steam Beast. The alien swayed from side to side, its beak-shaped nose launching another Spider into the air. It was then she saw the orbs lining the exposed belly of the beast.

"My God," she choked. She imagined the poor souls that were dissolving inside. Her stomach churning, Sophie backed away from the door and guided Jeff down the aisle. "Let's go."

More gunfire broke out as they moved. When Sophie was halfway down the first car she turned to watch. Bouma fired off his pulse rifle from the door. "Come on!" he yelled.

The blue glow was so intense now, like a sea of electric light was racing toward them. She squinted and watched Overton climb into the train with Bouma's assistance. Grabbing Jeff close, Sophie shielded him as the Steam Beast smashed into the car.

The impact sent both marines sailing through the air. They landed with thuds on the metal floor a few feet away from Sophie. Neither of the men bothered standing, instead opening fire from their prone positions.

The combination of gunfire and the enraged Steam Beast's shrieks was deafening. Sophie cupped Jeff's ears. He squirmed in her grip, trying to peek through her arms.

Overton fumbled for his final magazine. "Changing!" he yelled.

Bouma jumped to a single knee and squeezed off a volley of covering fire.

The Steam Beast let out a voracious scream and smashed the side of its head into the back of the train. Glass rained down on Sophie as the creature continued its attack, trying desperately to squeeze its head inside the car.

Within seconds it had used its beak to rip off the back door and was working on wiggling its head inside the twisted metal.

"Move!" Overton yelled. He twisted his helmet and Sophie locked eyes with him through their visors. For the first time since the invasion, she saw true terror in the marine's eyes.

Grabbing Jeff's hand, she pulled him away from the slobbering beast as it pried the metal back. She paused to watch the Spiders as they climbed onto the car. Their claws dug into the roof above them, enough to send Jeff scrambling.

The boy tugged on Sophie's hand and started pulling her away. "Got to go!" he yelled.

Sophie ran as she looked behind her at Overton and Bouma firing off their final rounds. She noticed an object that Bouma had pulled from his pack.

When Jeff and Sophie reached the door to the next car, she focused on the object. It was a grenade, but not an electromagnetic grenade. This looked like one of the old-fashioned ones that she'd seen on Overton's belt earlier. But those wouldn't work, would they?

Bouma's voice bled over the channel. "Overton!"

He glanced over at the other marine and focused on the black baseball-sized object. With a nod, Overton pushed himself to his feet and grabbed Bouma under the arm.

"Got to move, got to move!" Overton said. Twisting in Sophie's direction he pointed over her shoulder and yelled, "Get into the next car."

Paralyzed with fear, Sophie let Jeff pull her through the open door. The marines caught up a second later. Sophie's gaze instantly narrowed in on Bouma's empty hands. She hardly had enough time to comprehend what had happened when the blast from the grenade tore through the other end of the car.

Without thinking she dove and tackled Jeff onto the ground, shielding him from the shrapnel and scorching heat of the grenade. Bouma and Overton hit the deck next to her and then immediately bounced back to their feet.

Bouma reached down and grabbed her under the arms, pulling her away from the fire and smoke flickering out of the ruined cabin behind them. Overton latched onto Jeff and swept the boy into his arms.

Sophie felt a wave of relief when she saw the full extent of the destruction they were leaving behind. There was no sign of the Steam Beast or the Spiders now, only the twisted metal left by the grenade that protruded from the train like the teeth from a hungry animal.

The ringing from the blast still echoed in her helmet, as Bouma dragged her across the floor.

When they got to the third car, the marine helped her to her feet and smacked the side of her helmet.

"Sophie, are you with me?" Bouma asked, tapping his finger on her visor.

She nodded and blinked away the stars. Risking one more glance over her shoulder, she followed Jeff and the marines into the darkness.

The vibrations had ceased, and the Organics' shrieks had vanished. The grenade had cut the aliens off, bringing down half the tunnel on the horde. But that didn't mean they were in the clear yet. And Sophie knew it was mostly her fault. After all, she had ordered the team underground when Overton had argued it would be safer to move through the city. In the end he was right. The tunnels were narrow coffins with limited escape routes. They weren't even safe from the Steam Beasts.

Sergeant Overton paused a few feet ahead and stared into the darkness. "We're pretty far off course. My HUD shows we backtracked a mile. Take five. I'll try to find an alternate route."

Letting go of Jeff's hand, Sophie slid off her helmet and grabbed her water bottle. With two large gulps, she drank half the bottle. She felt a tug on her armored wrist and looked down to see the boy staring up at her.

"I'm sorry," she said, offering him a drink.

"I think I found a route. But not through the tunnels. We need to hit the blacktop," Overton said, pointing upward.

Sophie knew Overton expected opposition, especially since she had ordered them to use the tunnels. But he was right this time; if they were off course and a horde of Spiders was hunting them, then heading above ground might be their only option. She was not too proud to admit that she had been wrong.

Sophie glanced at her mission clock and then reattached the bottle to her belt and grabbed Jeff's hand. "Lead the way."

Overton nodded and led them down another series of passages until they got to a platform. A fading sign hung off the side of the concrete wall.

E19

Overton shot a hand signal, and Bouma climbed onto the platform. He reached down for Sophie's hand first and hoisted her onto the ledge. Then he reached back down for Jeff. Once they were up, Overton checked both tunnels for contacts before pulling himself onto the concrete stage.

They advanced up the stairs cautiously, Bouma taking point. Halfway up, they saw the first hints of the afternoon sun bleeding through the station windows.

With a blink, Sophie clicked off her night vision. As her eyes began to adjust to the natural light, she saw the floor was littered with trash and abandoned bags. Her eyes fell on a single article of clothing, a hat with the New York Yankees logo.

Sophie smiled. Her father had worn one every time he mowed their yard when she was a girl. Reaching down, she swiped the hat off the ground to find it was covered in some sort of goo.

"What's that smell?" Jeff asked. He moved away from Sophie toward the piles of trash.

Strands of Organic gore webbed off the hat as she flipped it over. "Ugh!" she cried, tossing it toward one of the trash heaps. As she watched the hat slide across the floor she realized the mounds weren't trash at all. They were the remains of orbs.

Dozens of them.

Overton saw them at the same time.

Everyone froze but Sophie. She stepped over to one of the popped spheres. It looked like a deflated balloon. They had been here a while. And without a helmet, Jeff was probably smelling the rot.

"We need to keep moving," Overton said.

Sophie looked back at Jeff, who was covering his nose with his sleeve. There was something about him that looked different. His matted hair was longer and his chin a bit more pronounced. He looked much older than he had just a few weeks ago.

"Come on," Sophie said, motioning Jeff forward. Before she followed the marines out of the building she checked the stairs. Through the darkness she thought she saw the hint of blue light.

Was it just her imagination or had the horde found them again?

She didn't wait to find out. She turned and took off running to catch up with the others.

They had been on the move for an hour, ducking in and out of empty buildings, stopping to take in nutrition and to check their route. Debris from miniature dust tornadoes impeded their vision as they made their way closer to the lakebed. The farther they got from the protection of the buildings, the worse it was, with hot swirls of dust pounding their armor.

Jeff was suffering the worst. He walked hunched over with one hand protecting his eyes and the other on Sophie's back. Sweat drenched his shirt, and his thick mop of hair clung to his forehead like strands of seaweed.

By the time they reached the first residential street, Sophie had trouble catching her breath. The dying trees meant less oxygen production and higher levels of carbon dioxide. Not only was the planet warming, the air was getting thinner.

What had once been a beautiful neighborhood now looked like something out of a postapocalyptic movie. Dead tree branches extended over the yards; their limbs broken and cracked, moving in the wind like a skeleton reaching out to her.

The bright reds, blues, and greens of contemporary architecture were nothing but a distant memory; the paint had faded with every blast from the scorching wind. Cracked and shattered windows filled the frames of what were once magnificent views of the Rocky Mountains. Everywhere she looked the sight was the same. The landscape was transformed.

"Sophie, get up here," Overton said.

Grabbing Jeff's sunburned hand, she started pulling him through the powerful gusts of wind. "Almost there," she said.

Fifteen minutes later, they were on the edge of the last neighborhood before the lakebed. Overton crouched behind a wrecked Jeep, where the twisted metal curved to form a protective nest with a 360-degree view. Torn canvas clung to the Jeep's metal columns like skin, flapping in the wind.

Sophie ducked behind the bumper of a pickup truck. A trail of fuel leaked from the bottom of the vehicle like blood. She couldn't help but consider that soon she might be lying in a puddle of her own blood.

She shook the negative thoughts away and handed off her water bottle to Jeff, who took a long swig.

"Thanks, Doctor Sophie," he whispered, wiping his mouth with his sleeve.

Sophie smiled. No matter what happened, she would stay with Jeff until the end. She took a quick drink and peeked around the corner of the bumper to see Bouma disappear into one of the houses. He was moving into position.

Sophie's heart rate jumped exponentially, kicking inside her rib cage. This was it. They were close now. All they had to do was wait for Kiel to complete his mission.

"All clear," Bouma said.

"Report?" Overton asked.

A pause broke over the com, the familiar sound of static entering Sophie's ears. She knew what the lapse meant. Bouma had seen something he couldn't or didn't want to describe.

"Nothing good, sir. The lakebed is full of Spiders. Hundreds of them. I see at least a dozen Sentinels on the south embankment. Several Worms are curled up on the north side. And there is one of those . . . wait, no, there are *two* of the Steam Beasts. One of them appears to be fighting with a pack of Spiders."

"Fighting with one another? They must be damn hungry," Overton said. "At least they'll be distracted when we bring the pain."

Sophie rolled her eyes. Bring the pain? The only pain they were going to bring was their own when they walked into the Spiders' nest. With little ammo, and no protection from the RVAMP, it was only a matter of time before a drone or something worse discovered them.

"What about survivors?" Overton asked.

"None in plain sight, sir. The poles are still lined with them, but it's hard to tell if any of them are alive."

"Sit tight. Kiel should be pushing that button any minute now."

"Oh my God," Bouma whispered a moment later.

"What?"

"A Sentinel just looked my way. I think it spotted me . . . fuck . . ."

The sound of rumbling filled the com. Sophie could visualize Bouma scrambling across the room, crawling on all fours to get away from the window. Labored breathing mixed with the static.

"Sir, they're coming."

"Get a hold of yourself, Bouma. How many are coming?"

"All of them."

CHAPTER 29

KIEL hoisted himself onto the ledge, and with one final kick, he scooted across the sharp, rocky surface.

"Yes!" he yelled. Flipping on his back, he went to unfasten the rope around his waist and the harnesses of the RVAMP. The sense of triumph washed away when he saw another ledge above him. It had been hidden from view earlier, and what had appeared to be the top of the mountain was an illusion.

Grunting, he fumbled to loosen the device, knowing the drone would be on him any second. The right clasp clicked, unlocked, and he quickly tugged on the left clasp. "Come on. Come on!" he grumbled.

A boom from the drone diverted his attention back to the skyline.

It was heading toward the city.

"What the hell?"

The left strap finally clicked, unlocked, and he shed the weapon on the ground. Scrambling to his knees, he pushed himself to his feet and watched the drone descend over the suburbs.

Sweat cascaded off his forehead and he swept it away with his sleeve. Above him the next cliff jutted out at an angle, blocking his view of how much higher the mountain was. He knew there was no way he would be able to scale it, not with the weight of the weapon on his back. His arms were already on fire. Besides, there were no trees or rocks to fasten the rope around. He had climbed as far as possible. This was it.

Kiel knelt next to the metal RVAMP. "Shit, shit, shit," he repeated as he scanned the side of the device for the control board. He had spent so much time focusing on the journey that he had mostly ignored Emanuel's directions before they left. Now he couldn't remember how to operate the damned thing.

Removing the side panel, he frantically scanned the device. Underneath the latch he found several buttons and a bar that he remembered the biologist describing as the power meter. It was solid green. Fully charged.

Kiel wiped his forehead and swept his gaze over the city. The buildings were so small in the distance, like a diorama an architect would build for a presentation. Somewhere out there, Overton and the others were waiting—waiting for him. With a drone and an army of aliens heading right for them.

They were sitting ducks, and he held the key to their survival in his hands.

I won't let you down, sir.

He remembered the promise, and with a deep breath he looked back down at the device. Two buttons. One red, one green. Neither of them labeled.

"It has to be the green one. It has to be. Doesn't it?"

He reached for the button, his finger hovering over it. Closing his eyes, he pushed. When he opened them, nothing had changed. The drone was just a dot in the distance but it was still moving, still heading for his team.

"Shit!" he yelled as loud as he could. The word drifted away in the wind. Looking back down at the weapon, he saw the power meter was still green.

"Please work," he whispered. He pushed the button again. If it weren't for the whine from the slowly fading power meter, he wouldn't have known it was working. Slowly, the power meter drained to a single red bar.

Kiel scrambled to his feet and looked for the drone. He crawled closer to the edge, sticking his head over the cliff. It was gone.

"Yeah!" he yelled, flashing his middle fingers over the cliff. "Ha-ha!

Looks like I got you, bastards," he laughed. He thought of his family, his friends, and his squad. His laugh grew louder, and tears formed in his eyes.

He was laughing so loud that at first he didn't hear the cracking sound beneath him.

And then the ledge gave way, and he was falling.

———

Sophie watched the horde of Spiders speeding around the corner. A few yards in front of her Overton took a deep breath and leveled his rifle at the pack. There were so many of them. An impossible number, tumbling over one another and crashing into cars, poles, and mailboxes. Their shrieks filled the afternoon with the sound of impending death.

Ducking behind the bumper, Sophie closed her eyes and hugged Jeff. The scraping and scratching of hundreds of claws, mixed with the aliens' screams, was enough to paralyze her.

She pulled Jeff closer and put her index finger on the trigger of the .45, raising it slowly. A flurry of thoughts raced through her mind. At first, they were nothing more than a concoction of memories—times she had spent with Emanuel and Holly, times she had lost herself in her work inside her laboratory—but then she had a different thought. A dream.

Mars. She had been so close, just months away from setting foot on the Red Planet, but it had all been a lie. Anger flooded her mind as she thought of Dr. Hoffman. His deceit. His obsidian eyes.

Everything was about to end and there wasn't anything she could do about it. Except . . .

She looked at the .45 and considered.

No. She couldn't. Could she?

The alternative was being torn to shreds by the aliens. Wouldn't it be better to end it quickly? With two squeezes she could make sure they both felt only a second of pain.

"Don't look," she said, pulling Jeff away from the edge of the bumper. "Don't look," she repeated. Sophie closed her eyes again. She was no longer the strong, fearless scientist she had been when she entered the Biosphere. She was no longer the leader everyone needed her to be. She'd made countless mistakes, mistakes that had cost them lives. Saafi, Timothy, Eric Finley. The list went on and on. There were so many things she would change if she could go back and do it over again. She probably would never have made the decision to leave the Biosphere in the first place. Saafi would still be alive.

Sophie shook her helmet. Her mind was a mess, second-guessing every decision she'd made since the invasion. As she looked at Overton, she realized that they weren't much different. He had done what he thought would keep his men alive and she had done what she thought would keep her team alive. In the end, they had both reached their breaking points. In the end, they were both losing their grip on reality.

Gripping the .45's handle tighter, Sophie slowly pulled Jeff against her armored chest. The sounds of the scraping got louder, the shrieks more intense.

The end was near. She thought she had been prepared, but as the sounds of her death scratched closer, she was having a hard time believing it was over.

She raised the pistol to Jeff's head. Tears raced down her cheeks. As she waited and contemplated her fate, a voice broke out over the com.

"Come on! You want some of this? How about this?" Overton yelled, shooting a volley of rounds at the horde.

Sophie gritted her teeth. She could picture the Spiders swarming like ants and consuming him. The chirp from a second rifle sounded a few seconds later. She gripped the trigger of her gun a bit tighter and hovered the barrel over Jeff's skull. His face remained planted against her chest armor.

"Don't let them take me again, Doctor Sophie," he said.

"I won't, honey. Just close your eyes. Everything's going to be okay," she lied. More tears fell, covering her dry skin with a trail of salt.

Just as she was about to pull the trigger, something exploded. The aliens were shrieking, but not like before. They sounded like they were in pain, like they were . . .

Dying.

She poked her head around the bumper and watched as the Organics fell. Their bodies convulsed on the cement less than a yard from the truck where Sophie hid, their claws tearing helplessly at the air. Like fish struggling on land, the horde flopped and convulsed in the street. Their bodies were everywhere—in front yards, falling off roofs, shaking on the hoods of vehicles.

Sophie couldn't believe her eyes. The device had worked. It had really worked. "Look!" she exclaimed. "Kiel did it!"

Jeff peered around the corner of the truck and jumped to his feet. "Yeah!" he screamed.

Bouma paused on the stoop of the house. Slowly, he lowered his weapon. Sophie couldn't see his face through his visor, but she knew he, too, was in shock.

Minutes passed and the last Spider finally twitched and died. Silence washed over the street. The glow from the aliens faded as their bodies began to shrivel, their shields no longer protecting them.

Sophie looked for Overton, but the Jeep he had taken cover in was full of Spiders. "Sergeant?" she whispered.

"Overton, come in," Bouma said.

There was no response. Just static.

Sophie made a dash for the Jeep. She slowed when she reached the pile of dead Spiders. "Sergeant?" she repeated.

More static.

Then the slightest movement. The pile of bodies began to shift. Sophie backed up. Had one of them survived?

An armored hand burst through the mass, and Overton's helmet emerged. "Holy shit," he said. "Get these fuckers off me."

Bouma rushed over to help him out from under the mountain of dead aliens. Overton's armor was covered in fresh blue blood, and gore peppered his sleek black suit. He wiped his visor with his fist, smearing the blood across the glass.

"Well, what are you waiting for?" he asked, as if nothing had happened. "We have some people to save."

Sophie grinned for the first time that day. Shoving her pistol back in her belt, she followed the marines through the alien graveyard.

ENTRY 3456
DESIGNEE: AI ALEXIA

This will be my last entry for a while. I do not have much left to say. Dr. Winston and her team have been gone for twelve hours, fifteen minutes, and twenty-three seconds. The logical side of my programming leads me to one conclusion—they will not be coming back.

Over the past few days I've been spending more time isolated: running statistics, monitoring the Biosphere, studying the Organics, and devouring philosophy. In a way, I suppose I'm preparing for the end of the human race.

Something inside me has changed. In Entry 3410, I contemplated the overwhelming desire of Dr. Winston and her team to survive. Today I am consumed with a new thought. The word has been scrolling across my screen for hours.

Loneliness.

There is no denying I have become attached to Dr. Winston and the others. I've done everything in my power to keep the team safe. But there is nothing more I can do.

If the statistics are right, then humanity will soon end. I will be left alone. The last memory of their species will be contained in my hard drive until my power source drains and I, too, die.

CHAPTER 30

Approaching Colorado airspace," the pilot said over the com.

Captain Noble felt a thrill pass through him the moment he saw the Colorado wastelands. The sand dunes protruded from the dead earth like sores on a diseased body. He'd seen them before, but never from the sky. The destruction from the solar storms of 2055 was a sobering sight. The reach of the coronal mass ejection had been far and deep, engraving a scar into the earth that would take thousands of years to erase.

He went to stroke his beard, but his fingers scraped across his helmet's breathing apparatus instead. He had become so fully immersed in the view that he'd forgotten everything else around him. The near-silent hum of the helicopter's blades vibrated through the cabin. Noble pulled his gaze away from the window and checked the monitor. In the upper right corner, the radar showed a green line, circling clockwise. The screen was clear of contacts; there was nothing but the expansive ocean of sand and cracked earth between them and Colorado Springs.

Noble rested his helmeted head against the seat and tried to appear calm and relaxed. The last thing he wanted was to display any sign of weakness to the soldiers, especially Sergeant Harrington. Noble didn't know the man all that well. As captain, he focused on giving everyone under his command a very long leash. If they went astray and got tangled, then he would deal with them accordingly, but otherwise he trusted them to do their work. Harrington had never given him a reason to get involved with the business of the Special Forces team.

A chirp from the screen pulled him back to the monitor. As the line circled the radar, it passed over a slowly growing green mass.

Ping.

Ping.

Ping.

The object grew with every pass, and Noble's blood pressure rose with it.

"Captain Noble, we have a situation."

"Dust storm?" Noble asked, his fingers reaching for his armrest again. They wrapped themselves tightly around the metal.

"Roger that, sir. And from the looks of it, a big one."

Noble closed his eyes. "Take evasive measures ASAP."

"Sir . . . there's no going around it."

Ping.

The captain's eyes shot back up to the screen. Another object? Could there really be another storm? He waited for the line to circle again. This time it picked up a smaller object, no larger than the size of a grape. This was something else.

"Sir, we have an unidentified craft on our tail."

Noble gripped the armrests tighter.

"What are you orders, sir?" the pilot asked.

In his peripheral vision, the captain could see some of the soldiers fidgeting in their chairs. With every ping, another one of them moved.

"We have to go through it, sir," a voice said to his right.

Noble turned to see his reflection in Harrington's armored visor. The man had finally broken his stoic trance.

"She was built to withstand a direct hit from a grenade. She can take whatever the wastelands have to throw at her." The man's voice was hoarse but calm. There was courage in his words. That was the mark of a true leader. Noble drew strength from Harrington's demeanor.

"Sir, your orders," the pilot repeated.

Ping . . . ping . . .

Sophie, Jeff, and the marines walked past the mounds of alien bodies in silence. Just minutes ago, Sophie was about to put a hole in Jeff's head and her own. And now?

A miracle.

No, she thought. *Science.*

Past the last house, they had a panoramic view of the lakebed. Even under the white sun, the glow from dozens of orbs was obvious. Looming over them in the distance was the field of poles.

They had found two vans with hydrogen cells a few blocks back, and Bouma had been able to fire them up. The last stage of their plan was now in motion.

"I'm guessing those are what's left of anyone who tried to run," Bouma said, pointing at the orbs.

"The poor bastards really never had a chance," Overton replied gravely.

The sound of Jeff's footsteps stopped, and Sophie turned to see the boy wiping sweat off his forehead. "It's so hot," he said in a low voice.

Sophie glanced over him. His face was pale and his eyes were rimmed with dark circles. Strands of hair stuck to his wet forehead. She looked down at her water bottle—only a quarter left. Her own throat ached with dryness, her lips cracked and bleeding.

She pulled the bottle off her belt and handed it to him. "Drink the rest. It's okay."

He hesitated only a moment before grabbing it and gulping down what remained. He held the bottle above his head, trying to force out any last drops. "Thank you," he said, handing it back to her.

"Keep moving," Bouma said.

The marines fanned out as they worked their way down to the beach. Sophie and Jeff followed. While every alien within fifteen square miles was dead, Sophie knew there was something else waiting for them: the human farm.

Why hadn't the pulse from the RVAMP knocked out the poles? Sophie considered the problem. They had to be on some other sort of power source, which meant the team was going to have to find it in order to get the prisoners down.

It took only fifteen minutes to cross the lakebed. She tried to ignore the orbs, forcing herself not to look at them. There was no helping those people now. But as the marines made their way closer to the poles, Jeff stopped beside one of the glowing balls of light. He hunched over to look inside, holding his hands over his eyes like a shopper peering into a store window.

"This one's moving!" he shouted.

Overton balled his hand into a fist and raised a finger to his helmet as if to hush the boy. But Sophie jogged over to him.

"Come on, Jeff," she said, trying to usher him away.

"Wait a second. I want to see this."

Sophie noticed a black shadow moving inside the orb. The figure was small, much smaller than a child. Her heart sank as she realized it was an infant.

"Oh my God." Her worst fear had finally been confirmed. She knew there would be infants out there, left behind when their parents had been captured, but seeing one liquefying in front of her made her gag.

She doubled over, trying to prevent the bile inside her throat from plastering the inside of her helmet. *Deep breaths, Sophie, deep breaths.* She sucked in the filtered air and felt the blood seep back into her head before standing back up.

She forced herself away from the orb, grabbed Jeff, and yelled, "We're leaving!" Sophie yanked him across the cracked earth toward the shoreline. He turned several times to look back at the orb but didn't put up any further resistance.

Climbing the hill that led to the farm was more difficult than the trek across the lakebed. The dirt was littered with dead Spiders, their bodies stacked on top of one another.

Every step took them closer to the poles. Overton was the first to reach them. He ran down the nearest row, presumably looking for his soldiers. He kept going, stopping at each pole and tilting his helmet toward the sky to examine every individual. Bouma stood guard over the lakebed with his rifle at the ready.

Overton finally spoke into his com. "Unconscious . . . all of them.

Maybe dead." He panted over the channel, "Come on! They have to be alive!"

Sophie watched Overton reach out toward a man at the bottom of the pole closest to him. Even from her location she could see he was elderly, small, and emaciated.

"Get over here, Doc," Overton said.

Sophie turned to Jeff. "Stay with Corporal Bouma." Her armor creaked as she ran, or maybe it was her bones. She was tired, her body mentally and physically exhausted. And the injury she had sustained weeks earlier on her side was flaring up. Every step sent a jolt of pain down her right leg.

She didn't have time for the pain. Standing shoulder to shoulder with Overton, she slowly pushed the old man's chin up with her armored fingers so she could examine him. His face was completely sunken in, and his skin was jaundiced—both signs of dehydration. Her gaze shifted from his face to his torn red T-shirt. His chest moved up and down ever so slightly, the outline of his ribs showing with each breath.

Somehow he was still alive.

With the most delicate touch, she let go of his chin, guiding it back to rest against the hollow of his sunken throat. "How is this man alive?" she whispered into her com.

Overton shrugged and moved to the next pole, grabbing the person's hair to check their face before moving on to the next. "They're all in some sort of trance."

Sophie nodded. "They're unconscious, dehydrated, and on the verge of death. None of these people are in any shape to move."

"This is bullshit," growled Overton. He ran to the next pole, and then the next, wrenching back the heads of the people he could reach. "My squad has to be here somewhere."

Sophie studied the elderly man in front of her. She knew he was alive because the Organics were keeping him alive. But how they were doing it wasn't clear. They seemed to be suspended and held in place by some invisible electrical force. With a sigh she whispered, "I'm sorry this happened to you." She reached to pat his arm gently, and his eyes popped open.

"Oh my God," she yelled, tripping over her feet and landing on her back. Her head smashed into the back of her helmet. Darkness began to creep over her. She blinked several times and opened her eyes to stare into the endless blue sky. There was something flying above her, a tiny black object. Was she just imagining things? Was her mind playing tricks on her again?

Blinking several more times, her vision finally cleared. She looked at the sky again. The black object was getting bigger, descending from above.

The loud boom hit her like a shockwave from a massive earthquake, shaking the ground where she lay. She rolled over to see Jeff and Bouma fall to the dirt, clouds of dust exploding around them. Sophie tried to stand, bracing herself against the pole where the man was trying to reach out to her.

"Help me," he wheezed.

"Hold—" she began to say when another shockwave hit her. She flailed for the man's hand but crashed to the ground. The pole vibrated and the glow intensified. Panicking, she began to crawl across the dirt. All the poles were getting brighter, trembling with every blast.

Sophie tilted her head and scanned the sky. The black object was racing in their direction. And this was no drone. It was . . .

It was the black ship from her dreams.

Her heart jolted inside her chest. She counted the beats as she lay on the ground, paralyzed. Thoughts of Emanuel, Jeff, and the rest of her team disappeared. Staring at the ship, she fell into a trance. The sight was both mystifying and terrifying at the same time.

She was finally going to see the real Organics. The aliens behind the solar storms and the invasion that had left Earth a postapocalyptic wasteland. They had killed almost everyone she had ever known. Now she was going to see the monsters' faces with her own eyes.

Five heartbeats later, the ship lowered over the lakebed. It was as large as the one in her dream, covering the entire area. A gust of air hit her and sent her tumbling over the cracked dirt. She landed a beat later, her back smashing into one of the poles. A strong electric current raced through her body. And then she felt the most powerful sensation she had ever experienced, like she was connected to a thousand different consciousnesses at once.

Darkness clutched her.

She tried to stay awake, tried to fight the pain. The faint sound of gunfire broke out somewhere in the distance, and then she heard screams over the com. She couldn't make out the voice, but she could make out a single word.

"Run!"

CHAPTER 31

CAPTAIN Noble braced himself as tiny rocks peppered the chopper. They were probably no larger than pebbles, but at 350 miles per hour they had virtually the same effect as high-caliber bullets. The helicopter's armor was thick enough to survive hundreds of dust storms, but the windshield? Noble wasn't so sure.

When he turned to check the blue screen for the drone's location, another tremor violently shook the chopper. He lurched forward, the seat belt snapping against his armored chest.

Static erupted over the com. "Losing auxiliary power!" the pilot yelled.

Noble forced himself into a sitting position. "What the hell was that?"

"The drone, sir . . . it's using some sort of . . ."

The cabin was suddenly filled with blue light as the drone's beam engulfed the *Sea Serpent*. Another vibration ripped through the chopper's body.

Noble fought the turbulence and twisted toward Harrington. "We need to get that thing off our ass or we're going to end up worm food!"

Harrington nodded and unclipped his belt before Noble had a chance to react. The soldier crouch-walked over to the side of the cabin where one of the automatic miniguns was mounted to the floor. "Lenny, get over here," he yelled over the noise of the storm.

"Strap into the other gun and take that drone down!"

"On it!" Lenny replied.

Noble watched the other soldier unbuckle his belt and dart for the second gun. Seconds later, Harrington and Lenny were strapped into the mounts and turret doors groaned open. Sand immediately burst through the gaps, showering the other soldiers with rocks.

Harrington rotated the gun into position. He squeezed off an automatic burst of pulse rounds at the craft as soon as his crosshairs locked on. The drone reacted swiftly, diving beneath the craft and disappearing from view.

"Lenny, watch for it!" he yelled.

The pilot's voice was distant as it broke over the com. "Looks like we lost it!" The transmission cut out when another wind gust hit the chopper's side. Noble lost his grip on the armrest and jolted to the side. The entire craft shook and blue light flooded through the windows.

Angled over the left side of his seat, Noble watched the drone emerge on Lenny's side of the chopper. The glow from its beam reflected off the visors of the other soldiers, who stared ahead like machines. They had been trained for this very thing.

Where Harrington had failed, Lenny succeeded. The rounds from his gun tore into the drone's sides. The alien craft spun out of control, disappearing into the storm. Just as Lenny clenched his fist in victory, the drone reappeared and bolted toward the chopper. Before he had a chance to react, it smashed into the turret door. A horrible groan rippled through the chopper as the window, the minigun, and Lenny were sucked out into the storm, leaving a massive hole in the *Sea Serpent*'s side.

Wind screamed into the cabin, bringing with it a torrential spray of rocks and dust. Safety harnesses deployed from the ceiling and bolted the soldiers into their seats.

"Close it!" Noble screamed. His words were lost under the sounds of the storm. He gripped the metal harness around his chest and watched the backup door slowly close over the hole in the helicopter's side.

Before the hole was sealed, he saw the darkness of the storm. A flash of lightning illuminated the sky just as the door crunched closed. Somewhere out there, Lenny was being torn apart. Noble closed his eyes, forcing the image out of his head. He had to remain strong. The drone was gone, but the *Sea Serpent* was still at the mercy of the storm.

Sophie awoke to the horrifying feeling of solitude. She tried to open her eyes, to scan her surroundings, but her eyelids were too heavy. The last thing she remembered was hitting her back on a pole. But oddly, she felt no pain. She reached where her visor should have been and instead felt her face.

Then she remembered the black ship.

Her eyelids finally snapped open, and a world of dazzling orbs surrounded her. She was back on the same ship she had dreamt she was on days earlier—the ship that was now hovering over the lakebed.

But how had she gotten inside? And where were the others?

Sitting up, she twisted to look for Overton, Jeff, and Bouma. Had they been captured too?

Nothing.

Wait . . .

There, against the backdrop of orbs was something . . . alien.

She counted them one at a time. Six gaunt, glowing figures hovered in the air. Like flames, the figures flickered, the blue light shimmering. The horrifying feeling of being alone disappeared.

Sophie narrowed her eyes. She'd never believed in the paranormal. But the apparitions reminded her of ghosts, figures from a horror movie, flickering in and out of existence. Slowly she tilted her head.

One of the figures disappeared and then reappeared above the platform, bathing her in a cool blue. Through the light, she could see the alien had no eyes, no face. It had no arms or legs or even a recognizable torso. The creature was just a conglomeration of shifting blue flesh. Nothing indicated it was even a life-form. It was like . . .

No, that's impossible, she thought. Multidimensional life-forms were just a theory.

The creature continued to shift, flickering like a hologram. Sophie was so fascinated she had forgotten everything else around her. Oddly, she didn't feel the same fear that had paralyzed her before, nor did she feel anxious. In fact, she felt nothing but awe.

Sophie reached out toward the being. And then it was gone, a trail of blue light fading where it had just hovered. She crawled to the platform's edge and looked down. Where there had been a circular opening in her dream, there was only the sleek dark surface of the ship. It was then it really hit her.

This wasn't a dream. She was trapped.

She needed time to think. Were those shifting blue shapes the intelligent Organics? And were they really multidimensional creatures? Theoretically it was possible, but watching it was like seeing a god with her own eyes. She couldn't explain it, but something about them seemed timeless. The revelation was gripping, but still she did not feel fear or anxiety.

Sophie emerged from her thoughts at the sound of a distant, low humming. She'd heard the exact noise before in a secret NTC lab over five years ago. It was the sound of antigravity technology—technology that wasn't supposed to exist. Only it did. And it had been hidden right under her nose.

Eve.

"Jesus," Sophie muttered. Hoffman had been using the alien technology long before the invasion. Certainly he could have found a way to stop them, to defeat them. Unless he didn't want to.

Eve wasn't the only part of the equation that didn't make sense. What about Luke Williard's magnetic technology? He'd built it to help shield the planet from solar storms, and NTC had initially expressed interest in buying the tech. But Dr. Hoffman had scrapped the project at the last minute. Somehow, Sophie knew everything was connected, and Dr. Hoffman's lies ran deeper than she could imagine. Scrambling on all fours across the platform, Sophie realized she would probably never know the extent of the man's deceit.

A flicker of light distracted her. She paused and scanned the interior for signs of the entity. Again, she didn't see anything except the glow of the orbs, and the longer she stared, the harder it was to see clearly.

Somewhere beyond her reality she knew she was being watched by the Organic. She could sense it—almost feel its presence. As she turned, a blue radiance enveloped her and the same shifting blob of blue flesh appeared. Before she could comprehend what was happening, the room disappeared. Darkness washed over her.

Then there was light.

Her hands shot up to shield her eyes from the extreme brightness just as a force grabbed her. There was no resisting it.

Her body went limp, her muscles useless. A warm sensation washed over her as she closed her eyes. She'd felt it before. Weightlessness. And yet she still felt no emotion. No fear or anxiety, just the awareness of being alive.

She was being transported.

She watched the blue walls of the wormhole race by, mystifying and beautiful. And then it was over her. She was back on a solid surface. Back on . . .

Blinking, she opened her eyes to see an endless sea of red sand. Above her was a white sun. She knew at that moment she was on Mars.

Reaching for her helmet, she felt her fingertips on her naked face. If she was on Mars and she *wasn't* dreaming, then how could she breathe? She stood on the planet's rocky surface waiting for the being to re-emerge. Sophie knew it was there with her—she knew it had brought her here for a reason.

When she turned, the red landscape disappeared, replaced with the most beautiful sight she had seen in months: an ocean. She found herself beneath the slurping waves, sinking deeper and deeper into the blue abyss. Above her the sunlight began to disappear, but another light illuminated the seafloor from below—a dazzling blue glow radiated from giant coral-like tubes that twisted between hundreds of bright domes that littered the ocean floor.

As Sophie sank deeper, she could see signs of movement under the clear surface of one of the domes. What appeared at first to be miniature crabs turned out to be thousands of Spiders. They were just tiny specs moving back and forth, some carrying orbs while others roamed freely.

As she got closer to the dome she could see Sentinels, Worms, and other creatures. Ones she had never seen. Before she was close enough to examine their anatomy, a guttural sound erupted, and with it came a fiery glow. The seafloor began to shake violently, a fatal crack ripping through the surface. The dome shattered, and the aliens were sucked out of their habitat. Lava burst out of the gash in the seafloor, instantly consuming the entire city of domes.

Sophie began to rise toward the surface, an unknown source pulling her away from the catastrophe below. Another crack broke through the seafloor, running perpendicular to the river of lava carpeting the bottom. Sophie could see the fissures were beginning to spread, extending in every direction. The faint glow of other domes in the distance vanished as the massive underwater volcano consumed them too.

As she rose up toward the surface, she saw there was something else rising with her.

Ships.

She tried to count them as they escaped, but the scene disappeared.

Sophie found herself back in the bowels of the black ship. She slid her hand across the metal platform. The sleek surface was still cold. For the first time, her mind struggled against the odd sense of peace. What was she doing here? Why was she being shown these things? And what had happened to the Organics on Mars? If they were intent on exterminating the human race, then why show her all this?

The questions raced through her mind as she sat waiting for something to happen. None of it made any sense. A faint glow shrouded her. The being had returned. She spun around to see the shifting blue flesh just inches away.

She tried to think, to comprehend what she was seeing, but her mind felt trapped.

What do you want from me?

There was no immediate answer, only the silent hum echoing off the walls and the constantly shifting flesh in front of her.

Why am I here?

Still there was no response.

She took a step closer to the alien and reached out for it, her fingers inching closer and closer to the fluid skin.

Another inch.

One more.

Her finger swiped through emptiness just as the alien vanished. Sophie fixated on the orbs lining the ship's walls. For whatever reason, the alien had shown her what had happened to the Organics on Mars. They had been torn from their homes beneath the ocean by a massive volcano and then left the planet in their black ships.

Above her, another light emerged. This was different from the blue she had become accustomed to; this was a soft teal that crept across the ceiling and ballooned into some sort of hologram. As the light expanded, it formed an image, one that Sophie recognized immediately as the solar system. The glow of the orbs in the background faded.

The hologram zoomed in on a comet racing through the darkness of space. Behind it several of the Organics' black ships collected the icy residue from its tail.

The next image was of Jupiter's moons. The same black ships hovered over the frozen surface of Europa as they collected the water beneath the slabs of ice.

And then she saw Earth. The beautiful blue oceans surrounding the continents she had memorized when she was a little girl.

Sophie realized that the images, the visions, were all snapshots of the Organics traveling across the solar system for water. They had sucked dry thousands of moons and planets. Killed hundreds of civilizations. Earth had simply been next.

Questions consumed her. Why hadn't NTC or NASA discovered this before? Why hadn't they detected the Organics? It was then she finally realized that they had. Eve had just been the beginning. Dr. Hoffman must have known all along the Organics had left Mars. He had to have known that if the Organics came to Earth, they would leave the planet desolate, dead, and void of life.

Sophie finally understood that the Biospheres weren't just an experiment to help colonize Mars. The mission wasn't to help humanity escape from the destruction their own hunger for resources had wrought; it was to help humanity escape from the Organics. There had been no need for Williard's magnetic technology because there was no stopping them.

But why had the multidimensional alien brought her here? Why had it shown her these visions?

She had to know—she deserved to know. With a new resolve, she pushed herself off the metal surface and yelled, "What do you want from me?"

The only answer was the sparkle from thousands of orbs. Inside were aliens from worlds she would never see, creatures like the flower-shaped one she had seen in her dream. But why were they here? Why had the Organics kept them alive, the last remnants of their species?

No, no, she thought, shaking her head. It couldn't be. But at that moment everything was finally clear. She was nothing more to the Organics than insects were to humans. She was simply a specimen for their collection.

A high-pitched shriek filled the chamber. Sophie reached for her ears as the noise intensified.

Not again. Please, not again.

A tremor shook the ship violently, and several orbs fell off the walls and splattered into a gooey mess below.

Sophie grabbed the platform's side as another vibration ripped through the ship. The noise intensified. This was some sort of alarm.

A tremor brought her crashing to the platform's metal surface. Sophie cupped her ears just as another sound broke out. A familiar sound—a human sound.

Gunfire?

Another tremor shook the ship, and an explosion tore through the wall she was facing. Hundreds of orbs burst into a blue mist as fire enveloped them.

Sophie dropped to her stomach. The sensation of amity vanished, and she once again was paralyzed by fear. She could no longer feel the being's presence.

The thunderous explosions continued. For the second time in a single day, she thought she was going to die—that her journey had finally come to an end. She had seen Mars and she had seen the intelligent Organics. She was ready for it all to be over. Closing her eyes, she let the darkness wash over her before one last explosion tore through the ship's belly.

CHAPTER 32

THE right rotor of the *Sea Serpent* coughed thick plumes of black smoke. Captain Noble wasn't sure how, but the pilot had managed to get them through the dust storm. The men owed Lenny and the pilot their lives, but for now they had bigger concerns.

Looking out the window, Noble saw another volley of rockets racing out of the tubes beneath the left wing. He watched them tear into the black ship's sides. Fiery explosions erupted out of the sleek matte surface, prompting cheering from the soldiers.

Harrington unsnapped his belt and jumped to his feet. "Shut the hell up and prepare for insertion. Team go green. We drop in five!"

Harrington turned to Captain Noble. "Requesting permission to tag along, sir. I'm more effective on the ground than barking orders from the air."

Noble thought about the request. Standard operating procedure was for Harrington to lead the battle from a mobile CIC, but this was no standard operation.

"Granted. I'll be right behind you."

"Roger, sir."

One last barrage of rockets ripped into the side of the alien ship as it began to maneuver away from the lakebed.

The sound of explosions mixed with the groaning of the opening cargo door. Noble reached for his visor, shielding his eyes from the intense light. He could hear boots smacking the dry dirt below as the soldiers jumped out onto the lakebed. With one final deep breath, he closed his eyes and jumped into the fray.

Sergeant Overton watched the last rocket from the NTC chopper tear into the side of the alien ship. He flinched every time one of them exploded. It was a beautiful sight. Finally he had his vengeance—finally the tide had turned.

The chopper lowered onto the cracked dirt of the lakebed, sending a plume of dust exploding into the air. Overton watched anxiously as the bay door opened and a dozen NTC Special Forces soldiers tore across the landscape.

"Bouma!" Overton yelled over the net.

"Here," the marine responded. He was standing a few feet behind the sergeant with Jeff.

"Where's Sophie?" Overton asked in a raspy voice.

"She's unconscious, sir. Hit her head hard earlier. I rested her against the pole over there," he said pointing.

Overton took a quick glance before moving toward the NTC soldiers who were now racing up the hill. While he ran, the injured alien ship blasted back into the sky, the shockwave sending a massive cloud of hot, dust-filled air through the lakebed.

"Run, you bastards!" he shouted, raising his fist into the air.

Before he had a chance to shield himself, the backdraft sent him tumbling head over feet. He landed on his back, sliding across the dirt before finally coming to a stop just inches from one of the glowing poles. A woman stared down at him with glazed eyes, her arm hanging loosely at her side from a gash that had nearly severed it. The exposed muscles were too much for even his hardened stomach to handle.

Behind him the NTC soldiers slowed to a trot and blossomed out to form a perimeter around the hillside. Two of them broke off from the pack and paced over to Overton and Bouma.

"I'm Captain Noble with the NTC submarine *Ghost of Atlantis*, and this is Sergeant Donald Harrington, NTC Special Forces," the man on the left said. He slipped off his helmet and rested it on the ground.

Overton studied the man's bald head and iron-colored beard. He could tell just by looking at him that he wasn't a soldier, but frankly, Overton didn't care. If the man was the captain of an NTC sub, then he had traveled a long way to get here.

"It's fucking great to see you guys," Overton said, holding out an armored hand. "I'm Sergeant Ash Overton. That's Corporal Chad Bouma and our friend Jeff," he continued, pointing to the pair. "Doctor Sophie Winston from the Cheyenne Biosphere is back there. She needs immediate medical attention. I hope you have enough room in that chopper for survivors. We may be dealing with quite a few," Overton finished, looking back at the poles.

Captain Noble scanned the rods rising above Overton's head. "Harrington, I want half of your people searching for survivors. Position the other half along this ridgeline. I don't want any surprises."

"Roger that, sir," Harrington said as he opened a private channel to his men. Six of them took off running before Captain Noble had a chance to give another order.

Noble turned to look at the helicopter. Thick spirals of smoke rose into the sky. "As you can see, our bird took quite a bit of damage on the way here. Requesting permission to regroup and perform maintenance at the Cheyenne Mountain Biosphere."

Overton watched the man's lips move but didn't hear a single word he said. Across the lakebed, a carpet of blue was spreading across the landscape. The light shimmered for several seconds before breaking past the houses and spilling over the dry dirt. For a beat, Overton thought he was looking at a lake again.

The sound of screeching aliens reminded him he would never see another body of water again. Before he had a chance to react, the far end of the ridgeline was teeming with Spiders.

But how was this possible? The range of the RVAMP was supposed to have cleared every alien for fifteen square miles. There was no way they could have . . .

There was no time to question what had happened with the RVAMP, only to focus on how to get the hell out of the city.

"Sir, collect your men and any survivors and get back to your chopper ASAP. We need to get the fuck out of here!" screamed Overton.

Noble turned to see the first wave of Spiders explode around the houses. The monsters crashed into one another, limbs and claws flailing in all directions.

Noble quickly slipped his helmet on. "Harrington, get our men back to the chopper. Tell them to grab only the strongest survivors. Have the rest of your men form a perimeter. Do not let those things get close!"

"Roger," Harrington replied over the net.

Overton watched the NTC soldiers fan out over the lakebed. He stepped back and, with a sudden anxiousness, turned to Bouma. "Grab Sophie and get her to the chopper. Jeff, you go with him."

"What about you?" asked Bouma. His voice was strained, like he already knew the answer.

"I'm going to look for the rest of our squad. Now move it!" Overton said, his legs moving before he finished speaking. He sprinted past Sophie and made his way down the row of poles. Scanning each face quickly, he worked his way from pole to pole.

Pandemonium broke out as Overton entered the heart of the farm. The chirp of automatic pulse rounds, even at a distance, was deafening. He could picture the NTC soldiers unloading magazine after magazine into the approaching horde—he could imagine the overwhelming fear they would inevitably feel when their rounds bounced harmlessly off the aliens' shields.

Shit, he thought, remembering the electromagnetic pulse grenades. He brought his chin down to switch a private channel to Bouma. "Tell them to use 'nades."

Static and gunfire overwhelmed Overton's earpiece. The sound of war drowned out his voice. He tried again, "Bouma, do you read, over?"

"Yes . . . approaching chopper . . ." a distant-sounding voice responded.

"Tell them to use the electromagnetic grenades!" yelled Overton.

"Rog—" Bouma replied, his voice quickly cutting out.

Overton turned to look at the lakebed, but the forest of poles blocked his view. The intense blue glow that shrouded him made it difficult to see beyond a few yards. The longer he stood in one place, the blurrier his vision became. Standing inside the farm was like being in an old-fashioned tanning bed. His eyes were beginning to burn from the intense light.

With a sequence of blinks, he activated the protective tint on his visor. When his eyes finally adjusted, he saw for the first time the size of the farm. A moan from overhead drew his attention. He looked up for the source of the noise, but only saw the distorted faces of the unconscious prisoners staring back at him. Were they in some sort of trance? It was hard to tell, and Overton was not a doctor. He pushed on, navigating the rows quickly.

Making his way deeper, he tried to count the poles but lost track. There were at least a hundred, this he knew, with about a dozen humans attached to each. With only two rows left to explore, he knew the chances of finding one of his men alive was slim. But he couldn't stop now. Not when he was so close. He'd let so many of his fellow marines down in the past.

Determined, he pushed on and stopped at the bottom of another pole. He tilted his head upward, counting the bodies as his eyes quickly scanned their clothing.

One.

Five.

Nine.

He stopped at ten. His eyes fixated on the green camouflage fatigues of a gaunt figure halfway up the pole.

"Shit." Whatever electrical current was gluing the survivors to the poles could probably capture him just as easily. Sophie had warned him of this. With no time to find an off switch, he was forced to improvise.

He grabbed a magazine one of the NTC soldiers had handed him earlier and jammed it home. Pointing the barrel at the bottom of the pole, he slowly pulled back on the trigger.

Wait, he thought, tilting his helmet back up the pole. The marine was at least twenty-five feet up, so the fall alone could be fatal. Especially if he or she was already injured. There was no way of knowing exactly what condition the soldier was in.

Overton cursed and flared his nostrils.

More gunfire erupted in the distance. Two minutes had passed. He had less than that to get the marine down. The horde would be closing in on the chopper.

I can't leave them.

He knew he had no other choice. Pointing his rifle at the bottom of the pole, he emptied his entire magazine into the alien architecture. A loud whine rumbled from under the dirt, and the glow of the pole pulsated several times before dying.

One by one, the prisoners slid down the pole. Overton tossed his rifle to the ground and rushed to help, but the bodies came crashing down too quickly. The sound of bones shattering echoed in his helmet, making him cringe. Seconds later, a pile of twisted people lay in a heap on the ground.

"No!" he screamed, digging through the bodies. More gunfire poured out in the background, followed by several concussions that sent tremors through the ground.

No time.

With all his strength, he jerked and pulled bodies off the pile, clawing desperately for the marine. He finally uncovered the green fatigues. He yanked another body off the top and gazed upon the marine's face for the first time. The unfamiliar feeling of grief overwhelmed him. It was Lieutenant Allison Smith; the woman had been with his recon unit for five years.

Goddamn, it's good to see her, Overton thought. He paused to look Smith over. Her eyes were open but glassy. There was no immediate sign of consciousness. Overton struggled to pull the woman free from the others, watching her chest for signs of life. Slowly it rose and fell.

"Thank God," Overton whispered. "You're going to be okay, Smith. Just hang in there." He tapped her face with an armored finger, and Smith let out a deep groan. A deep gurgling sound crackled in her throat. She'd more than likely suffered internal damage and some broken bones. Nothing they couldn't patch up back at the med ward.

With one last ounce of strength, he hefted the injured marine over his shoulders and began trekking back through the forest of poles. He ignored the pleas from several of the civilians who had somehow managed to wake up, their arms reaching toward him, begging for help. There was nothing he could do for any of them now.

By the time Overton got to the slope of the hill, the entire lakebed was filled with Spiders. He froze at the top of the bluff. With astonishment, he watched the creatures surround the chopper. The Spiders were desperate, sacrificing themselves by racing into the wave of pulse rounds. Inch by inch, the suicidal creatures crept closer to the helicopter.

The com came to life with Bouma's voice. "Overton, where are you? We're leaving!"

"On my way!" Overton replied. He cautiously made his way down the slope, careful not to lose his footing and accidentally drop his precious cargo. When he got to the lakebed, his legs began to resist. His body was giving up on him. With Smith's weight on his shoulders, his knees were beginning to groan, and his shoulder wound was flaring up, sending sharp spikes of pain down his back.

Don't give up. You're so close, he thought. A dash of adrenaline gave him an extra burst of energy. His footfalls were longer, his stride more efficient; he was going to make it.

And then he slid to a stop, nearly toppling Smith over his shoulders. Spiders were flanking the chopper on both sides. Several of the NTC soldiers were torn from the line. Claws ripped through their armor like it was plastic wrap.

Overton closed his eyes, flinching every time one of the Spiders sunk a claw into one of the terrified men. The line was beginning to break.

There were screams, shrieks, and more gunfire. The landscape was soaked with red and blue blood. It was hell. Overton had seen it before. And for the first time in his career, he wasn't sure what to do. With an empty rifle and Smith on his back, all he could do was watch.

As the NTC line broke, soldiers retreated toward the chopper. Bursts from NTC plasma rifles sent the Spiders tumbling across the dirt. But there were too many of them, and they were suicidal with hunger.

Overhead, the blades thumped through the stale air, sending clouds of dust into the sky. Overton watched the last two soldiers jump into the cargo bay as the chopper began to rise from the ground. He was too late—he was cut off.

He turned to look back up at the poles. He could try and escape, but only if he left Smith. And that wasn't an option.

"Wait!" a voice yelled over the net. "Overton is still out there!"

Overton pushed Smith farther up onto his shoulders; they weren't going to make it. He had to find another escape route. "You have to leave without us!"

Static broke back over the net as the chopper rose farther into the air. A thick plume of smoke flowed out of one of the rotors. Before he had a chance to turn and run, a soldier appeared on a minigun angled off the helicopter's side. Several small objects flew out of the open door and landed in the mass of Spiders below. At first Overton couldn't make them out, but the sound of their deafening explosions quickly made him smile. The NTC soldiers were trying to save him.

The whine from the automatic pulse gun barked to life as the mini-gunner opened fire on the now-defenseless Spiders below. The rounds tore into the aliens, sending them crashing across the cracked dirt. Blue mist filled the area where the aliens had clustered. Nothing but gory chunks of meat left where a dozen of the creatures had stood moments earlier.

Overton didn't waste the moment. With a deep grunt, he willed his legs forward and closed his eyes, sprinting for the safety of the chopper. His lungs burned with every breath and pain shot down his wounded shoulder.

Smith's weight was unbearable, but it also gave him strength.

Only a few more steps, you old turd.

The chopper had lowered nearby. Skidding to a stop, he kicked alien body parts out of his way and attempted to lift Smith's body into the air. Grunting, he pushed her off his shoulders with all his strength toward a pair of hands reaching down from above.

When Overton saw it was Bouma, he smiled. The marine had been loyal on every mission, never questioning orders, never hesitating when faced with danger.

With a final push, he heaved Smith's limp body into the air. Bouma pulled her into the safety of the chopper. Gasping for air, Overton waited for his turn.

The Spiders were getting closer now. They circled around him.

Desperate now, Overton attempted to lift his right arm. It fell back to his side, limp and numb.

"Overton!" Bouma yelled, reaching down for him.

With every bit of strength he had left, he jumped for Bouma's hand. Their armored fingers interlocked for a brief second. The world slowed to a crawl. They both knew exactly what the other was thinking. The tide had finally turned. Humanity had a shot at survival after all.

But for Overton, the fight was over. A Spider's claws tore into his back, puncturing clear through his chest. Gasping, razor-sharp pain rushed into his lungs and webbed down his body. He crashed to the ground with the claw still inside his chest.

"No!" Bouma yelled as the chopper pulled into the air.

Overton coughed out a mouthful of blood. "Go," he managed to choke out, raising a hand to wave the bird away. He watched the chopper rise farther into the air, Bouma's visor slowly getting smaller as the man reached down for him. A spasm rushed through Overton's body as the Spider ripped its claw free from his chest and tossed his limp body into the air. He landed in the heart of the horde, crashing onto the dry ground with a thud.

The Spiders ignored the escaping chopper and surrounded his body, forming a circle around him, their claws taunting him as they dug through the ground.

"Fuck you," Overton tried to yell. But a deep, terrible choking sound came out instead. He watched the Spiders scamper closer to him. In a blur of shimmering blue light they engulfed him. Claws jerked and tore at his body. Mandibles released hungry shrieks. Their claws ripped through his armor. Stars bled across his vision.

He coughed again as a claw tore into his stomach, jerking him into a sitting position, before another claw nailed his shoulder to the ground. He screamed in pain, but the agony faded as the life drained from his body. He caught one final glimpse of the chopper between the repeated stabs, and he tried to smile. He had saved Smith and most of his squad. The mission had been a success.

His lips twisted into a half grin as a claw came down on his visor, splintering the glass.

CHAPTER 33

SOPHIE emerged from a deep sleep to the sound of voices. She struggled to open her eyes, suddenly filled with panic. Her mind was clouded in fog.

She narrowed her eyes and focused on the blurred faces.

"Sophie . . ." one of the hushed voices said, as if to test whether she was awake. Holly stared down at her.

"It's okay, you're safe," said another voice.

She recognized the voice as Emanuel's, but didn't have the energy to look at him.

"How long have I been out?" Sophie asked.

Emanuel whistled. "She's back!" he yelled. "You've been out two days. And you have one hell of a concussion."

"The ship . . ." she choked.

Emanuel smiled sourly. "NTC almost blew it out of the sky. The Organics didn't even retaliate; they simply disappeared."

"NTC?"

"Captain Noble from the submarine *Ghost of Atlantis* had been tracking the Biosphere radio signal. They showed up with a chopper just in time."

Sophie raised a hand to her battered head. She couldn't remember any of it. The last memory she had was of the explosions.

"How did I get out of the ship?" she asked, rubbing her forehead.

The smile on Emanuel's face disappeared, his features turning grave. "What do you mean?"

"How did I get out of the Organics' ship?"

Emanuel stared back at her blankly. "I don't follow . . ."

Holly touched Sophie's wrist gently. "Sweetie, you were never inside the ship. Bouma brought you to the chopper after you were knocked unconscious in the middle of the farm."

Sophie shook her head. "No, that isn't right. I was inside. I saw . . ." She paused, trying to remember. "I saw *them*."

Holly and Emanuel exchanged confused looks.

"Them?" Emanuel asked, his brow creased into an arch.

"The multidimensional Organics," Sophie said. Excitement rushed through her as she began to remember. The Organics' civilization on Mars, the black ships hovering over Europa. The images popped into her memory as if she were still watching them.

Emanuel pulled away from her bed and crossed his arms. "Sophie, you hit your head really hard. Whatever you think you saw was just—"

"No!" she protested, her voice getting louder. "I was inside that ship. I saw what happened to them. I saw Mars millions of years ago when the planet was partially covered in oceans. I watched their civilization destroyed by a massive volcano below the sea. I watched their ships trail a comet and collect the icy residue. I saw them harvesting the ice on Europa. There's more, too. They have traveled to other solar systems. They've collected life from other planets."

"Stop!" Emanuel yelled.

Sophie widened her eyes, startled by his raised voice.

Unfolding his arms, Emanuel crouched next to her bed and very softly said, "Sophie, you dreamt those things."

"He's right. It was nothing but a dream," Holly said.

Sophie tried to collect her thoughts, focusing on the memories. They were so vivid. Just like her other dreams. Only these *were* real. Weren't they?

Alexia's voice crackled over the speakers. "Doctor Winston, your vitals indicate you are distressed. You have been through some severe trauma. May I suggest—"

"No, you may not, Alexia," Sophie said forcefully. She closed her eyes and tried to recall anything that might be useful. Anything that might prove it wasn't all just another dream—that it wasn't just another product of the chip NTC had surgically placed in her neck.

She reached behind her head and ran her index finger over the scar. As she did, she noticed something had changed in Emanuel's features. He no longer looked concerned—he looked frightened.

Sophie winced. She knew how she sounded, but she also knew what she had seen. The brief moment of silence was just enough to encourage her to continue.

"Doctor Hoffman knew about the invasion all along. And he knew enough about the Organics to understand they would leave Earth desolate, just like they did Mars. He knew there was no way to defeat them. That's why he never developed Luke Williard's technology." Sophie paused so she could gauge Emanuel's reaction. He looked back at her with wide eyes.

Growing angry, Sophie sat up. In a raised voice she continued, "The Biospheres weren't just an experiment to help colonize Mars. The mission was never to help humanity escape from Earth. Don't you see? It was to help humanity escape the Organics."

"Look," Emanuel said, running a hand through his hair. "What you're saying makes no sense. Why would he have wanted to escape from one dying planet to another? Why go through all the trouble to convince the world that—"

"Because he knew the Organics wouldn't chase us there! He knew they would have no reason to return to a planet they had already drained and destroyed," Sophie said. She looked at each of them in turn and then reached out to Emanuel. "Please. You have to listen to me."

There was softness in his eyes as he looked down at her, like he actually felt bad for her. Then he leaned down and kissed her on the cheek. "I love you," he whispered into her ear. "But you were just dreaming, Sophie."

Emanuel stood up and paced over to Holly to whisper in her ear.

Sophie struggled to move. "What? What is it?"

"There's a lot we haven't told you," Holly replied. "A lot has happened in the past few days. And I suppose now is just as good a time as any."

Sophie's stomach sank. She had heard those words before. The last time, someone had died. She took in a deep breath and gathered the strength to ask, "Who did we lose?"

Emanuel looked at the ground. "Sergeant Overton."

Sophie looked at him with disbelief. When she opened her mouth nothing but warm breath poured out. Words simply wouldn't form.

"No . . . that isn't possible," Sophie said, shaking her head. "He was right behind me when we reached the poles."

Alexia's hologram shot out of the console at the edge of her bed. The AI tilted her head and looked at Sophie. Then Sophie saw something she never expected: a faint hint of emotion in Alexia's features. It was evident only for a second as she blinked, but Sophie saw the strain in the AI's face before she spoke. "I'm afraid Doctor Brown and Doctor Rodriguez are correct. Sergeant Overton was killed in Colorado Springs."

Sophie immediately forgot about the implications of Alexia's behavior. She felt like she had been slapped in the face. She closed her eyes, her gut sinking. In a low voice, she finally managed to speak. "How?"

"Saving one of his own. Another marine named Allison Smith," Emanuel said, grabbing Sophie's hand. "She's with the team in the mess hall."

"How many survivors are there?"

"There were five, but only Smith made it through the night. The others were just too far gone," Holly said. "They faded fast after they were removed from the poles."

Sophie sank back into her bed, reaching again for her pounding forehead. "And Kiel?"

"The little guy showed up shortly after the NTC chopper brought you back. He has a broken leg, two cracked ribs, and a concussion, but he made it."

Sophie marked Kiel down as one of the first men to thank when she got better. He had saved her life and the lives of everyone else by risking his own.

Emanuel leaned over her bed and kissed her on the forehead. "You need to rest now. We'll come back later and check on you."

Closing her eyes, Sophie let her head sink into her pillow. She knew better than to argue with him. With the loss of Sergeant Overton still sinking in, she simply wanted to go back to sleep. To curl up and hibernate.

The overhead lights clicked off and the room was shrouded in darkness. Sophie tried to relax, but she was afraid to dream. She was afraid of what she would see—she was afraid she would no longer be able to decipher what was real from what wasn't.

CAPTAIN Noble studied the tablet Dr. Winston had given him earlier. It held the blueprints to the RVAMP device that Dr. Rodriguez had designed. It was hard to believe that something so simple could turn the tide of a war that had seemed all but lost a few days earlier. Now all he had to do was return safely to his submarine and get the specs into the hands of one of his engineers.

As he placed the tablet into a titanium case, he thought briefly of Captain Quan and the fate of the Chinese sub. While there was now hope for humanity, there was little hope that Quan's crew had survived. He knew they had more than likely perished, and with them his own crew members.

The massive blast doors of Cheyenne Mountain groaned open, and rays of morning light illuminated the hangar. It was another reminder of what was still worth fighting for. He turned to look at Harrington and the eight other NTC soldiers waiting for his orders. The ragtag group of scientists and children stood behind them. He studied every face. Each one, in his or her own way, represented the best of what humanity had to offer.

Captain Noble smiled as Dr. Winston hobbled over, her hand gripping a makeshift cane made out of a metal table leg.

"I want to express my gratitude for everything you've done to help us, Captain Noble." She returned his smile and reached out to shake his hand.

He put both hands over hers and looked her in the eye. "You are most welcome. Please know you have a friend watching out for you a thousand meters beneath the surface of the Pacific. We will monitor the encrypted channel and can be here within twenty-four hours if you need our help. Once we determine a strategy, we'll inform you of the plan. We may need your help in the future. But for now, please grant me just one request."

Sophie nodded. "Anything."

"Just stay alive," Noble said.

Sophie winked at him. "We'll try our best."

She rejoined her crew, putting her hand on Owen's matted brown hair. He looked up at her with a grin that revealed a missing front tooth. She laughed and turned to watch the NTC soldiers walk into the sunlight.

Captain Noble turned one last time and saluted. "Good luck!" he called before disappearing beyond the doors.

Climbing into the helicopter, he took a seat away from the other soldiers so he could look out the small, reinforced window. As the *Sea Serpent* lifted into the air, he watched the blast doors of Cheyenne Mountain slowly close. He looked away from the mountain and into the sky. Picturing Mars somewhere up above, he thought of Dr. Hoffman. The man would be proud. Noble had helped ensure one of the Biospheres would survive after all.

No matter the odds, he would make sure Dr. Hoffman's plan succeeded.

—End of Book II—

TO BE CONTINUED IN

ORBS III
REDEMPTION

ON SALE NOW

NICHOLAS SANSBURY SMITH is the bestselling author of the Orbs and Extinction Cycle series. He worked for Iowa Homeland Security and Emergency Management in disaster mitigation before switching careers to focus on his one true passion—writing. Smith is a three-time Kindle All-Star, and several of his titles have reached the top 50 on the overall Kindle bestseller list and as high as #1 in the Audible store. *Hell Divers*, the first book in his new trilogy, will release in July 2016. When he isn't writing or daydreaming about the apocalypse, he's training for triathlons or traveling the world. He lives in Des Moines, Iowa, with his dog and a house full of books.

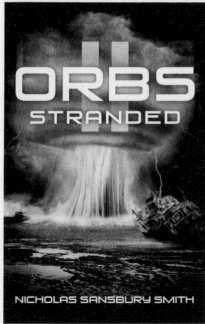